She had ~~to remain professional, no~~ matter what s~~...~~

No matter what h~~...~~

And yet, she ma~~...~~ there naked, stretching~~...~~ muscles of his…a~~...~~act in ways they absolutely shouldn't right now.

But scolding herself didn't help.

He accepted a vial of clear liquid from Patrick and drank it. He seemed to shoot one more look toward her. Then Denny lifted a large light from where it had been in his backpack, turned it on and aimed it toward Liam.

She knew what to expect—kind of. But she still couldn't help feeling amazed as his face lifted and its features began elongating into a muzzle, and his body grew smaller, furrier, more slender, shrinking closer to the ground.

And in a very short time, handsome, naked Liam had turned, as anticipated, into a wolf.

Linda O. Johnston loves to write. While honing her writing skills, she worked in advertising and public relations, then became a lawyer...and enjoyed writing contracts. Linda's first published fiction appeared in *Ellery Queen's Mystery Magazine* and won a Robert L. Fish Memorial Award for Best First Mystery Short Story of the Year. Linda now spends most of her time creating memorable tales of paranormal romance, romantic suspense and mystery. Visit her on the web at www.lindaojohnston.com.

Books by Linda O. Johnston

Harlequin Nocturne

Guardian Wolf
Undercover Wolf
Loyal Wolf
Canadian Wolf
Protector Wolf

Back to Life

Harlequin Romantic Suspense

K-9 Ranch Rescue

Second Chance Soldier
Trained to Protect

Undercover Soldier
Covert Attraction

VISIONARY WOLF

———

LINDA O. JOHNSTON

Recycling programs
for this product may
not exist in your area.

ISBN-13: 978-1-335-62966-1

Visionary Wolf

HARLEQUIN®
www.Harlequin.com

Printed in U.S.A.

Dear Reader,

Visionary Wolf is the ninth Alpha Force Harlequin Nocturne—and the last, since the Nocturne line is ending soon. It takes place where the first Alpha Force Nocturne did, in fictional Mary Glen, Maryland, and nearby Ft. Lukman, the headquarters of the covert military unit of shapeshifters, Alpha Force.

The story features the hero, Lieutenant Liam Corland, a visionary technology expert and shapeshifter who has the dream and hope that someday shapeshifters will be accepted by all humans. Then there's veterinarian Dr. Rosa Jontay, who's aware of shapeshifters, likes them in general and is happy to treat them while they are in shifted form. But getting to know them better? Not a good idea.

When troubles occur with some of the Alpha Force shifters in resuming their human forms after a shift—including Liam—Rosa is happy to help in any way she can. But why are such problems occurring? As the two of them work together to find out what is going on, they spend a lot of time together...and despite their misgivings, their attraction ignites.

I hope you enjoy *Visionary Wolf*! Please visit me at my website, lindaojohnston.com, and at my blog, killerhobbies.Blogspot.com. And, yes, I'm also on Facebook.

Linda O. Johnston

Visionary Wolf is dedicated to all Harlequin Nocturne readers, especially those who have enjoyed my stories about Alpha Force.

And yes, as always, my thanks to my fantastic agent, Paige Wheeler of Creative Media Agency, and to my wonderful Harlequin editor, Allison Lyons. There may be no further Alpha Force stories, but I look forward to more Harlequin Romantic Suspense.

Also, as always, I thank my dear husband, Fred, for being there, and for inspiring me.

Chapter 1

Good thing he was at Ft. Lukman, Lieutenant Liam Corland thought. At any other military facility, he would never feel comfortable walking calmly with his dog, Chase, across the nearly empty grounds, in his casual camo uniform, later in the morning than he should be reporting for duty. In fact, he wouldn't feel comfortable working at any other military facility, period.

But this was where Alpha Force was stationed. He had just left his apartment in the bachelor officers' quarters. Now he headed toward the building across the compound that contained so many important functions—mainly laboratory, cover dog kennel and offices, including his own.

Sure, he should have started his important assignment of this day an hour ago, so he didn't want to make his lateness too obvious. He avoided the most used pathways, hustling along behind buildings occupied by units other than Alpha Force. Chase and he would be picked up on security cameras when they sneaked in through a back door of the appropriate building, but no one would do anything about it, since they belonged there. Besides, he had a good excuse, and he probably wasn't the only one who slept in a bit. Not that he had gotten much sleep anyway.

There had been a full moon last night. He had shifted, of course—pretty much on his own terms, thanks to Alpha Force.

And thanks also to the help of his aide, Sergeant Denny Orringer, who now waited for him in the kennel and lab building. Covering for him, if necessary.

He'd talked to Denny earlier, and—

There. Chase and he had reached the back of that building, near the doors leading into the kennel area. The shapeshifters' cover dogs like Chase were kept there frequently, along with other dogs that helped this military base look like it had a lot of well-trained canines living here all the time.

Of course Alpha Force members who had cover dogs also kept them with them a lot as well, both at Ft. Lukman and when they were traveling—as long as there were some living here, too, to keep up appearances.

Liam, a tech expert, used the key card he had programmed himself to open the back door. He slipped in and enclosed Chase in one of several fenced areas, joining three dogs that resembled him.

Of course, Chase looked wolfen, resembling Liam himself while he was shifted…

"See you later, guy," Liam whispered to his canine companion, who was already being greeted by his fellows.

Heading for the stairway down to the most important floor of the building, which contained offices and the laboratories where the very special Alpha Force elixir was brewed, Liam walked slowly, figuring he was likely to run into someone else dressed like him.

But fortunately, he saw no one—so no one saw him, either, as he again used a key card to open a door, this time to the stairs.

He heard raised voices from down the hall when he slipped carefully into his own office. They sounded excited. With his special senses, even when he was in human form, he could easily have eavesdropped had he wanted to.

But what he wanted was to get to work.

First, though, he shot a quick text message to Denny to let him know where he was. Then he booted up his computer, a highly sophisticated desktop that was the epitome of today's technology.

A good thing, since it was used for such a critical purpose.

His phone made a text ping. Denny was probably just acknowledging what Liam had sent. He'd check it later.

A sudden urge for a cup of coffee shot through Liam but he ignored it. He'd get one later when he went to the meeting, but right now he needed to check his usual social media and other sources.

His job at the moment? Look for any and all mentions online of people claiming to have seen shapeshifters last night, in this area first of all, then other locales in this country and the world where Alpha Force members were stationed. And, finally, everywhere else.

He'd undoubtedly find some mentions. Perhaps a lot. He always did, and most appeared to come from people who loved what they considered paranormal—fiction lovers who wanted to see if others, unlike them, had spotted shifters during a night of a full moon. They were easy to deal with.

But Liam needed to deal with the reality of those who didn't have the kinds of backgrounds to have been introduced to Alpha Force and what it did, but had caught glimpses of possible Alpha Force shifters on that night of the full moon—or claimed to.

Liam had to find their posts, then kid around online. Make them look foolish to the rest of the world, and maybe even to themselves.

That was one of the things Liam, vying, at least in his mind, for tech champion of the universe, did best. But he wasn't a geek. Oh, no. He loved being a member of the military. Of Alpha Force. He both looked and acted the part.

Except at the computer.

Using one of his many false identities, he logged on to a favorite social media site—and gasped. "No!" he exclaimed aloud.

He read the post more carefully, then jumped onto several other sites—and got the same results.

Existence of a strange military unit of shapeshifters was mentioned more than once on this day after a night of a full moon. That wasn't unusual.

But claims of damage, destruction—and injuries to real people? The extent of what was described on so many sites was horrific.

And did not bode well at all for Liam's vision of shifters' acceptance someday by other people. Those lies were more of the reality now, though.

"I need to let the others know." Liam was barely aware he was talking aloud. He picked up his phone, then realized this was critical enough that he wanted to tell his superiors in person. One in particular— Major Drew Connell, their commanding officer who had begun Alpha Force and remained in charge.

Drew's office was on the opposite side of this floor, past the lab areas, and Liam immediately headed there. If he hadn't had this important assignment, that was where he would have gone first, since nearly all Alpha Force members present on the base attended informal meetings in Drew's office the morning after a night of a full moon. Liam would have headed there eventually anyway to let the others know what he found.

But with these horrible allegations… Liam had to let his unit members know right away. Then he had to dig further online to learn their truth—or, hopefully, not.

If not, though, how had so many unheard of references and accusations been put out there?

He put his computer to sleep, then hurried out his office door, down the halls whose plainness would never suggest the amazing things that went on in the laboratories beyond them, to another hall lined with closed doors. The last one was to Drew's office.

Without knocking, Liam burst in, expecting to see Drew there holding court with the other shifters and their aides.

But though the room looked busy, he didn't see that officer in charge. Nor did he see Captain Jonas Truro,

Drew's close friend and aide, a medical doctor like Drew, but, unlike him, not a shifter.

That was strange for a post–full moon meeting in Drew's office. Did they know what Liam had learned online? Were they trying to deal with it themselves?

But Liam might just be allowing his own angst over what he'd seen on the computer to lead him to false conclusions. Drew and Jonas could be down the hall in the restroom. Or checking something in the lab. Or—

"Oh, there you are, Liam." Denny, in a folding chair near the doorway of the small, crowded office, stood and looked at him. "I'm glad you read my text." Which Liam didn't always do quickly, and he wasn't about to tell his aide he hadn't this time, either. Denny was younger and shorter than Liam, and he had a slight growth of facial hair. Liam kept his own dark hair closely shaved—when he was in human form.

He wondered what Denny had said in that text, but he wasn't about to check now.

"Come in, Liam," Captain Patrick Worley said, also standing. He was tall, dressed in camos like the rest, and the expression on his face looked grim. Had he heard about what the Alpha Force shifters were alleged to have done?

Had Alpha Force shifters actually done any of it? Any of them in this room?

"Glad you're here," Patrick continued. "Have you checked out any online references to shifters yet?"

"Yes, and—"

But Patrick didn't let him finish. "Good. We'll want to hear about it. But first there's something you need to know that we've been discussing. Something bad."

Liam swallowed hard. "I definitely want to hear

about it." Hopefully, none of it was true and he could find a way to calm all the comments that had shown up online. Or—

"It's about Major Connell," Patrick said. "Something went wrong with Drew's shift. Really wrong. He hasn't shifted back from wolf form yet, and he's not doing well. Right now, Jonas is with him at the veterinary clinic in Mary Glen. Drew is being cared for by Melanie."

Drew's wife, a veterinarian. Not a medical doctor.

This was definitely bad. Very bad. Certainly more important than the false claims Liam had seen online.

What was Alpha Force going to do?

"How is Drew now?" demanded Dr. Melanie Harding Connell. Dr. Rosa Jontay's boss faced her at the back of the Mary Glen Veterinary Clinic's main hallway, arms crossed, head tilted.

Rosa understood her concern, of course. Major Drew Connell wasn't just the head of that highly special military unit known as Alpha Force. He was also Melanie's husband. Father of her adorable four-year-old daughter, Emily, and two-year-old son, Andy.

"He seems tired," Rosa said softly, looking into Melanie's sad but pretty blue eyes. "I just came out of the room for a short break and to get coffee, but I'll be heading back in there soon. Jonas is still with him."

That was Captain Jonas Truro, also part of Alpha Force, and from what Rosa understood Jonas was additionally a medical doctor—and Drew's aide when he shifted. She had seen him a few times in the year or so she had been here, but, as with most of the Alpha Force members, she didn't know him well. Jonas had

apparently been hanging out with his superior officer
earlier that night—and later.

"Thank you. And thank Jonas." Melanie also
seemed tired. Stressed. But that wasn't surprising.

As the only veterinarians at the clinic, they both
wore white lab coats. Rosa was the taller one. They
both had brown hair pulled up in back by clips, with
Melanie's darker than hers.

Not that she was comparing herself to Melanie,
Rosa thought. She considered them both exceptional
vets, and that was what really mattered.

But she did wonder what it was like to have as
strange a relationship as the one between Melanie and
Drew. Committed and deeply caring—but yes, strange,
since Drew was a shapeshifter.

"Everything okay with the rest of the clinic?" she
asked Melanie. "Do you need me for anything else?"

"Fortunately, we're not very busy today. What I
need you to do is—"

"I'm going back into that examination room right
now," Rosa finished. "But with this kind of situation…
it's so different, and other than to keep an eye on him
I'm not sure what to do."

"That's all I want you to do. Having Jonas there
helps, but the kind of medical assistance Drew might
need now—"

"Is veterinary. Right. I understand."

The door to the reception area down the hall opened,
and the senior receptionist, Susie Damon, came out and
looked toward them. "Our eleven o'clock Yorkie ap-
pointment is here for an exam and shots," she called.
"Okay to bring him in?"

"Fine," Melanie responded. "I'll be right there."

Melanie was handling all the cases that came in, for now at least. She was clearly upset, and Rosa assumed she feared breaking down if she was the vet to spend time with Drew.

And that might make things worse with him.

Melanie looked back toward Rosa. "Just so you know, I did get a call a few minutes ago. So far…well, I gather there are no more answers from Ft. Lukman yet, but one of the Alpha Force members is on his way to relieve Jonas. Maybe whoever that is can shed some more light on what's going on there, and when…"

She didn't have to finish. Especially not with the newest look of pain that flashed across her face.

"That's fine," Rosa said. "I'll still hang out with Drew, but I'll also see what I can learn from whoever that is and report to you if it…if there's any indication of what they're doing and how long it will take."

"Great. And maybe Jonas can help more by doing something at the base. I'll check back with you soon." Melanie headed down the hall toward the reception area as Susie led the tiny Yorkshire terrier and his not-so-tiny owner toward one of the closest exam rooms.

Which left Rosa to go grab two cups of coffee from the break room at the end of the hall and take them with her to another exam room, the one where Drew had been brought by Jonas and Melanie early that morning, before anyone else had arrived—but after dawn had broken.

Rosa looked around the hallway once more, but it was empty. Then she slipped into the room.

It was a fairly ordinary exam room for a veterinary clinic, with the back wall covered by a cabinet containing shelves for supplies like bandages, exam gloves and disinfectant, and a sink in the middle for washing hands and more. There was a closed trash can nearby, and a couple chairs sat along the outer wall. In the middle was a substantial metal table.

One of the chairs was occupied by Jonas, who stood when she entered. He was a large guy, dark-complected and dressed in a camouflage uniform. He was around her own age of thirty, she figured.

"Here's some coffee." Rosa handed him one of the cups.

"Thanks," he said as he accepted it.

Rosa turned then. On the table with legs adjusted to keep it close to the floor lay a large canine that resembled a wolf. And he was a wolf—of sorts.

That canine was Major Drew Connell of nearby Alpha Force, its lead officer, from what Rosa had heard.

She had also heard that Alpha Force was a highly covert military unit of shapeshifters, which was fascinating to her. There had been a full moon last night, and Drew had shifted into his wolf form. But he hadn't shifted back at dawn or beyond.

He'd been home when the sun rose, and the Connells' home was next door to the vet clinic. Melanie had brought him here after taking their daughter to preschool and making sure the sitter was there for their son. Rosa could only guess what Mommy had said to their kids about where Daddy was, and about the wolf in their house.

Or maybe the kids were shifters, too...

Melanie had also called Jonas, who had arrived at the clinic even before Drew and had stayed with him, along with Rosa, from early morning. It was around ten o'clock now.

Rosa realized she had been standing in the doorway after closing the door behind her. The wolf on the table hadn't moved—before. Now, he made a soft growling sound and, moving slowly, carefully along the towels that had been secured around the metal top, repositioned himself into a canine sit. His fur was long, an almost silvery brown, with patches of darker coloration. His eyes were amber, and he seemed to stare at her over his long, pointed muzzle.

"It's okay, Drew," Jonas said. "It's just Rosa."

In his current situation, Drew looked a lot like Grunge, a wolflike shepherd-malamute combination that Rosa had been informed was his cover dog. That meant, she'd been told, that Grunge could be pointed out to people as Drew's pet, the canine they supposedly saw when he was changed, not him. She assumed Grunge was hidden at home at the moment, or maybe at the base.

"Hi, Drew," she said. "How are you feeling now?"

He couldn't answer by speaking to her, of course. But from what Melanie had told her, the members of Alpha Force took some kind of medicine—an elixir, they called it—before they shifted that helped them keep their human cognition. He most likely understood what she said.

But they also were supposed to turn back into human form once daylight began after a night of a full moon, unless they had drunk that elixir and chose not to shift back then. She gathered that Drew hadn't chosen to stay a wolf when daylight arrived that morning, but still hadn't regained his human form. And judging by the reactions of Melanie and Jonas, that wasn't good.

He apparently did understand her, though. Maybe. But he aimed his gaze down at the table and shook his head slowly, as if communicating to her that he wasn't feeling well.

"I'm so sorry," she said.

And she was. The fact that she had known about shapeshifters, and had, in fact, helped to treat some shifted wolves and other creatures at her home in Michigan, had been the main reason Melanie had hired her here. Apparently the shifter community kept in touch with each other, or at least some did, and Melanie had been hunting for someone like her. And Rosa had been thrilled by the offer of this kind of job.

"Is there anything I can do to help?" she asked, not for the first time, looking from Drew to Jonas and back again. She had sat in here with the two of them pretty much since she had arrived at work that day. Melanie had tearfully explained the situation, including her request that Rosa stay with Drew and make sure he wasn't suffering.

Or, even better, report to Melanie when he finally started to shift back to human form.

But that hadn't happened. Not yet, at least.

Right now, Drew didn't even look at her, let alone attempt to communicate something he wanted her to do. Jonas didn't offer any suggestions, either.

"Would you like some water?" she asked Drew.

He looked at her and nodded, so she removed a clean metal bowl from the sink, filled it partway and placed it on the table in front of him. He lapped up maybe half of it.

A knock sounded on the exam room door.

Rosa glanced at Drew, who was once more lying on the towel-covered table, head between his paws in a fully canine position, the bowl off to his side.

"Come in," she called.

The door opened and Susie popped her head in. "There's a guy here from Ft. Lukman who says he's come to help out."

To take over for Jonas, Rosa assumed, from what Melanie had said before.

She figured that Susie and the others who worked here had some knowledge of the ties Melanie and her husband had to Ft. Lukman, and probably even knew there were shapeshifters there—and possibly that Drew was one of them.

But they'd also been instructed to remain totally discreet, even among themselves. To Rosa's knowledge, they never talked about it—or at least they'd never done so around her.

"Thanks, Susie. Let him in."

In a moment, a tall guy dressed in a camouflage shirt and slacks like Jonas entered the room, and Susie shut the door behind him.

Jonas rose again. "Liam," he said. "Glad you're here." He turned to Rosa. "This is Dr. Jontay, one of the vets here. Rosa, that's Lieutenant Liam Corland."

"Hi, Dr. Jontay," the guy said in a deep, masculine voice. He held out his hand and gave hers a quick, substantial shake. The contact made her feel fully aware of this man's presence. He was wide shouldered, and his face was angular—and gorgeous. His hair was black and military short. Dark brown eyes looked straight into hers, but only for a moment.

"Hello, Lieutenant Corland," she said as matter-of-factly as she could manage, considering how oddly her mind was reacting to this guy.

"Liam," he gently corrected, making Rosa regret she hadn't done the same. He turned to Jonas. "I'm assigned to relieve you here."

"Got it. Thanks. I'll run now, and keep you informed about how things go at the base." Jonas bent toward Drew, who was sitting up once more on the table, and said something into his ear, which twitched canine style. Then he exited the room.

"Well," Rosa said, not exactly sure how to handle this. What was this Liam going to do here?

As if she had spoken aloud, he looked her directly in the eyes once more. "Do you know and understand the full situation?" His tone was demanding. She didn't like it, but she did understand.

"Yes, I think so," she said. Then, more brazenly, "Do you?"

"Of course. I'm a member of Alpha Force, too. One of its…special members." Again, he caught her gaze, as if attempting to ensure she knew what that meant.

"Then you're like…" She tilted her head toward the table, where the canine Drew remained seated, clearly watching them and presumably understanding. "Like Drew," she finished.

"That's right. I'm here to help Drew out as much as possible from the…from the military angle. Watch over him while members of our unit try to figure out how to help him in their way." Something to do with that elixir that helped shifters? Something else? Maybe she would find out more. "And discuss if you think there's any veterinary way to help him…help him get over his current condition."

"I see." This seemed so odd—and yet, since Rosa had grown up with both real wolves and shifters in her area, she could deal with it. Right?

Of course. But the part of all this that made her somehow feel worse at this moment was that she couldn't help focusing on how this Liam had admitted to her right away what he was.

And she felt terrible to think that this gorgeous hunk of a military man was also a shapeshifter.

Chapter 2

"Hi, Drew," Liam finally said.

There his commanding officer was, in canine form, sitting on a bunch of towels on a lowered table in the middle of this veterinary examination room. Watching them. And now he nodded his head as if in greeting.

Liam turned back to Dr. Jontay. Rosa. This vet was fairly special, from what he had been told before he left Ft. Lukman. She had apparently been found after a long hunt for a good, smart backup by Melanie Connell, who'd been seeking a vet who knew about shifters, had provided medical care to them in the past and would keep her mouth shut about working with more in the future.

Rosa was one pretty, hot woman, to boot.

But checking her out wasn't why Liam was there. Seeing, taking care of his friend, his mentor, his superior officer—that was his reason for coming to this clinic.

Sure, he'd told his fellow Alpha Force members at Ft. Lukman about the accusations he'd found online. That was important, of course. But not as important as ensuring that Drew returned to normal. Fast.

And when the topic of needing Jonas to get back to the base to help find a solution arose, Liam volunteered to hang out with Drew here for as long as it took to get him cured.

The rest of the team had argued, since the idea of having so much garbage out there online about shifters and Alpha Force was horrendous, and Liam was the best tool they had for countering it. But he'd told them he had taught Denny how to start his critical counter–social media games. Plus, he would work on it himself as Drew's condition here permitted.

They'd finally agreed, since most of those at the base would be focused on how to deal with what had happened to Drew, and keeping one of their own with him was critical, too. But if what Denny accomplished, with Liam's backup, wasn't enough, they would send Denny to trade places with him so Liam could focus on his job—which was now ridiculing all the ridiculous, and not so ridiculous, claims that had appeared on the internet.

So Liam's giving a damn about his mentor and wanting to do something about it had worked out—at least for now.

"Okay if we sit down?" Liam asked Rosa. "I've got a few things to update for Drew." Assuming that the elixir Drew had first developed, and had worked with over the years of Alpha Force's existence, still allowed him to keep his mental acuity—his *human* mental acuity—hours after he should have shifted back. And his nod before had indicated that, at least, hadn't been affected.

"Would you like a cup of coffee before we talk?" Rosa asked Liam.

Nice lady, or at least polite.

Or did she have an ulterior motive?

"Yeah, thanks. I'd love one." But he'd love finding out what was on her mind even more.

"It's just down the hall." She motioned toward the door with graceful fingers. Probably skilled fingers, too, since she used them to cure animals around here.

He wondered what those fingers would feel like on him… Heck, just because she was a pretty brunette with shining brown eyes and full lips didn't mean he should allow himself to feel any attraction toward her. She wasn't a shifter. She might work with shifters, but he had no idea how she felt about them.

He followed, as she apparently wanted. Well, he wanted it, too.

A guy in blue scrubs walked past them in the fairly long hall—probably a vet tech, Liam figured. He waved to Rosa. "Everything okay?" he asked.

"Everything's fine, Brendan," she replied. "Are all our patients being handled okay?"

Liam assumed she asked that because she wasn't caring for anyone besides Drew right now, or at least it looked that way.

"Sure. Melanie's got it covered, and Dina and I are helping." The guy waved and walked through one of the doors off the hall. Liam assumed Dina was another vet tech.

"Good," Rosa said softly. Then, more loudly, she said, "We've got coffee brewing in the break room, right here." She walked a few more steps, then opened a closed door and motioned for him to follow, which he did.

"Coffee's fine with me," he said right away, "but why am I really here?" He looked around. The room was a bit larger than the exam room and had a few small tables clustered in its center, a fridge on one side and a counter on the other where a large coffee maker sat.

The smile she sent up to him was pretty, as well as ironic. "I'm that obvious? Well, you're right. I don't want us to leave Drew alone for long, but I wanted to ask how things are going at Ft. Lukman. Does anyone there know why Drew hasn't shifted back? What are they doing to help him? I figure that, since they wanted Jonas there, they must be working on that elixir, since I know he's a medical doctor and has helped Drew before with that stuff."

"You're right, and I know they're hoping to come up with some new formulation of the elixir that'll help." But from what Liam had heard, no one had any good ideas yet about why Drew hadn't shifted back despite clearly wanting to, or what kind of adaptation could be made to the elixir to help him. They'd even given him some more of the current version of the elixir to lap up, but that hadn't helped.

"Okay." Rosa turned her back and headed to the coffeepot, where she poured some into two foam cups that she got out of the cabinet below. She handed one to him. "Milk? Sugar?"

"Black," he said. "Thanks."

She went to the fridge and added a few drops of milk to her cup. She turned again toward him. "We'd better get back to Drew." She seemed to hesitate. "Do you know anything about the formulation of the main elixir?"

"Just generally," he said.

"Then what do you do in Alpha Force? For one thing, I assume from what you said before that you're a shifter."

She said that very matter-of-factly, as if she knew about and accepted their existence, as she'd implied earlier, which fit with the little Liam knew about Melanie Connell's assistant vet.

"Yes," he said. "I am." He thought he caught just the tiniest hint of a reaction in her expression. Maybe he was wrong, and she was good at hiding what so many regular humans who knew that shifters were real actually thought about them. Just to bug her, he asked, "Are you?"

Her brief laugh sounded genuine. "No, though I've worked with quite a few over the years." She paused. "Do you do anything special for Alpha Force? I mean, do you handle some of their special ops–type assignments, or do you do something besides train for the future at the base?"

Somehow, he wanted to impress her, which made no sense. He had no intention of flirting with her. But it wouldn't hurt to tell the truth. "Well, I do train for the kinds of special assignments we're sent on," he said. "But I'm also the chief technology officer."

Those pretty brown eyes of hers widened. "Really? What does that entail?"

He didn't want to tell her about the stuff he had seen

online making claims of injuries and worse, caused by shifters last night during the full moon. From the little he'd seen here in Mary Glen it had all been false, anyway—he hoped. If all was going well, Denny was continuing with the solution.

So instead of being fully honest, he said, "I just scout around to see what technology is out there that Alpha Force may be able to use to enhance its already fantastic and covert abilities." That probably sounded good, and it wasn't entirely false, since he did that along with the rest.

"Interesting." Rosa pulled her gaze away from his face. "Now, let's go back and check on Drew."

Checking on Drew was exactly what Liam wanted to do. And he was glad to see that the wolf with the silver-tipped, thick brown fur sat up on the towel-covered table as they entered and began observing them with his wide, golden eyes.

What was he thinking? Liam would try to find out.

"Hi, boss," he said. "Rosa and I just got some coffee, but the caffeine wouldn't be good for you right now. But I want to bring you up-to-date on what was going on at the base."

That everyone in Alpha Force was scrambling around trying to figure out what happened to him. Liam would tell him that, but word it a bit differently.

Also, as the commanding officer of their unit, Drew would be the first person Liam would normally tell about the kind of online social media fiasco he'd discovered—under other circumstances. He wouldn't now, of course. Giving Drew further information that would torment him wouldn't help him shift back any faster.

And would it do any good at all for even a tech expert like Liam to do research online about what had happened to Drew? Shifters weren't likely to post anything about problems in their shifting, let alone what to do about it.

Plus, Alpha Force had its own unique take—and elixir—that would render most comments inapplicable.

Just in case, though, Liam would take a look later.

"How are you feeling now?" Rosa moved around Liam as if taking charge. She approached Drew and patted him gently on the head between his pointed, moving ears as if he were a pet canine. That irritated Liam a little—although he had a passing thought that if she wanted to touch *him* that way, or any other way, he probably wouldn't mind at all, shifted or not.

Drew actually did seem to try to communicate with her some, growling slightly, then shaking his head.

"Do you feel bad physically?" Rosa asked. He stopped moving. "Or are you just frustrated that you haven't changed back?" He nodded.

Good. At least he seemed to be using human cognition and showed no sign of growing wilder, wanting to attack. He was a human in the guise of a wolf, but for a much longer time than Liam was aware any shifter had remained that way without choosing to stay shifted.

So how were they going to bring him back?

Almost as if he heard Liam's thoughts, Drew gently pushed Rosa away with his head. He lay down on the table and stared at Liam.

"I think he wants you to bring him up-to-date, as you said." Rosa looked at Liam with a wry grin on her lovely face, her brown eyes looking both interested and sad. She seemed to really care about her veterinary patient. She probably knew him as a person, too, since she worked for his wife. Liam wished he had something to say that would make her smile.

And Drew, too. Wolves could smile, after all. At least shifters could, somewhat, while in wolf form.

"Okay." Liam sat down on one of the chairs. Rosa remained standing beside Drew at first, her eyes examining him as the wolf regarded the other man in the room. "Now, here's the situation—and if you have any ideas we'll have to figure out a way for you to convey them to me."

Drew nodded as he continued to lie there. Rosa moved to the chair beside Liam.

"First," Liam said, "Jonas and Melanie—and maybe Rosa, too—" he looked at her for an instant and saw she was regarding him steadily "—may already have asked you this, but do you know why you haven't shifted back? I gather this wasn't your choice. Was anything different this time from one of your regular shifts?"

The response was no, based on the low, grumbling noise he made and the slight shake of his head.

"Okay, then. Here's what I learned from the conversations at the base before I left."

Liam started talking about all he had heard and participated in once he had joined the meeting in Jonas's office. No other shifter had had any problem, so they didn't believe it was the elixir—the most current version of the tonic that Drew had begun brewing with the changes that had been suggested and tried by other shifters and seemed to work best for everyone. It allowed for all-important human cognition while shifted. There were slightly different versions now being used outside the full moon to give more choice about when to shift into wolf form and when to shift back. A version that wasn't being used much, if at all, allowed for shifting back to human form when the moon remained full, but it had never been as perfected as the unit members hoped for.

"So," Liam said, "did you drink the regular elixir we're now using during the full moon?"

Drew nodded.

"And did Jonas use the light on you?" That was still preferred by Alpha Force members even under a full moon to ensure the timing.

Again, Drew nodded.

"I assume the elixir looked and tasted like it always did, right?" Rosa asked. Liam was impressed that she was jumping into the discussion, as if she knew what she was talking about. And most likely she did, considering who her boss and her boss's husband were, as well as her own apparent background of at least knowing about shifters.

Shifters other than those in Alpha Force also sometimes attempted to develop their own formulas to help them change when they wanted to. Even some members of Alpha Force besides Drew, including second in command Captain Patrick Worley, and Lieutenant Simon Parran, had brought their own versions when they had joined the unique military unit, or so Liam had heard.

Rosa might have known something about that even before joining this clinic as a veterinarian.

Liam, though, hadn't brought anything like an elixir

with him when he'd joined the unit. As always, he'd been focused on his technological skills. He had been online when he'd first learned such stuff actually existed, beyond the stories and legends, and so did a special, covert military unit that used it.

That was how he had learned about Alpha Force, and the rumors about what and where it was. Why he had shown up at Ft. Lukman one day with a résumé in hand, and had asked to speak with the officer in charge, who happened to be Drew.

Drew had apparently been as impressed by him and his techie skills as Liam had been impressed by Alpha Force. The result had been Liam enlisting and joining the unit—and being taught and mentored by the man before him, the shifter who now couldn't shift back.

Liam had to figure out how to help him, by assisting the others working on the same problem to succeed or otherwise.

"Well, it would be easier if I could report back to the rest of the gang that you admitted to drinking something besides, or in addition to, our regular elixir," Liam said, pursing his lips a bit. "But I know they're all trying hard, without knowing what they're looking for, to research how this could happen."

"I'm trying, in my own way, too," Rosa said, standing again. "I gave him a brief physical before, but would like to do more now, although under these circumstances I'm not sure a regular veterinarian, even with some knowledge of shifters, can help."

"But we appreciate your trying." Liam also rose and looked at her. This, at least, was a different angle. "What do you want to do?"

"A blood test, for one thing. And I'd like to take a closer look at Drew's body to see if there's something visible, a cut or growth beneath his fur...anything that may be different. Maybe an X-ray, too."

"Great," Liam said. "I'll help."

Drew appeared to be okay with it as well, since he just stayed limp on the table, which Rosa adjusted to be closer to her waist level. She did the exam first, saying she would draw blood when they were done, then take it into the clinic's lab to analyze.

"Many vets send blood out to a specialized laboratory for analysis," she told Liam. "But with this kind of patient I've learned to conduct the analyses myself. It's safer that way."

Liam wanted to hug this attractive, smart, careful vet, but of course he didn't.

Instead, he helped her work with Drew, moving him on the table so she could use her stethoscope to check his heartbeat—normal for a canine, she indicated. Also to feel his chest, his limbs, his back, his skin, seeking any kind of lump or other abnormality, but she found none.

With Liam's help—and also that of Brendan, the vet tech he had seen in the hall before—they moved Drew into another room where the X-ray equipment was kept, but once again nothing unusual was discovered.

Brendan took charge of the move back to the same exam room. There were others in the hall then, including a woman also dressed in blue scrubs like Brendan, whom Liam assumed was the other vet tech Brendan had mentioned before.

Melanie, too, came into the hall just as Brendan got Drew inside the room. "How is he doing?" she asked in a thick voice.

Rosa, who'd been following them, said, "We haven't found anything yet. He seems tired at times but he—" her voice lowered "—he seems to know what's going on and communicates with us when we ask questions."

"That's good," Melanie said. "I just wish…" She didn't finish, but instead hurried away from them, down the empty hall.

Liam looked into Rosa's lovely brown eyes. She looked sad. No, worse, tormented. He had another urge to hug her in empathy. Better yet, to come up with an immediate answer.

He did neither. But he also didn't look away from her.

Odd, but he felt they'd somehow bonded over this difficult situation. They both wanted to resolve it. Fast. For similar, but not identical reasons.

Alpha Force needed Drew back the way he was. And Liam needed his friend and commanding officer.

His wife, head vet at this place and Rosa's employer, mother of Drew's daughter and son, undoubtedly needed him most of all.

Brendan came out the exam room door. "Okay, he's situated on the table again. He looks tired."

Rosa immediately pulled her anguished gaze away from him and Liam felt a pang of…sorrow? "Thanks, Brendan. I'm going to draw some blood now."

Which was what she did, after entering the room again accompanied by Liam, who helped to keep Drew resting despite the prick of the needle.

But there wasn't a lot he needed to do. Drew appeared exhausted.

What was wrong with him?

And how were they going to fix whatever it was?

Chapter 3

In a way, Rosa appreciated the break from hanging out with Drew and using her veterinary skills to watch over him for any illness symptoms that the wolf he was now might evince.

She was of course happy about his apparent understanding of what she, and other people, were saying. That tended to be true with shifters she'd had as occasional patients around here, unlike before she moved here, when the shifters turned fully into the animals they were. And despite his apparent exhaustion, Drew seemed to be doing all right.

But of course he wasn't.

So, after drawing his blood using a needle, she said, "I'll be back soon. I need to analyze this." She waved the tube containing the red liquid just slightly. She felt sure that both Drew and Liam understood what she meant even without saying so.

But notwithstanding the pressure caused by her worry, she felt even more concerned as she left the room. Drew was her patient, and as a veterinarian she was always anxious about her patients, who generally couldn't tell her what their ailments were.

In Drew's case, she might not know all he was feeling, but she knew what his most important condition was.

Plus, oddly, she felt a bit apprehensive about walking away from Liam at the moment. Not because she thought leaving him with Drew was inappropriate in the least. But she recognized that, in the short time since she had first met him, she was relying on him to at least acknowledge, and possibly approve, what she was doing with his commanding officer to make him well.

"Ridiculous," she muttered, as she reached the door to the lab, next to the room where Drew's X-rays had been taken. She was the vet. Liam just worked—and shifted—with her patient.

Yeah, and probably had more knowledge than she did about how to deal with this situation. But Rosa would do all she could.

As she'd told Liam, if blood work was needed for most patients of the vet clinic, they sent the sample to a nearby lab for analysis. But the blood of shifters in wolf form was different from that of other canines.

Rosa had learned those differences where she had first obtained her veterinary license and begun practicing, in an area of Michigan where wolves of both types were prevalent.

That was one of many reasons why she had fit in when Melanie had conducted a hunt for the right type of vet—one with knowledge of what, in shifters, remained the same and what didn't.

Not that Rosa was a doctor for humans, but from what she understood, shifters' blood and other characteristics remained the same as other people's when they weren't shifted.

Now, as she entered the lab, someone was already in there: Dina, the clinic's other vet tech besides Brendan. "Hi, Rosa," she said. "Anything I can do for you here?"

"Not now, thanks," she responded to the short young woman in the typical blue scrubs.

"Let me know if that changes. I just checked out the discharge from a wound of one of our canine patients. Fortunately, the bacterial count was low."

"Great," Rosa said, as Dina left the room.

Sometimes Rosa did have one of the techs handle the blood work, often preparing it to be sent to the official lab. Other times they analyzed other kinds of liquids or discharges from the animals.

But the very rare times there were samples from shifters in animal form, either Melanie or Rosa handled it herself.

Not that the techs or other people who worked here didn't know, or at least suspect, that some of the patients were not exactly regular pets. Still, though they talked about it a little, everyone around here seemed to understand the need for tact and confidentiality. Now, at least. Rosa had heard that there were some rumors after Melanie had taken over this clinic, as a result of the death of the former veterinarians—parents of one of the officers at Ft. Lukman, Captain Patrick Worley, who happened to be a shifter.

Not wanting any interruptions, after placing the

tube of blood carefully on the table, Rosa locked the door and muted her phone.

She then washed her hands carefully once more, as she'd done before extracting the sample.

Finally, using a microscope and other appropriate equipment, she began the process of analyzing the contents of the sample, including the red blood cell count and the blood type. As anticipated, both were quite different from a normal canine's—even though canines had more blood types than humans did.

But there was more that she didn't anticipate. She had done only a few analyses of shifters' blood, since they generally remained in shifted form for only a short while. She figured that those around here might have extra chemicals in their blood thanks to their imbibing the elixir to help them with their shift.

That didn't explain, though, the additional contents in Drew's sample. Stuff she couldn't really analyze. It seemed a darker red than usual, somewhat thicker than the blood cells surrounding it.

She was knowledgeable but not an expert in chemistry, and what she saw might mean nothing.

But she realized that, whatever it was, this might be the evidence of whatever was keeping Drew in his shifted form.

She needed someone else to check it out, though. Someone more skilled in this than she was.

She placed the samples into airtight containers for now. Then she hurried back to the exam room that contained Drew—and Liam.

She slipped in without knocking, which was a good thing. Drew was asleep.

Liam had his smartphone in his hands and seemed

to be concentrating as he typed something into it. He heard her, though. He probably would have even with normal ears, not just those of a shifter in human form. He looked at her right away.

She gestured for him to follow her, which he did after aiming a glance in Drew's direction. Evidently he thought all was well, since soon they were out in the hall together with the door shut.

Fortunately, the hall was empty. Rosa looked up at Liam, into his face. Her concern must have been written on hers since his handsome masculine features tightened into a frown. "What's wrong?" he asked quietly.

"I guess my worry is obvious." She kept her voice low, too. "Are any of your Alpha Force people experts in chemistry? I assume they are because of putting together your elixir, right?"

"I think so, but since that's not my area I can't tell you much. Why? Is there something wrong with Drew's blood?"

The guy was apparently smart and astute. But then again, he'd known she had drawn blood and gone off to try to analyze it.

"I'm not sure, but there's something different about it. I still don't want to send it to the standard outside places, so I wonder if anyone at your base could take a look and figure it out."

"Let me check." He walked to the closest end of the hall, which was a good thing, since Melanie exited one of the exam rooms, and a couple followed her, the man holding the leash of a good-sized boxer. Melanie aimed a quizzical glance in Rosa's direction, and Rosa just smiled back.

She didn't have anything to tell Melanie except to report her question.

When she turned back, Liam was just pressing a button on his phone, evidently ending a quick call. "Yes, a couple of our guys, Jonas Truro in particular, may be able to help. Let me take the sample you have to him. I've already got Sergeant Noel Chuma, one of the Alpha Force aides, on his way to relieve me here." He looked up, over Rosa's shoulder.

Rosa realized she must have looked worried to Melanie, or maybe her boss was just curious—or wanted to see her shifted husband. But from behind her she heard, also in a soft voice, "What's going on? Why are you both out here?"

She didn't want to alarm Melanie—or give her false hope that they were about to find any answers. Turning, she said, "I just need a little advice about Drew's blood test. And Liam checked and found that some of the guys out at the base might be able to help. Unless you'd rather I didn't do it…"

"No, I'd rather you do it. How is Drew?"

"Sleeping," Liam said. "But I think we need to wake him up, at least briefly. My contact said to bring the samples you already have, Rosa, but also another one that hasn't been separated or analyzed at all."

"Fine," Melanie said. "I'll go in with you while you draw that sample and wait with Drew till Noel arrives." She looked pale, but the expression on her face appeared…well, a little hopeful, if Rosa was reading it right.

"Good," she said. "And I'm going to the base, too, to talk to your guys there." She looked at Liam, half expecting him to object.

"That'll work," he said. In fact, was that a touch of relief on his face? Admiration? Or was she reading too much into it? "You can tell them what you found and your take on it, and they can do their own kind of analysis."

"Good," she said again. "Now, let's go get that other sample."

Liam wanted more information about blood tests in general, and this one in particular.

At least that was the reason he gave himself, and Rosa, as he told her he would drive her to the base and back.

He had no other reason to be alone in this smart vet's presence for the twenty minute trip to Ft. Lukman, or the return trip. She could drive herself, of course.

But she seemed okay with the idea of riding in his black military-issued sedan. Maybe she wanted to talk more about the blood test. Or maybe she felt uncomfortable with the idea of appearing by herself at the military facility.

Or maybe he was reading things into her attitude.

They were on their way now, just exiting the town of Mary Glen on the way to Ft. Lukman. The distance was only about five miles, but it always felt longer, thanks to the two-lane roads lined by tall trees of the surrounding woods.

Liam figured the site of the military base, with its particularly covert unit, had been chosen because of the obscure location.

"So you said you're not a shifter," he began, aiming a brief glance at her in the passenger seat, a box containing the carefully wrapped blood samples on her

lap. That statement didn't address the blood tests—
but he'd get there. He had other questions he hoped to
get answered first.

Their eyes met for an instant before he looked back
toward the road. The grin on her face looked wary.
Even so, she was still one pretty lady.

"No," she said, "I'm not. But where I grew up in
Michigan there were quite a few wolves, and I learned
early on that a few of my school friends and their families happened to be shifters. The existence of real
wolves in that area gave them a bit of cover."

"Makes sense. My family lived in Minnesota for
the same reason. But not being a shifter yourself, how
did you end up learning that your friends were?" All
the shifters he knew were taught from a young age to
keep that critical fact to themselves.

"Well, I always wanted to become a veterinarian.
I love animals. I always had a dog or two, visited the
nearest zoo a lot and—well, I realized at a fairly young
age that I heard more wolf howls in the distance on
nights of the full moon than otherwise." She leaned
toward him a little. "Did you howl then as you were
growing up? Turned out my friends did. One of them,
a guy I guess I had a crush on in seventh grade, hinted
to me about where to show up at sundown on one of
those special nights. He knew I was there, hiding behind a tree, when his family and a couple of others
went out into the forest together. It was really amazing to watch when the four of them went from being
a regular human family to a small pack of wolves.
I never forgot it, of course, though that guy stopped
talking to me. Guess his family caught my scent and
bawled him out."

"But you knew then," Liam stated. He couldn't help smiling. It must have been quite an experience for a young non-shifter.

"I knew then," she confirmed. "I hardly ever talked about it—but I just happened to snoop around on more nights of the full moon and saw that a few other friends shared that characteristic."

"And did they stop talking to you, too?"

"I tried to be a lot more careful. If they knew about me, they never said so, and I never said anything to them, either."

"But you still wanted to help them as a vet?"

"Sure. When I went to veterinary school I made sure to learn about all canine anatomy as well as volunteering to help the vets who worked with the local zoo. And then, as I learned enough to help, I visited that first guy's mother one day—he was off at a different college by then—and told her what I knew about them, and how I was learning a lot about working with feral creatures like wolves, in case anyone needed medical help while shifted. She pretended not to know what I was talking about, but—"

"But sometime near then she called on you in her wolf form to come help another shifter who needed medical help that night, right?"

"Exactly."

Liam could hear her big smile in the tone of her voice. He looked over and grinned back at her. "And from then on they knew you were there to help."

"Yes, I was. I helped them and myself, and they were the ones to give recommendations about me to Melanie when she put word out—very discreetly, I might add—about how she was a regular veterinarian with…interesting contacts who sometimes needed medical assistance. Since the shifters around me made a point of not admitting their true nature, I thought that the type of organization Melanie hinted about—the US military, of all things—might be a fascinating group of potential patients."

As he was growing up, Liam had known a couple local people who seemed to recognize what he, his family members and others in the area were, but although they were mostly polite, they didn't attempt to get to know any shifters better.

He was impressed with this lovely lady who not only accepted the idea of shifters in her life, but actually seemed to appreciate them. Worry about them. Want to heal them.

"I'm sure Melanie is really glad to have your help," he told her, then shared a brief smile with her before he made another turn on the twisty road.

"And I'm really glad to help her. And the others." A tone he didn't quite recognize modified Rosa's voice.

"Especially Drew," Liam guessed.

"Especially Drew," she agreed. "But…I just hope we really can help him."

"We will," Liam asserted—hoping it was true.

Chapter 4

Even though Liam had asked her to ride with him so he could ask questions about blood and blood types, Rosa was somewhat amused that they never really got into that topic much. And when they did, all she needed to do was go over a bit of what she had already been thinking about.

Yes, she told him when he finally asked, the blood types of people and regular canines had differences. So did the blood types of wolves in general from shifted wolves. People and their unshifted counterparts, not so much.

And the differences she saw from the blood she had drawn from Drew? Well, she didn't exactly know what they were, except for the odd consistency and darker coloration. That was why she hoped for someone else's advice.

She didn't let him know how concerned she really was, although since she was looking for guidance he probably gathered that.

Would those at Ft. Lukman know whether that blood issue was the cause of Drew's not changing back? If so, would they know how to fix it?

Liam didn't seem inclined to talk much more about it, which was fine with her. It allowed her to avoid revealing how inadequate she felt, and instead gave her time to ask him about what he did as a technology expert for Alpha Force.

That got him going immediately—and what he had to say about the online claims worried her, too, as someone who had friends and patients around here who were shifters.

Sure, she had met actual shifters at home when she was young. She had also seen sites on the internet, mostly blogs or social media posts, that speculated whether there actually were such things as shapeshifters, as depicted in horror movies and otherwise. Sometimes people claimed to have seen the real thing, and maybe, like her, they had.

She had even found some references to oddities that had allegedly gone on here in Mary Glen a while back. But she'd also seen posts about how all that got resolved when it was discovered that one member of an offbeat group of people who claimed shapeshifters exist had made unsubstantiated claims for his own benefit. Discovering who it was and stopping him had helped quiet things down in this area—at least as far as the rest of the world was likely to know.

But what Liam was describing could be a lot worse for the ongoing peace of shapeshifters—and Alpha

Force in particular. Rosa now lived near downtown Mary Glen, not far from the vet clinic. She had heard nothing at all regarding the claims Liam described about how shifters around here, under the last full moon, had hurt some regular people in this area—badly.

Neither had Liam, he assured her. It was simply untrue.

And it was his job to make sure that anyone who saw those ridiculous posts didn't believe a word.

He'd already checked on how his aide, Denny, had started dealing with the situation, and believed he was doing a good job. But Liam would take over himself later that evening.

After driving through the thick woodlands, they finally arrived at the gate to the military base. Even Liam had to provide his ID to the guards despite being stationed there, and of course Rosa had to provide hers, as well. Then Liam drove across the base to a building she had visited once before to check on an injured animal Melanie had explained was a cover dog, resembling one of the shifters in canine form.

Most of the time, those cover dogs that needed shots or exams were brought to the veterinary clinic, like all other pets in the Mary Glen area. That was how Rosa got to meet and treat them.

However, they'd chosen not to move that dog, Spike—Seth Ambers's cover dog—without getting him treatment first. Fortunately, though he'd been bleeding profusely, he'd had nothing worse than a fairly minor cut from a broken bottle he'd stepped on.

When Rosa had arrived, Spike was in a special fenced pen by himself in the upstairs area where the cover dogs were housed when not on duty, his leg bandaged, and one of the aides continuously changing the dressing. Rosa had been able to follow Drew as he carried Spike downstairs to what he'd referred to as the base's primary lab area, where she'd been able to snip off fur from around the cut, wash it well, soak it with disinfectant and wrap it in sterile bandages after providing topical anesthetic, a few stitches and a larger cover bandage and temporary cone collar to make sure he didn't chew too close to it. He'd healed just fine.

The poor dog's injury had given Rosa not only the opportunity to see part of the military facility that housed the amazing Alpha Force, but also to increase her already good reputation, thanks to Melanie's verbal recognition of what Rosa additionally did to help those shifters who needed medical assistance while in their animal forms.

Liam parked his car and used a key card to get them both inside the building. The guy was either a gentleman or he didn't trust her not to drop the critically important box containing Drew's blood samples, since he carried it inside. He then led her to the stairway to the area where Rosa knew the labs, and some offices, were located. He unlocked that door and she followed him downstairs.

A lot, maybe all, of the members of Alpha Force were gathered in a room past the labs where Rosa had been before.

"This is Drew's office in this building," Liam told her, "although he's got another one in the main admin building at the other side of the base."

It wasn't a large room, but there were many chairs in rows facing the desk, all occupied. Rosa recognized a few of the people there who'd sometimes brought their cover animals to the vet clinic or had come to visit Drew and Melanie in their home next door.

Even so, Liam introduced her to them all—and most important to her now were Captain Patrick Worley and Captain Jonas Truro, whom she'd already met. They were both medical doctors, but only Patrick was a shifter.

Then there was Lieutenant Seth Ambers, also a doctor, Staff Sergeant Jason Connell, who was Drew's cousin as well as a member of Alpha Force, aides including Staff Sergeants Ruby Belmont, Piers Janus, and more. Rosa hoped she would remember names, but even if she didn't right away, she would try to have as good a relationship as possible with all of them, easiest if a solution was found quickly for Drew's problem.

When he was done with the introductions, Liam told Rosa to join him standing behind Drew's desk facing the group. "Rosa has come here to give a rundown, especially to everyone who's a medical doctor, regarding what she found when she conducted Drew's blood test. I've mentioned that to some of you." He gestured toward the box they'd brought, which now rested on Drew's desk.

Rosa wondered if the entire group needed to hear this, since she figured only a few would know anything about blood and blood tests and the different blood types of regular people and shifters and all. But considering the fascinated and concerned way they stared at her, she assumed they were all highly worried about their commanding officer and what was going on with him. They wanted him back, as normal for his type as he'd been before.

Plus some of them were shifters, too, and would want to ensure, if possible, that the same thing didn't happen with them. And fellow Alpha Force members who were aides would need to know how to help the shifters they worked for.

So, yes, for their own reasons they all needed to be there.

She first described how she had been put in charge of Major Connell by the head veterinarian at the clinic—his wife. "Melanie did her own exam first, of course, and I've been keeping her up-to-date. But I'm sure it was hard on her to have to check out poor Drew in this situation."

Rosa then talked about how she had examined Drew, had kept him under her care, had looked for any abnormalities in his canine form—and had, of course, taken a blood test.

"I don't know that I need to get into much detail here," she told the group. "I did find what appears to be some irregularity in the consistency and color of the fluid and, not being a chemist beyond the skills needed to be a damn good veterinarian—" she smiled a bit sadly at that, realizing that her own fears of inadequacy were showing in her irony "—I wanted to see if anyone here could help analyze Drew's blood and determine if it's the cause, or an indication, of what's going on with him."

"We'll take a look." Patrick was the first to stand, then Jonas did. "Come into the lab area with us, Rosa, and we'll start checking things out, okay?"

"Of course."

She glanced toward Liam, who nodded. He apparently wasn't joining them, but he was her ride back to town. She suspected she'd be able to find another one, though, if necessary.

Patrick picked up the box. She wasn't surprised when Seth joined them. It wouldn't hurt to have all the doctors who knew human patients' traits getting involved, or at least that's what she surmised.

Patrick led Rosa next door to the lab areas, where he asked Seth to start the analysis process, getting slides ready for the microscope and more.

"We really appreciate this," Patrick said, standing with Rosa in the middle of the main room, which was lined with shiny metal cabinets with glass doors. Some had equipment on top—a lot of microscopes, for one thing.

Patrick was a tall guy, dressed in camos like all the people around here but Rosa. His hair was light and short, his face long and nice looking, with a cleft in his chin.

He didn't resemble Liam except for his height and outfit—and for an instant Rosa missed Liam's presence. Ridiculous.

"I appreciate it, too," she said to Patrick. "I just hope you can figure this out."

"I'm sure you know we want to," he replied. Seth was already removing the various vials of blood from the padding in the box. Rosa had labeled them with the time collected and whether she had done anything to attempt to examine each particular sample, so she figured they at least wouldn't have any questions about that.

But what they all really needed was answers.

She hung out in the lab for a while, mostly watching the others, listening to them discuss what to do next.

Then Patrick said, "You know, Rosa, this is going to take a while. Why don't you go back to your clinic, and we'll let you know what we find, okay?"

In other words, her staring wasn't making them go faster, but might be causing them some discomfort.

She didn't want that. Besides, back at the clinic she'd be able to bring Melanie up-to-date, such as it was with no answers so far, and maybe do something helpful there before the day ended. "Sounds good," she said.

She just hoped that Liam was ready to leave.

Liam was champing at the bit.

He had gone to his own office, upstairs in another part of the building, but only briefly to check on how Denny was doing.

He'd promised to return Rosa to town, and though he figured he could get someone else to do it, he wanted to be the one.

He also wanted to get on his own computer and get busy doing his own thing to start fixing all the absurd and detrimental rumors.

"Here's what I've done," Denny had told him, and good guy that he was, Liam's aide had followed his prior instructions and started with one of the social media sites where the posts were among the most awful and accusatory against shapeshifters the night before, including an unnamed military group containing shifters. Oddly, as Liam had previously noted, a few had signed their posts with the names of Greek or Roman gods, like Zeus, Hera, Orion, Diana and Poseidon, and even Cerberus, the three-headed dog. They could be a group of anti-shifters, or just one person pretending to be a bunch. Which frustrated Liam. He hadn't had the time to start figuring that out yet.

Still, Denny had used one of his own fake identities to make fun of the stupid stuff. That needed to be started even before they attempted to figure out the sources of those posts.

"Good job," Liam had told him, making his short, young helper grin widely.

"Thanks. You want to take over?"

"Soon," Liam assured him. "Meantime, keep up the good work."

He returned to Drew's office, where some of his fellow Alpha Forcers remained. Could he text Rosa to see how much longer she'd be? He felt a duty to do as he'd promised her.

He also felt eager to see her again, and not entirely to get her update on what the others were doing to assess Drew's weird blood.

He was delighted when she came back almost immediately after his reappearance. "They're working on it now," she told Liam and the others in the room. "Not much I can do to help, so do you think…" She looked at Liam, who just nodded, reading the question in her eyes.

"Yep," he said. "I'll take you back to the clinic now. Right?"

"Thanks." She smiled at him.

He got a promise from the clearly worried Jason that he'd keep Liam informed about anything the doctors found and revealed about his cousin Drew's bad blood. Then he told Rosa, "I've a stop to make before we leave."

"Oh. Okay." The way she looked at him, he assumed she thought he meant the restroom.

"Pit stop first is fine," he agreed, "but that's not what I meant."

In a few minutes, he met her to go upstairs. Instead of heading for the door out of the building, he turned and said, "Time for some cover dog attention."

"Really?" She sounded delighted. "Then you're going to get yours?"

"Yep, that's my Chase."

"Is Spike there, too?"

He knew that was Seth's dog. "Sure. That's right— you took care of his wound, didn't you? I've heard a lot about it."

"He's still okay, isn't he?"

"He sure is."

They'd reached the door to the large room where the cover dogs were in enclosures. For fun, Liam let out a brief howl as if he was shifted, and several of those inside responded in kind. He grinned at Rosa's pleased smile.

"Gee, these guys sound a lot like wolves," she said, "and so do you."

"I wonder why."

He asked her to wait outside while he went in for Chase. She agreed, but asked to peek in the door and see all the canines hanging out there behind the low fences.

When he returned with Chase, her smile was even broader.

"So this is how you look when you shift?" she asked.

"Yep, that's me—or close enough to me for now." He asked what she knew about cover animals. From what she told him, Rosa had already learned from Melanie that the shifters in Alpha Force all had cover animals who resembled them when they were shifted. That way, if a non-shifter happened to see them while they were in shifted form and claim they must be werewolves or whatever, they could later bring out their cover animal—mostly wolves here at Ft. Lukman these days—show the non-shifter, and tell them they'd simply seen the Alpha Force member's pet. That seemed to work well, Liam thought, since Alpha Force members didn't need to wait till a full moon to shift.

Now Rosa and Liam walked outside toward his car, then into the warmth of the midday air, and he soon tethered Chase in the back seat. His look-alike cover dog-wolf sat up and looked around expectantly. Chase always enjoyed attention and was probably eager to see what the rest of the day held in store for him.

There'd be one stop he might enjoy. After they dropped Rosa off at the vet clinic, Liam had promised a visit to his family in town—his brother, Chuck, and sister-in-law, Carleen. They had moved from Minnesota to Mary Glen just a few months ago and bought an existing restaurant that was a franchise for the Fastest Foods chain, planning to stay here a while.

That was the result of Liam learning about a possible experiment that would involve allowing limited individuals related to Alpha Force team members to occasionally use the elixir on nights of a full moon, with results to be examined by the unit. Those people had to be shifters, close in both relationship and distance, although if all went well, the program might be expanded.

Liam's family were shifters like him, and were

eager to have more access to the elixir. That's why they had considered their move here worth it, even if they wound up only being closer to Liam. But of course they hoped things went better than that—and they had, at least somewhat. His family members had been allowed to use the elixir once now, during this most recent full moon, as part of the experiment. And more? That remained to be seen, but the ongoing experiment might help.

Liam had received a text message from Chuck a short while ago, as he waited for Rosa. He hadn't seen his family since their shift last night, nor had he had a chance to speak with the Alpha Force member who'd acted as their temporary aide for the occasion, Sergeant Kristine Parran. Though he'd talked to them briefly on his way downtown before, and they'd sounded thrilled, he wanted to know more about how it all went, and apparently they wanted to talk to him, too. But he couldn't stay long at the restaurant.

So first he'd take Rosa back to the veterinary hospital and dash in with her to see how Drew was doing. Then he'd stop to see family—quickly.

And finally, he would fulfill his obligation—and do what he really wanted to. He'd hurry back here to get on the computer at last.

As Liam pulled his car past the base's front gate and onto the road secluded by trees, Rosa took her phone from her purse and looked at it. "I was hoping to get a call right away saying they'd figured out how to help Drew."

"That would be a nice thing." He looked at her briefly and nodded. And had an idea.

He could easily drive past the restaurant on the way

to the clinic. That would give him a great excuse to keep his visit quick. He trusted Denny, but the aide was too new at this to fully accomplish what Liam needed to do. If he stopped with Rosa to buy a fast-food burger and coffee—and ask in more detail how his family had enjoyed last night—he could leave quickly to return Rosa to her clinic.

Besides, he would get to stay in her presence just a little longer. That wasn't important, of course—no matter how much he knew he'd enjoy it. But the idea seemed to work well in all ways.

"I'd like to stop to pick up a meal to go, from the Fastest Foods shop," he told Rosa. "My treat, if you'd like anything."

The look she shot at him was one of surprise. "Good idea," she said. "You don't have to treat, but I'll pick up a few things for the clinic staff...and also get Drew a burger to help keep his spirits up."

"Good idea," he said in turn. "We'll be there soon." Then he had to ask. "Did you get a sense that my superior officers knew what they were doing when it came to analyzing Drew's blood and determining if that had anything to do with his non-shifting?"

"I liked those guys," she hedged. "And I'm hopeful...but not sure. I just wish there was more I could do."

He hated to hear the sad tone in her voice, and to see the dejection in her expression when he managed another glance toward her.

"I've got a feeling," he said to cheer her up, "that there is more you can do, and you'll figure it out."

He looked at her again briefly as she shifted in her

seat. "Really? I can't make any promises, but I sure hope you're right."

Me, too, he thought, then made the turn from the woodsy road into town.

And if she figured it out—well, that would give him a good excuse to kiss those now happily smiling lips of hers in thanks.

Chapter 5

"There we are." From the driver's seat beside Rosa, Liam pointed just ahead along one of the town's main streets. Sure enough, a familiar large neon sign that resembled those in lots of other locations jutted over the sidewalk: Fastest Foods.

"Yes," Rosa agreed, trying to sound excited. And to her surprise, she was—a little.

A stop for a meal?

After all that had gone on today, Rosa wasn't really hungry, but the stop would give her a little more time in Liam's presence. Despite being in the same places a lot that day, they really hadn't spent much time together.

On the other hand, she barely knew the guy. Plus he happened to be a shifter. Not that she disliked shifters.

Quite the contrary…but she certainly couldn't be attracted to one, no matter how caring and sympathetic he happened to be about his commanding officer's medical—or whatever—problem.

The restaurant stood alone in the middle of a sizable parking lot that also had a drive-through line. "Are we going to go through there?" Rosa pointed toward the stream of cars slowly inching forward.

"No, we'll go inside, though we'll order takeout."

He fortunately found a parking spot right away in the busy lot and opened his door. Rosa opened hers, too, and hopped out. "I assume you'll roll down the back windows a bit for Chase," she said, looking into the back seat at the wolflike dog, who was now sitting up, panting a bit. Fortunately, the outside air was cool.

"No need," Liam said. "He'll come in with us."

"Into the restaurant? Is that allowed?"

"Of course. He's a soldier dog—and he's also kind of my service dog." Liam's grin, as he stood beside her near the car on the black paved surface of the lot, seemed proud.

"Oh. Okay." Rosa loved dogs, and other animals, enough that she wished they were all allowed into all restaurants and other places that served people.

Of course, shapeshifters were allowed anywhere—as long as they were in human form, as Liam was now.

And Rosa realized it was okay to bring Chase, too, when they walked in the door of the crowded, noisy restaurant and Liam was greeted right away by the people who seemed in charge.

A guy who'd been behind the service counter came out the door beside it and hustled toward Liam. They shook hands, then hugged each other. Was he a relative? The guy was about Liam's height, with similarly dark hair and angular features. He wasn't in a camo uniform, of course, but a blue denim shirt and jeans, with a white apron on top.

He looked down then and grinned at Chase, leashed beside Liam. "Can't pet him, bro, though I know he's family. You know that's why we keep our Louper out back, too, when he's here."

"Right. Not sanitary when you're on duty. But let me introduce you to someone." Liam turned toward Rosa and gestured for her to join them.

As she did, a woman who'd been cleaning tables in the busy place dashed over. She was dressed similarly to the man who'd hugged Liam. She was slender, with long, silver-blond hair pulled into a clip at the back of her head, a very attractive woman—who also hugged Liam.

Rosa knew she shouldn't feel jealous about that—especially when she looked down and saw a ring on the woman's finger.

"So good to see you, Liam," the woman said.

"I'll say," said the man.

Liam once more looked at Rosa. "I want to introduce you both to someone I'll bet you'll be very happy to know one of these days. This is Dr. Rosa Jontay, one of the town's veterinarians. Rosa, this is my brother, Chuck, and his wife, Carleen. They own this place now—and they're also owned by Louper, a dog who stays either in the enclosed backyard behind this place, or at home. He's home today with a dog walker visiting him. Louper resembles Chase."

Liam looked at her and grinned, and she read in his look the fact that these two people were also shifters who happened to have a cover dog, even though they weren't military.

"Very nice to meet you." She shook hands first with Carleen, then Chuck. "And I would be delighted to meet your dog sometime when he's here or otherwise, though I hope he has no need of a vet."

"My sentiments exactly," Carleen said. "Now, you two come over here and sit down, and we'll get you something to eat."

"Oh, but—" Rosa began, but fortunately, Liam took over.

"We just need some takeout right now," he said. "Rosa's going to get some extra stuff for some of her veterinary staff, and she needs to get back to her clinic."

"Great," Carleen said. "We'll get our staff moving on it right away. Just let them know at the counter what you want."

There were several people ahead of them in the line, and Rosa didn't want to butt in. "We'll take our time," she said. "But thanks."

Liam nodded his agreement, though he said, "It helps to be related to the owners when you're in a hurry. I agree with being polite to their customers, though. And if you don't mind standing here a few minutes to hold our place, I'd appreciate it. I've something to ask Chuck."

"Fine," Rosa said, and agreed to keep Chase with her. She watched Liam talking to his brother by the wall nearest the door into the order area and kitchen. It was one of the few times she wished she had a shifter's abilities—not to shift, but to hear things better than a normal person. The two brothers seemed to be talking animatedly, and she was curious about what they were saying.

The teenage guy at the front of the line stepped aside after placing his order. Rosa was glad to move ahead a little, particularly for the sake of the animals that might be needing her care back at the clinic.

Including, perhaps, Drew. She'd at least check on him, no matter what Melanie and the Alpha Force guy who'd taken over for Liam said about how he was doing—though she'd be absolutely delighted if he'd changed back during their absence.

Unlikely, though, or Melanie would have called her.

At least now there were only three more people ahead of her in line, and two appeared to be a couple. Rosa bent and patted Chase's head. The dog was definitely behaving well, leashed at her side.

Liam rejoined her. "Everything okay?" she asked.

"Real good," he responded, without more detail. In fact, he was quiet for a while.

"How long have your relatives owned this place?" Rosa asked finally, to make conversation. Besides, she was interested in his answer. "Did they follow you to Mary Glen?"

And did they want to become members of Alpha Force? she wondered. She figured that a lot of shifters might want to do so if they knew of the reality of Alpha Force, and its special elixir. With their relative, Liam, now a member, she had no doubt that Chuck and Carleen were well aware of the nature of that military unit.

She'd ask Liam more about them later, as she couldn't here, in public.

"They've been here about four months," Liam said. "They bought this franchise from the former owners and just took over. And yes, they followed me here."

"Got it." She looked around again. The restaurant

was filled with customers—and with the aroma of grilled meat. Even she could smell it, and she figured it must be many times stronger to Liam, even in his human form. Or at least that's what she'd heard from shifters in her past—and now. They all had enhanced senses.

And of course Chase stuck his nose in the air and sniffed, off and on.

The next person moved out of their way in line. As they started to edge forward a woman rushed out the door from the kitchen and threw herself against Liam, giving him a huge hug. "Liam, so glad to see you," she exclaimed.

"Good to see you, too, Valerie," he said, although his not-so-inviting expression, and the way he moved back, suggested he was fibbing a bit.

Somehow, that made Rosa feel a bit better about the woman's highly effusive greeting. But who was Valerie?

She found out right away as Liam introduced them. "Rosa, this is Carleen's sister, Valerie. And Valerie, Rosa's one of Mary Glen's wonderful veterinarians."

Carleen's sister—a sort of sister-in-law to Liam. That made Rosa feel somewhat better, although since they weren't related by blood that connection wouldn't keep Liam from getting into a relationship with her.

But that wasn't Rosa's business, though he hadn't appeared to care about Valerie in that way.

Valerie resembled Carleen. Her silvery blond hair was shorter, though, and loose. She had deep brown eyes like her sister.

"Welcome to town," Rosa said, to be polite. "Do you work here, too?" She gestured around the restaurant.

"I do right now," the other woman said. "Look, you go ahead and place your orders, and then we can talk."

She must have said that because Liam and Rosa had finally reached the front of their line. But Rosa didn't want to take the time to talk to Valerie, and hoped Liam felt the same way.

Fortunately, Valerie disappeared, heading back into the kitchen—but then reappeared behind the counter, next to the guy who'd begun taking their order. She was the one to start entering things on the computer, and her counterpart, a twentysomething guy with a scruffy beard, didn't look exactly thrilled about the help.

Rosa wasn't surprised that Liam's order consisted of a double burger, rare—lots of red meat. She asked for several sandwiches, including burgers and a couple containing chicken. The one with the most beef she intended to provide to Drew in his canine form.

When they were done ordering, Rosa immediately handed her credit card to Valerie over the counter. She'd already gotten it out and didn't want to argue with Liam about it. She didn't even look at him and was glad when Valerie took it from her and began to ring up their order.

"I'll pay you back," Liam growled from beside her. She just waved in a neutral gesture. This was another thing not to get into a discussion about here.

Valerie soon handed them the plastic bags containing their food. "Come back anytime, Rosa," she said. "Bye, Chase. And Liam—when are we all getting together again? You know I'm only planning on being here for a fairly short while, so I'd really like us to see each other as often as possible while I'm in town."

"I'll talk to Chuck about it," Liam said.

"Talk to Chuck about what?" said a voice from behind Rosa. Liam's brother was there, maybe to say goodbye.

"Having a family get-together," Valerie replied. "Soon, I hope."

"Sounds good to me," Chuck responded. "We'll invite you over to our condo soon, bro. You, too, Rosa."

She couldn't help but cast a sideways glance toward Valerie to see what she thought about that invitation. Carleen's sister remained smiling, and it didn't appear forced.

Maybe Rosa was wrong about this woman flirting with her kind-of brother-in-law. Maybe she just intended to keep the family in contact as long as she did stay in town.

"Thanks," Rosa said, not committing to anything.

But somehow the idea of spending more friendly time with Liam, not related to veterinary or Alpha Force issues, sounded good.

For now, though, she was glad when Liam said goodbye to Chuck, then Carleen, who also joined them, and waved to Valerie behind the counter.

Time for them to get busy with everything they each needed to do for the rest of the day.

Liam refused to feel embarrassed or uncomfortable about the attention Valerie had leveled on him. The woman was attractive, sure. She was also a shifter, like her sister. She'd made it seem that flirting with him was second nature to her, though he had never encouraged it.

But he always remained friendly toward her. She was, after all, a member of his family.

"Nice people," Rosa said from beside him in the car. Behind them, Chase shifted in his seat, clearly wanting to get into the bags of food that sat on the floor near Rosa's feet.

"Of course they are," Liam said. "They're family."

"Like Chase?" Rosa wasn't exactly jesting. She'd told him she considered pet dogs to be family, and she assumed the relationship between a shifter and his cover dog had to be strong.

"Yeah, kind of. Chase and I are pretty damn close these days." Hearing his name, Chase sat back on the seat and made a low sound that made Liam laugh. "Glad you agree," he said.

As they continued on, Liam thought a bit about his brief discussion with Chuck. Yes, both he and Carleen had loved the way their shift went. Yes, the Alpha Force person who'd acted as their aide for the night had been just great: Sergeant Kristine Parran. The elixir had been amazing. As far as he knew, all had gone well from Alpha Force's perspective. And, yes, both Carleen and he would love to do it again. Soon.

Almost as if she read his thoughts, Rosa asked, "Are your brother and sister-in-law shifters, too?"

"Yes," he acknowledged.

"Do they get to use your elixir?"

Good and appropriate question, he thought. Without saying too much, he told her they were involved in an experiment being conducted by Alpha Force, in which they could be given occasional doses of the elixir on nights of a full moon.

He was glad that Rosa and he had reached the vet

clinic, since he didn't want to answer any further questions she might have. Liam parked along the street. He intended not to just let Rosa out of the car. He planned to go inside and check with Denny about how things were going. And most especially, he wanted to see for himself how Drew was doing.

He opened his car door at the same time Rosa opened hers. Her expression seemed to register surprise as she turned back to look at him. "I thought you were just dropping me off so you could get to work."

"Not till I check on Drew. Besides, we can wolf down our sandwiches together." He grinned at his own pun, and she laughed.

"Fair enough." She bent down to get the bags as Liam got out to leash Chase and let him out of the back seat.

As Rosa headed toward the clinic's rear door, bags in hand, Liam let his dog sniff the curb and driveway, and when he was ready, hurried him to the entrance.

The street had been fairly well lined with cars, so Liam wasn't surprised, as he entered the waiting room, to see a lot of people there with their pets—everything from an English sheepdog to a couple mewing kittens in carriers.

They all carried scents of their own.

Since he didn't see Rosa there, he figured he'd better let the receptionist behind the desk know he needed to catch up with the vet. But Susie, whom he'd met before, smiled and motioned Chase and him through the inner door.

Rosa approached him from down the hall. "I just put our food in the break room, but let's go check on Drew."

"Great." Liam followed her to the room where he had last seen his superior officer. Rosa opened the door, but motioned for him to enter first, which he did, Chase right behind him.

The place looked the same as before, with wolfen Drew sitting on the towel-covered top of the lowered table. With him, on one of the chairs against the wall, sat Staff Sergeant Noel Chuma, who was an aide to whichever Alpha Force shifter needed him.

And no one needed help now more than Drew.

Noel wasn't a big guy, but he was strong, smart and dedicated to Alpha Force. He rose, and the expression on his deep-toned face worried Liam.

He couldn't ask detailed questions now, though. Not in front of Drew.

"So, how's our patient doing?" Rosa asked. She approached Drew, who regarded her with stony eyes that, on some canines—whether shifters or not—would have made Liam worry that he was about to attack.

He knew Drew wouldn't do that. But Drew's expression did indicate that he wasn't happy.

That he probably didn't have a sense he'd be shifting back anytime soon—and it was getting to be late afternoon on the day he should have retaken his human form early in the morning.

"He's mostly been resting," Noel answered for him. "We've been for a couple of walks and he seemed happy enough to be out of this room, but, well—*happy* isn't the best word. I think he's really frustrated."

"Understandably," Liam said.

Drew made a growling sound that didn't seem threatening, but might've connoted frustration. It was enough to get Chase, who had sat beside Liam, to stand again and watch his sort-of counterpart.

"Tell you what," Liam said. "Drew, are you okay with being here on your own for a few minutes? Dr. Rosa and I brought lunch back and we need to sort it out, but one of us is going to bring you a really good burger very soon."

Drew answered by making a noise that this time sounded like a sigh, then lying back down.

He didn't seem overly excited about the late, tasty lunch he'd get.

And Liam could understand why.

Chapter 6

"I don't want to leave him alone for long," Rosa said quietly, once they were back in the hall with the door shut behind them. "But we do have a sandwich for you, too, Sergeant Chuma."

"Noel," he corrected. "And I'm sure you want to talk with me about our CO and what went on while you all were gone."

Rosa watched the two military guys trade glances. She figured Liam would hear a lot more than she would, but not while they were all together.

And she appreciated that the sergeant had come here, to ensure that Drew was nearly never alone. His condition was such that no one knew what needs he might have, or when he might have them. And he certainly wasn't in any condition to grab a smartphone and call for help.

They all headed the short distance along the hall to the break room. Rosa motioned for the others to enter first, glad to see that Brendan had just come into the hall, ushering a young woman with her standard poodle mix from another exam room. Rosa waited long enough for Brendan to ensure that his charges entered the reception area, where the owner could pay her bill and they could leave. But when Brendan turned again, Rosa was right beside him.

"Is Melanie in that room?" She gestured to the room he'd just come out of.

"Yes. Want me to get her for you?"

"Please."

Brendan once more went through that door, and almost immediately Melanie, in her white lab jacket, strode out and faced Rosa. "You're back. Do they have any answers yet at Ft. Lukman?"

"They're working on it. I gave them the blood samples and discussed what I'd seen, and my concerns. They got right on it, so hopefully they'll figure it out soon."

"Yes. Hopefully." Melanie's hair wasn't pulled back as neatly as usual. Her pretty face seemed to be aging minute by minute. Rosa just hoped she was providing adequate care to their patients, despite the stress she was under.

"Meantime," Rosa said brightly, "Liam came back here with me, but I assume he'll be leaving Noel here, since he has to get back to the base right away. Or almost right away. We brought a late lunch from Fastest Foods, a few sandwiches. That includes a really nice big, rare burger for Drew." Rosa made herself smile broadly, then motioned for her employer to follow her as Brendan reappeared in the hall, followed by a large man hugging a moderate-size golden cat.

She was glad when Melanie did as she hoped and joined her, Liam and Noel in the break room. Given a choice, Melanie picked out a chicken sandwich among those laid out on one of the tables in the middle of the room, as did Rosa. That left burgers for the guys.

Including the large one for Drew, which Liam was holding. "I'd like to go say hi to Drew, if that's okay with you," he said to Melanie. "I can give this to him then."

"Of course. And thank you both so much for bringing Drew a burger from Fastest Foods. It's one of his favorite places when...when..." Her voice started to drop off, and Rosa recognized her signs of sorrow.

"When he's not shifted," she finished brightly for Melanie. "And when he is shifted. I get it. Let's give him what we have now, and I promise that, when he's back to his unshifted self again, I'll go get him even more burgers there. Okay?"

She looked at Melanie's brave smile and almost broke down herself. Rosa had had a few relationships now and then, but hadn't met anyone she wanted to spend her life with. Melanie had, and she'd even gotten past whatever confusion she might have felt about falling hard for a shapeshifter.

She was clearly, deeply in love. And the man she loved was in distress. Ill. In the middle of a condition that no one knew anything about, so no one knew how to fix it. Fix him.

A wonderment about how she'd feel if Liam somehow became her veterinary patient flashed through Rosa. Ridiculous. Yes, she found him good-looking as a human. Kind. Sexy… No, she wasn't going there. She wasn't going anywhere with him, or with these ideas. She glanced at him, though—and saw that, for some reason, he was watching her.

She turned away and quickly stepped toward Melanie, then gave her a hug. "We'll figure it out," she promised, hoping she wasn't lying about something as important to her employer as that.

"I know," Melanie said hoarsely. "And thanks." She turned to where the two men stood behind her, eating their sandwiches. "And thanks to both of you, too."

"No problem," Liam said. "Noel, you said you'd give us a rundown of how Drew's been doing while you've been with him."

"Sure." The muscular guy chewed briefly, then described how things had been since he'd gone into the room. "Drew slept a lot. When he was awake, he seemed mostly comfortable but unhappy, getting off that table and pacing around the room, looking me in the face as if he wanted to tell me something, then shaking his head and lying down again. I wished I could understand what he wasn't saying."

Maybe this wasn't such a good idea, Rosa thought, even though it might be helpful in trying to figure out what was wrong with Drew, how he was reacting.

But how Melanie was reacting…that was hard. Sad.

For many reasons, they needed to get this all straightened out. Fast.

But what else could Rosa do?

She would continue pondering that till something came to her. Something useful—she hoped.

For now, though, she looked at the others and said,

"Great. Thanks, Noel. Now, let's all join Liam and go present Drew with his nice, meaty hamburger."

Liam, with Chase fastened in the back seat, was on his way back to the base—and felt somewhat bad about it.

Because he'd seen that his friend and mentor, his commanding officer, Drew, hadn't improved.

Because he was also leaving the woman he'd spent the last few intense hours with, attempting to help Drew—and becoming impressed with her tenacity and knowledge and caring. Not to mention her sexual appeal…

Enough. He needed to concentrate on the real issues. "Got it, Chase?" he called into the back seat, as if his dog would tell him to get his mind back on track.

He had seen most of his fellow shifting Alpha Forcers in their wolfen or other modes such as cougars and hawks while he was still human. They were always involved in training sessions and drills in both forms. Testing the elixir in its current standard mixture and in variations.

He'd been a member of Alpha Force for only about a year, but he knew that the brew of their special potion was always undergoing potential changes.

Fortunately, Drew, who'd been the originator of the elixir, was continuously thinking of ways to improve it, as had the others who'd come up with their own versions before joining the covert military unit. Drew and those others seemed always amenable to attempts to improve it even further.

But what would they do now, with Drew unable to even be human, let alone work to improve their elixir?

Liam was glad that wasn't his area of expertise. But he still wished he had answers.

Well, he hadn't any—but hopefully he would help Alpha Force get them. He'd received a call from Patrick earlier—and had agreed to be the subject of a test tomorrow night.

A test that involved shifting with a modified version of the elixir, in an attempt to help determine what had happened to Drew.

Liam had immediately agreed.

He also figured that the intensity of what was now going on with Alpha Force was likely to put at least a temporary halt to their experimenting with allowing family members to use the elixir sometimes during the full moon. The intent was to observe them now and perhaps eventually use them as extra assistants on limited unit assignments while they were in shifted form—and had more cognition thanks to the elixir. He liked the idea of his brother and sister-in-law being able to participate, but he'd understand if their one-time experiment remained just that, and knew they would understand, too.

And Liam and his membership in Alpha Force? Well, in addition to being a possible guinea pig tomorrow—guinea wolf?—he'd soon be right by that amazing contraption that was his area of expertise: his computer.

He'd take care of his own work as well as he could, and as fast as he could.

Then he might attempt to do some further digging into what was going on with Drew.

Yeah, right. As if the internet would, despite its vastness, have detailed answers to flawed shapeshifting.

Thanks to his background and love of technology he'd done a lot of research on many subjects, particularly shifting. And though its various aspects always seemed to have at least a reference or two, nothing really addressed this issue—at least nothing he'd seen so far.

As usual, there wasn't a lot of traffic in Mary Glen, so his drive back to the base wasn't taking long—a good thing. En route, Liam continued pondering what was next. Maybe he could figure out the answer to the non-shifting question himself somehow. While shifted. Thanks to the elixir, he could choose the time—like tomorrow night.

Tonight would be too soon, since he had work of his own to do. Plus he needed to undertake some preparation. He wanted to talk again to Melanie first, get her rundown about what Drew had been doing yesterday before moonrise. He'd rather do that in person, a good excuse to return to the clinic tomorrow. And if he happened to see Rosa there? Well, he could also ask about her latest insights into Drew.

He could further request that she hang around when he accomplished his shift, in case he needed a veterinarian's help this time because of the likely changes being tried.

He'd also check with the aide Jonas, who'd helped Drew with his shift into wolf form—and had been there to try to help him shift back.

By now, Liam had completed the winding drive through the forest and reached the base. He pulled out his ID, and as he handed it to the entrance guard, immediately started pondering what he needed to accomplish now.

Time to get on the computer.

* * *

Rosa exited the exam room where she had just given a fourteen-year-old shih tzu her annual checkup, including a few shots.

She always enjoyed caring for senior pets, making sure they were as healthy as possible for their age so they could hopefully remain with their owners for a nice, long time.

Younger pets, too.

All pets. And other animals, of whatever type... or origin.

Almost automatically, she turned away from where the owner was carrying the shih tzu to the reception area, and headed toward the room that housed Drew for the moment. The clinic's technician Dina walked out of it, staring at the door as she shut it behind her.

Uh-oh. Did that mean there was a problem? Rosa hurried in her direction, and Dina nearly bumped into her. Dina was shorter than her male counterpart, and older—late thirties, Rosa believed, compared with Brendan's early twenties. Brendan was thin, and Dina was heftier, but both were strong and muscular, as was best for carrying ill animals when necessary. Of course, they both wore blue lab jackets.

"How are things?" Rosa asked immediately, shifting her eyes toward that now closed door and back again to Dina's face. She was a pretty lady, prone to smiling, but she looked serious now.

"They're okay, but that wolf-dog seems to be getting more distressed all the time when he's not sleeping." Dina kept her voice low, but Rosa figured she knew who and what that animal was, and that if he was awake he'd hear what she said and understand it.

"I'm not surprised." Rosa considered making some kind of optimistic statement when she went in to see Drew, to cheer him up a little, but what could she say? Sure, his coworkers in his military unit were working on it, and even she hoped to come up with something more than just taking blood tests, but for now she didn't know what or how.

Maybe Liam would figure something out. If so, she hoped he'd let her know. Perhaps even allow her to participate. For Melanie's sake in particular, she wanted to make sure things worked out well.

And also so the other shifters, including Liam, would know what to do if such a problem ever arose with them.

"Anyway," she said to Dina, "I was planning on stopping in to see him now, too. I assume Noel's still with him, right?"

"Right. I think his presence helps."

"Glad to hear that," Rosa responded, not surprised. Hopefully, an Alpha Force member experienced at being an aide would know how to behave in the presence of a shifter in animal form—even one with a problem. "I'll go check on them both now. Thanks for looking in on our patient."

"Sure." Dina turned and hurried down the hall.

Rosa opened the exam room door and peeked in before entering. Drew was lying down and appeared to be asleep. But as she glanced toward Noel, seated on one of the chairs looking at his cell phone, Drew rose on his haunches to a seated position and stared at her expectantly.

"No news yet," she told him, as if he had asked a question. Then she did add something optimistic, as she'd been considering. "But everyone is still hard at work on finding you an answer."

Or so she hoped.

Liam had been on the computer for an hour now. *His* computer. Or at least the top-of-the-line system owned by the US government that had been assigned to him for his work.

He loved it. He also liked being alone here now, with Chase, in this solitary, quiet office in a remote area of Alpha Force's main building at the base. A small room, sure, but one with a comfortable desk chair, high quality shelving and even a large screen television mounted on the wall in case some of his technological research could be assisted by tuning in to news or other useful shows.

It was getting late. He had spent quite a while with Denny going over all the posts his aide had found about shifters anywhere, and particularly those with alleged military connections.

They were generally consistent with what Liam had already discovered and informed Denny about as a basis of his search. There weren't as many as Liam had feared, which was good.

But those that existed had been viewed many times, according to those sites, especially those alleging misconduct by the shifted wolves. They had collected a bevy of fascinated comments despite the general consensus, still, that it was all fiction, since shapeshifters didn't really exist.

As directed, Denny had used a couple of the fake identities Liam had helped him create to jump in and make fun of some of the nastiest comments.

Liam was about to do the same with as many others as he could. Grinning, he began. Let's see. Who should he be first?

He opened one of his favorite social media sites and signed in as Mite T. Maus. *Maus* was the German word for mouse. Several of his assumed identities used implied animal names, which worked well while he attempted to make fun of anything posted that suggested shapeshifters were real.

"Okay, now," he said aloud. "Let's see what we can do." He immediately asked for the supposedly injured townsfolk to contact him, let the world know how they were doing, and how much fun they had attempting to fight off weird creatures who supposedly were part human. Hey, he—or rather Maus—claimed, he'd done that once as a kid and now treasured the scar on his right arm. But, gee, that doggy had remained in his neighborhood and tried biting him again after the moon was no longer full. That was one reason he really tried hard to find proof of shapeshifters.

He got a response almost immediately—but the person, using the name Cerberus, only posted a picture of a bloody raised finger.

Hopefully, that would just make other readers laugh. It certainly didn't suggest proof of shapeshifters.

Liam did something similar under another name on another site, and the early responses there were more belligerent, suggesting there was something wrong with him for not believing in shapeshifters. Other people responded by apparently laughing at the believers. Interestingly, as he'd seen before, some of them also used the names of Greek or Roman gods—Hera, Zeus, Diana and Orion.

He also checked out similar social media posts by Denny. They, too, made fun of the whole idea of shapeshifters.

Did all this help quash what the suggestion of attacks had begun last night?

At least it was a start, and Liam kept it going for a while. Some names, like Orion, seemed to pop up a lot.

He wondered more than once what Rosa would think of all this. Her job was saving animal lives. His was protecting shapeshifters in this quirky way.

"Hey, Rosa," he said aloud, after finding her picture on the Mary Glen Veterinary Clinic website. "What would you think of this?"

Maybe he'd actually ask her. But at the moment, he needed to work.

Finally, though, he'd had enough of this—for now. But his night wasn't over.

Nope, next thing he'd do would be to check out who'd done the original posts, attempt to learn their real identities. That could take a tremendous amount of time. But somehow, he had to get at least some sleep that night.

He wouldn't be able to sleep all day tomorrow. No, he would need to report in to his current commanding officers about what Denny and he had learned, and what they'd done about it.

Then he would need to do that additional checking to see if he could learn more about Drew's day before his critical, and faulty, shift.

Which would, as Liam had already figured, involve going to the vet clinic. Get what info he could from Melanie. And Rosa.

Rosa. She was on his mind too much.

But for now she had to be. He definitely wanted her present when he shifted tomorrow night. Melanie might be too emotional. Besides, she had her kids at home.

And Liam was relatively certain that, however he decided to conduct his shift, it wouldn't hurt to have a veterinarian in the background.

And it certainly wouldn't hurt if that vet was as kind, caring—and sexy—as Rosa.

Chapter 7

"So how are you feeling this morning?" Rosa asked early the next day.

The shifted wolf who was Drew sat on his table-bed and looked at her, ears erect. He'd been alone when she walked in. Melanie must have been okay with it, as he had apparently spent the night by himself here in this room.

Rosa felt certain Melanie would have popped in on him now and then as she sometimes did at the clinic when they had patients staying overnight, especially if they were badly ill. But then Drew was always around to watch the kids. Not last night. At least their house was next door, but Melanie wouldn't have spent much time away from the children.

And though Melanie sometimes had Rosa visit those ill animals instead, she hadn't asked her to come here last night, either.

"I gather you're as okay as possible under these circumstances," she continued, knowing Drew wasn't going to answer—at least not by talking to her. He did move his head a little, as if in a nod. That was good. He apparently still maintained his human cognition despite the time that had passed.

Melanie hadn't arrived for the workday yet. Of course, Rosa's boss had to follow her usual routine of taking her daughter to preschool for the morning, after the babysitter arrived for their son.

Rosa had beat the two vet techs to the clinic, too. Susie, at the reception desk when Rosa arrived, had confirmed that so far she was the only staff present. Rosa could have gotten here earlier than Susie, too, but had somewhat taken her time getting ready.

She was up early, hadn't slept well that night.

Too much on her mind.

At least she didn't have to worry about shapeshifters running around under a full moon, as she had the night before. But she did have to worry about at least one shapeshifter—this one, who was her patient.

"So," she said, "are you hungry? We don't have any fresh burgers here that I know of, like we did yesterday, but I'm sure we have some good, premium dog food. Or if you'd prefer people food, we can work that out, too. I'm not sure what you ate yesterday besides that burger."

Was that a touch of amusement on the wolfen face? Rosa knew she was blathering a bit. The two techs, when they arrived, might have a better sense about what Melanie had told them to feed Drew. The visitors from Ft. Lukman who'd hung out with him probably did, too, especially Noel Chuma, who'd been here for quite a while. Was he awake at his quarters yet? Should Rosa call him?

Almost as if she had actually called him, there was a knock on the door, which opened immediately. Noel entered, followed by Liam. Chase wasn't with them.

"So how's our patient today?" Noel approached Drew, who stood up and nodded as Noel stroked his head.

Liam, closing the door behind him, looked at Rosa, his head cocked at a slight angle. "How's our patient?" he repeated. "And how's his excellent veterinarian? You're here early this morning, Dr. Jontay."

"So are you, Lieutenant Corland. In fact, that's even more surprising. I work here. But why have you come?"

"Well, that's somewhat obvious, since we have a common issue here." He looked toward Drew. "We're going to figure this out, sir. Soon. But I do wish we could get your input."

The expression on the wolf's face darkened. Rosa had the impression that he was upset, certainly. But she also believed he would have done something else to try to communicate with them if he actually had answers.

Which in a way made things worse. His optimism, if he'd had any, might be waning. And, she'd gathered, he was the number one expert on formulating that elixir in its various permutations over the past few years. As a medical doctor, would he know anything about why his blood was different while he was shifted?

Were there answers to be found?

There had to be, even if Drew himself couldn't participate in fixing things.

"But don't worry about it." Liam must have read the same emotion on the wolf's face. "We're making progress on working on a solution. It'll come soon. I promise."

Rosa glanced at him, and saw that the large smile he sent toward his commanding officer didn't look exactly happy...or promising.

But keeping Drew optimistic was vital. "We trust your Alpha Force team on that," she said, "and we'll be doing everything here that we can to help and support them, to make sure what Liam said comes true."

Liam looked toward her, and for a moment his smile did appear genuine. She felt a warmth circulate through her that had little to do with the hopefully true promise she was backing. He was clearly appreciative of her support—and more, she believed. She had a sudden urge to go shake his hand. Well, hold it, and draw him closer for an encouraging hug, and—

Ridiculous. Sure, they could, and should, work together for this important common purpose. But the fact that she found the guy appealing, despite his being a shifter, was totally foolish.

Yes, they could reinforce each other in what they were saying to this man-wolf who needed to hear it. And for it to happen.

But that was the only thing they should do together.

"Well, this is quite a crowd." The door had opened again, and Melanie walked in. Like Rosa, she was dressed in her white lab jacket. Her pale face barely contrasted with the color, and the dark circles beneath her eyes, despite the makeup she'd put on, didn't disguise that she mustn't have slept well, if at all. "I assume you're all here to give my husband a new elixir formulation or whatever that will bring him back to human form."

She looked first toward Liam and Noel, then at Rosa.

"Soon," Liam said, but despite his upbeat tone Rosa assumed he was just attempting to cheer Melanie. "We've a few questions first, though. Could we go to your office?" He looked at Melanie. "All of us, including Noel."

"Fine." Melanie didn't sound especially agreeable, and Rosa assumed she was trying to not only do as Liam apparently wanted, but also attempting to be nothing but positive in Drew's presence.

Rosa followed the others out the door and down the fortunately still-empty hallway to the office. Although Rosa figured it was late enough now that Melanie could have one of the other staff members hang out with Drew, she didn't stop in the reception area or break room to set that up.

Liam closed the door behind them. Melanie remained standing behind her desk, and though Rosa wanted to sink into a chair, she didn't choose to be the only one sitting down. She was between Liam and Noel.

"Now, what's really happening?" Melanie's tone was sharp, almost accusatory. Rosa hardly ever heard her boss be anything but pleasant and encouraging.

But this wasn't a usual situation.

Liam sat in one of the chairs facing the desk, as did Noel, and Rosa was glad to do the same.

"I wish I had some really great news for you, Melanie," Liam said. "But so far all we have is ideas—and, well, a little more. Before we can stir them together and implement a cure, we need more information to be sure we're not missing something. Noel, we've already talked, of course. You weren't Drew's aide that night. Jonas was."

"Right," he agreed.

"Thanks to Jonas, I've received nearly a minute-by-minute rundown on all Drew did before and during his shift, till he headed home still in shifted form." Liam turned toward Melanie. "Did you see him that evening before his shift?"

"No," she said dejectedly. "I didn't even have the chance to wish him a good time while shifted. And then when he came home when the sun rose... I wondered where Jonas was, Noel. Did you see him?"

"Yes, he was trying to find Drew. Drew started out on base, of course, and the shifters were just doing a few maneuvers that night. Nothing particularly stressful. I was just observing and helping generally. We all had an early dinner, then got the gang together in a secluded area, had them undress, and the aides shone the lights on them—nothing unusual for the night of a full moon or other nights when shifting was scheduled."

"That's right," Liam said. "That was how it worked for me, too."

Rosa pictured the scene in her mind—and forced herself not to think too graphically of how Liam might have looked nude after taking the elixir so he could have more control over his shift and maintain his human cognition. She'd heard that was their standard procedure.

Including getting undressed to have those lights turned on the shifters... She sighed silently.

Her purpose here was all she should be thinking about regarding shifters.

Including that handsome, smart—and sexy—Liam.

"Okay," Liam said. "That's what I figured, or you'd have told us otherwise. Just so you know, our medical guys don't have answers about the unusual quality of Drew's blood. They're still working on it. They're also working on modifying the elixir, and we're going to test a new formulation tonight—one that should make me remain in shifted form longer than usual—as well as a possible antidote that'll let me shift back when I want to. Those will be variations on some of the formulas used before, and if the one letting me shift back works okay, then they'll enhance it and give it a try with Drew."

"Really? That sounds great!" Melanie's sudden grin also suggested she was optimistic.

Rosa not so much. Still… "Yes," she said. "But in case you have any issues while shifting—"

"You go with them, Rosa," Melanie said, "in case they need any veterinary help."

That wasn't where she'd been going with her comments—was it?

Well, maybe so.

If she did as her boss said, she'd get the opportunity to watch Liam's shift.

All of it.

"That's okay," she said. "Although I know you can't go, Melanie. But I doubt that Alpha Force will want someone who's not a member of their military unit to barge in that way."

"It's not barging in," Liam contradicted, "and I was planning on asking if you would come along, just in case, since we'll be playing some unusual games here."

Games? He considered it a game?

Maybe so—from his perspective.

From hers? It was serious.

And what if he really did need some veterinary care as a result of what they'd be doing that night?

"Okay," she said. "Count me in."

This had to be a mistake, Rosa thought a short time later as she drove her car to the base, following Liam. But it promised to be a fascinating one—and maybe helpful, too.

After some discussion, they'd left Noel at the clinic to watch Drew again and provide more food to him, since Melanie would be busy taking care of the day's veterinary patients. The knowledgeable aide would be useful during what was going on that afternoon at the base—and night—but Noel could catch up with them later.

Was she going to learn a lot more today about Alpha Force—and its shifters' methods, even outside of a full moon?

Was she actually going to see Liam shift? He'd said he'd be doing so that night as a test. That way, his fellow Alpha Force members would be around to help him shift back after attempting to imitate, somehow, what Drew had done.

Was she going to need to use her vet skills to help him while he was in wolf form, if whatever the test they were conducting ran into glitches?

Just in case, she had brought her veterinary bag filled with essential items in case she needed to examine, and possibly treat, Liam for illness, injuries or whatever.

She felt a bit guilty leaving Melanie on her own to

care for patients, but her boss was one very good veterinarian. Plus the two techs would be able to help out with the general stuff, particularly after being given instructions.

Part of a day away from her beloved job—and for a very good cause, to help her boss's husband—should be fine.

After reaching the gate, Rosa figured that Liam had informed the guards about who was in the car behind him. Getting their okay to go through was quick.

She followed him to a parking lot and got out as Liam also exited.

He strode toward her, somehow looking all handsome, proud soldier. His camo uniform didn't hurt, but Rosa had a sense that anticipation of what was to come helped to ramp up his attitude.

"You ready for this?" he asked, as they met on the pavement near the building's back entrance.

"Sure," she asserted, with as much confidence as she could muster. And in actuality, she was ready—to see how things worked out.

To actually see a shift today? Heck, yes! She'd known shifters for quite a while, but this promised to be a first for her around here.

As they reached the building, Liam brought a key card from his pocket and swiped it in, then opened the door. But before either of them entered, he took her hand.

Somewhat startled, she looked up into his amazing deep brown eyes. "We'll figure this out," he said. "We'll help Drew."

"I know," she said, but she had the sense that he was asserting that aloud to try to make it come true.

Well, that was fine with her. That assertion made her feel even more confident, too, than she had before. Liam was, after all, a shifter and a technology expert and a military man. He had to know what he was talking about.

She hoped it wasn't just the way her insides warmed as they exchanged glances that was revving up her confidence.

He squeezed her hand tighter, drawing her closer. Was he going to kiss her? She hoped so and remained looking up at him in readiness.

But then he released her. "We're going to go visit Chase first, then head downstairs to see how the gang is progressing with playing with the elixir formulations."

"Right." She stepped back, all business once more— or at least she hoped she appeared that way despite the regret inside her.

He preceded her into the low-slung building, leading her down a hallway to the really nice kennel area she'd visited before, where the cover dogs were housed when not with their closest allies—the shifters they resembled. There were only four present now, and a couple started barking when Liam opened the door. Rosa just laughed at their eagerness to be noticed.

Chase was in the closest fenced-in area with one other wolflike dog. Nice, fluffy bedding lay on the tile floor for them, and the place looked almost elite enough for military officers to hang out when not on duty.

Maybe these dogs were considered officers of sorts.

"Hi, guy," Liam said, after letting Chase out of his enclosure. "Miss me?"

The dog's tongue came out and licked Liam's arm as if he'd understood what his master had said and was answering affirmatively.

"Good." Liam didn't leash him, but gave a gesture that told Chase to come with him. He then led Rosa back out the door. As he shut it, she stroked Chase's head.

She would see tonight, she believed, how much Chase resembled Liam when he was shifted.

And would Liam fail to shift back like Drew? Would he remain looking like, being like, his cover dog for a longer time than just that night—as Drew continued to look like his cover dog, Grunge? Rosa had seen Grunge at the clinic sometimes, since he, too, mostly lived next door.

"Okay," Liam said, as they walked down the hall. "Let's take Chase out for a minute, then we'll bring him back and head downstairs."

Their visit outside to the nearby small patch of lawn was quick and productive. Soon they'd brought Chase back to his enclosure and were walking down the stairs to the lab and office area. Rosa walked beside Liam, who had a hand on her shoulder as if to guide her.

She was aware of it. Very aware. Appreciative of the contact.

More appreciative than she should be.

When Rosa had been on the lab floor recently, she had mostly been in Drew's office—although not with him. Now, Liam led her into a vast laboratory area.

She had seen similar places in veterinary school and otherwise, but knew this one was amazing. There were quite a few shiny metal cabinets along the perimeter, with metal counters on top that held a lot of different kinds of equipment. Unsurprisingly, that included electron microscopes, as well as items that appeared intended to test humans for things like respiration and circulation.

Was there any apparatus to check out canines and other animals when the humans were shifted? Most likely.

Patrick and Jonas, whom she'd seen the last time, when she was here to give a rundown about Drew's blood test, stood with Denny near one of the counters on which large containers of liquids had been placed, as well as some smaller vials.

Were some or all of these that incredible and all-important elixir?

"Welcome," Patrick said, and Rosa knew from before that Captain Patrick Worley was the highest rank-ing officer in this small group—and apparently the second highest in Alpha Force, after Drew. He was a medical doctor, dressed like the others in a white lab coat. "Put on one of those jackets over there—" he pointed to a coat rack that had a lot of lab coats on hangers "—and join us."

Rosa complied immediately, as did Liam.

This was the group she had kind of anticipated, since she had learned that Lieutenant Jonas Truro was also a medical doctor, and Sergeant Denny Orringer was Liam's aide while shifting.

All of them, except maybe Denny, would be ap-propriate to attempt to modify the elixir for its cur-rent purpose, and Denny would need to be there for Liam's test shift that night.

Assuming she was correct about the skills of each of them. But in the day since Drew's problems had begun, and based on her visit here before, she believed she was accurate in this, at least.

But what had they been doing?

And had they come up with the necessary answers to allow Liam to test their latest brews—and ensure that they could get Drew shifted back to human form soon?

She hoped she would find out.

Chapter 8

Liam had been watching Rosa's face—her lovely, animated face—since they arrived down in the lab.

He wanted to read Rosa's mind right now. What questions did she want to ask those who were now re-doing the elixir? But he'd find that out soon.

In a way, he was relying on her. Sure, he was a member of Alpha Force and these guys would have his best interests in mind.

Sort of. Drew's best interests would come first, and that was fine. As long as Liam wouldn't wind up unable to shift back for any prolonged period of time, like his poor commanding officer.

"So," he began, looking at Patrick. "Can we talk about—"

"I know the elixir's formulas, all of them, are confidential," Rosa interrupted, leveling a quick glance at him before turning toward Patrick. "I don't need to know much. But could you tell me in general what you've been working on—what formulations will help Liam shift into wolf form, and how he won't be able to shift back right away, and, most important, how you intend for him to be able to shift back soon? Oh, and where are you with figuring out what was in Drew's blood? Is that a factor in what you've done?"

Great questions, Liam thought. And he liked that Rosa was sort of taking over, as he'd hoped.

She would be the vet in charge when he was shifted, of course. He hoped he wouldn't require her services. But it would be better if she was fully informed, just in case…

"You're right," Patrick said. "We've been working on all of that. And we'll tell you what you need to know. Thanks for coming, although we hope it'll just be a waste of your time."

"Me, too," Rosa responded. "But just in case…"

"Of course."

As the officer in charge of Alpha Force with Drew out of commission, Patrick was worth quizzing—and listening to. He gave the appearance of being in charge, too, Liam thought. His eyes, a light shade of brown, looked determined and assessing under his furrowed brow, as though he was attempting to figure out how much he could trust Rosa with. He stood right beside one of the shiny metal counters that held lines of microscopes with vials of liquid between them, probably the most important location in the lab today.

Liam just hoped what was in those vials had been mixed and vetted and perfected as well as possible before any of it was finally tested—on him.

"First of all," Patrick said, "most test work so far

was done in our inner lab over there." He cocked his head toward the side of the room, where a small area was secured behind a metal wall—not someplace Liam had ever been invited into, but he knew what that room was. "If we're going to talk, though, let's go sit in the lounge area." That was another part of this large room, also behind walls, but glass ones.

"Good idea," Liam said, and after seeing Rosa nod, too, he followed Patrick, as well as Jonas and Denny, to that area. Denny might be his aide, but he seemed to be doing a good job of toadying up to the officers in charge here. That was fine. Maybe he'd learn more than Liam did and be able to use it that night.

They were all soon seated on the couches in there, and Patrick started talking, with occasional input from his other colleagues. Apparently they still had no answers about the change in Drew's blood, but were still working on it. The conversation about the development and constant updating of the original elixir was long, but didn't really give much in the way of detail, since it was primarily confidential.

Rosa continued to acknowledge the confidentiality—mostly. She did ask some specific questions at times and received a little more information.

Finally, they got to the crux of what was important today.

"Yes," Jonas said, "the elixir has been modified a lot since it was first used by Alpha Force, sometimes because new members bring their own versions with ingredients that are then incorporated. We've experimented with it for specific kinds of shifts or issues, and we're always working on more. Like now." As a medical doctor as well as an Alpha Force aide, he was bound to know a lot of the details, maybe as much as Patrick, who was also a doctor. Jonas leaned forward on the sofa, clasping his hands in front of him. He appeared concerned, ready to do what was necessary both to answer questions and to attempt to fix the situation. He was, after all, not only Drew's chief aide, but also his friend.

"So what you've been working with now is just variations of formulas you have already developed?" Rosa asked.

"Pretty much so," Patrick acknowledged. "We can't discuss the various contents, which are sometimes derived from human or canine bodily fluids and are other times chemicals we purchase, but you get the general idea."

Rosa nodded. "I don't want or need to know what those contents are, but I understand you've been working with them for quite a while and test those permutations on shifters both during full moons and otherwise, right?"

"Exactly." Patrick nodded as he settled in his seat, as if feeling less stress now with this conversation.

"And I gather that part of your research includes attempting to come up with formulations that allow shifters to remain shifted for long periods of time."

"Yes. We've had something like that for a while, but it always allowed the shifter who drank it to choose to change back at will. What we're working on now won't give the shifter that choice, but will definitely give his or her aide the ability to trigger the change back."

"And that's what you'll have Liam test tonight?" There was a catch in Rosa's voice. Liam wasn't sure that the others would have heard it, and he certainly didn't know her well, but it still made his insides warm a bit. She gave a damn.

But maybe not about him. Maybe about the issues with all shifters.

In any case, he appreciated her caring.

"Yes," Patrick said, "and before you get too worried, we've worked with it as much as we could over this brief period of time. We're pretty certain it'll do what we need it to."

Pretty certain?

Rosa caught that, too. "Are you certain enough to really test it on an actual shifter this soon? What happens if Liam winds up like Drew?"

Jonas laughed aloud, which surprised Liam—a bit. But the medical doctor/aide had been a member of Alpha Force for a while and had seemed to give a damn about the unit and its members for as long as Liam, more of a newcomer, had known him. "We've considered that in our preparation, and if anything, erred on the side of caution. Our concoction will definitely allow us to bring Liam back to human form. But even so we won't be certain about Drew until we test it on him afterward. We don't want to try it on Drew first, though, since we don't know for sure what caused his failure to shift back, and we feel we have more control about testing this first with Liam."

Rosa seemed to hesitate, then said, "I have to assume you guys know what you're doing—even without the assistance of the person who, I've heard, has done the most to create and modify the elixir, Drew. But—"

"But I'm going to let them give it a try," Liam said, softly but firmly. "I appreciate your concern, but I trust these guys." He had to, if he wanted to remain a member of Alpha Force. And he'd been the one to volunteer to shift that night, with the intention of helping Drew.

"It's of course up to you." But Rosa's gaze remained on him for only a few seconds before moving on to Patrick, Jonas and Denny in succession. "I just hope you're right. Otherwise, I suppose I'll have the veterinary fun of treating another shifter in wolf form for a while."

There wasn't anything she could do about it, Rosa realized, but fret and worry.

They remained sitting there, talking in generalities about the very specific issues they could run into that night with Liam using those new elixir formulations for shifting—and shifting back.

Would she be so worried if someone else was going to be the test subject?

Sure, she told herself. Yes, she had come to know Liam a little over the past short while, liked the guy, admired his intelligence both as a shifter and as an apparent computer and technology whiz. She also liked the way he seemed to really care about his commanding officer, enough to risk his own life, or at least its stability, to try to help him out.

But now, as Liam engaged more in the conversation about techniques they would use—apparently not much different from normal—she enjoyed watching the good-looking, serious yet droll shapeshifter trade questions, information and barbs with his fellow Alpha Force members.

And when they finally were through, Liam looked at her. "You know, Dr. Jontay, this may wind up being the only time I can give you a tour of this base. I'd like to show you around. Okay?"

The expression he leveled on her looked mostly amused—yet she somehow caught a hint of pleading in it. Maybe he just wanted to get away from this gang for now, before he had to meet up with them again for a test that hopefully would go well, yet could instead go very bad.

What could she do?

What did she want to do?

"Sure," she said, meaning it.

The group made plans to meet at the base's cafeteria for dinner in a few hours—all of them, for a final yet discreet discussion about what would happen afterward. Then, somewhat relieved for the moment, Rosa followed Liam out of the lounge, through the lab and up the stairs to the building's main floor.

She felt as if she could breathe better then. And when Liam told her his first target for their current outing, she could only grin.

They were going to visit the area where the shifters' cover dogs were housed—again. And not just to see Chase.

"A bunch of our dogs should be around today. I want to introduce you to some you haven't met yet, let you say hi to those you know." Liam spoke with an almost evil grin, stopping in the hall with the door to the stairway closed behind them. "I think they're all healthy, but it wouldn't hurt to have a quick vet check for each of them."

"It also won't hurt to kill a little time there so we don't have to think about our…plans for tonight," she added.

"There's that, too." Liam's voice had changed from teasing to almost gloomy.

"You don't have to do it, you know," Rosa said quickly. "They can figure out another method to test their new formulas. Or—"

"They need to try it on a shifter," he said. "I'm one of the lowest on their wolfen totem pole, one of the unit's newest members."

"But I thought they asked you to enlist in Alpha Force because of your special technological skills. You're the chief technology officer? Surely it would be better to have someone who doesn't have your abilities be the one to take chances tonight."

"Well, I've taught my aide enough to have him follow up on the social media stuff that's so important to deal with right now—although there are aspects that I'll need to take care of. After I've shifted back."

"But—"

He put a finger over her lips to keep her from continuing. And then, strangely, he glanced around the hallway.

What was he looking for?

Rosa figured that out nearly immediately, when he replaced his finger with his warm, sensual lips.

But only for a moment—long enough to shut her up, though.

When he pulled back she felt speechless—and disappointed that the kiss had ended so soon.

"Now," he said, "let's change the subject." He turned his back and strolled down the hall toward the room containing the dog enclosures.

Okay, maybe that hadn't been the wisest thing to do—although it was really, really enjoyable.

Including viewing the sexy look on Rosa's face as he backed away.

And it had accomplished what he'd wanted to do just then: keep her, for that moment, from addressing the subject of his upcoming shift.

Oh, he wanted to talk to her again, hold conversations on animal health and her take on shifting and—well, nearly anything…tomorrow. After he had shifted back.

And hopefully without needing Rosa to take any critical steps as a veterinarian to deal with his health while shifted.

They'd reached the door to the large kennel room and he pulled it open without looking at Rosa. Of course, the wolf-dogs inside began barking, and Chase stood up on his hind feet behind the fence enclosing him.

"Hi, guy," Liam said to his cover dog. Rosa, beside him, petted Chase briefly but caringly, then started visiting with some of the other dogs in their enclosures.

"Oh, hi, Spike," she said to one of them. "How are you doing?"

"Far as I know, he's doing fine," Liam said. "Your treatment of his injured paw did the trick. He's been acting just fine here and also when brought out to do his duty as Seth Ambers's cover dog. I know Seth's happy about his quick recovery."

"That's great. And how about the rest of you?" Rosa's intense gaze ranged over the other fenced areas. "Everyone feeling okay?"

As far as Liam could tell, they were. They all moved around excitedly on their bedding and regarded Rosa and him as if they wanted even more attention than the acknowledgment they were currently getting.

And why not? Rosa and he had a while before dinnertime. "I think they're all fine, but eager for walks. Let's do it, okay? Short ones. We'll leave Chase here for now."

"Love it!" Rosa grinned at him, making him feel all gushy inside. He turned and headed to the wall where leashes were hung.

They had some time to kill that afternoon, so they wound up taking their time on the walks, just for fun. These walks really weren't necessary, since the dogs were well cared for and often spent active time with the people they worked with. But in the afternoon, like now, usually those people were doing other things, so the idea was that these dogs could bond together here in their own kind of pack.

But aides and others came in often to talk to them and walk them.

Grunge, though, was a different matter. Drew's cover dog spent afternoons here, but was generally the only one to pretty much live off the base, at the house next to the veterinary clinic with Drew, Melanie and their kids.

Grunge was here now. Liam assumed that was because Melanie chose to let him stay here while she dealt with Drew's issues. Rosa clearly understood the situation, for as soon as Liam handed her a leash she went over to where he was enclosed with Shadow, the cover dog of Staff Sergeant Jason Connell, Drew's cousin.

"I'll get Shadow," Liam said. "You take care of Grunge. I'm sure he knows you from the clinic and next door."

"He does," Rosa agreed, kneeling to pat the wolf-dog she had taken from his enclosure. He nuzzled her, clearly recognizing her and liking the attention. "Poor guy." Rosa gave him a hug, then stood. "Getting Drew changed back is important for many reasons—and Grunge's best interests are among them. I'm sure he'd rather be home with his human family."

Telling them all, particularly Chase, that they'd be back, Liam motioned for Rosa to walk Grunge out the door while he followed with Shadow.

Both dogs seemed excited to be outside on the base's nearby grassy grounds, and Liam was glad that Rosa seemed perfectly happy running with her charge, as he did with Shadow. They spent around twenty minutes giving the dogs, and themselves, some exercise.

Returning to the building, they put the two canines back in their enclosures. Rosa chose to walk Spike next and seemed delighted that the dog whose injured paw she'd treated seemed as well now as Liam had told her. Liam elected to take Rocky, Lieutenant Ryan Blaiddinger's cover dog, out this time.

And when they brought those two back, Liam told Rosa, "It's time for me to show you around more. I'll just bring Chase along with us."

"That sounds great." Rosa smiled at him. "It was delightful to hang out with these dogs for a while, and in case you're wondering, though I did no formal checkups, I saw nothing wrong with any of them. Looks like they're well cared for here."

"Of course. They're not just wolf-dogs. They're our alternate personalities."

Rosa laughed. "Of course."

With Chase leashed beside him, Liam took Rosa on a nice, long walk around the base, pretty much sticking with the narrow driveways. He pointed out where he lived, in the bachelor officers' quarters at the far side of the property, with the main office building nearby. "I don't know whether you've ever met our highest-up commanding officer, General Greg Yarrow, but he maintains an office in that building. He mostly hangs out at the Pentagon, but visits us here often. I know he sticks up for Alpha Force with the higher-up muckety-mucks, though he's good at maintaining our secrecy where it matters."

"I don't know him, but I've heard of him."

Rosa seemed to have no trouble keeping up with Chase and Liam. She of course wore civilian clothing, not too casual but not particularly dressy, either. And she fortunately had on athletic shoes, although perhaps she always wore comfortable shoes, as a vet who'd likely be on her feet a lot during the day.

The May day was warmish, but not too hot. Liam enjoyed the walk and he hoped Rosa did, too. She seemed to. She often pointed to something she saw, such as the base's auditorium, where programs were sometimes held with outside military folks, or even those stationed on base who weren't part of Alpha Force. It was small and attached to the rear of the main admin building.

They discussed Alpha Force in low voices. They discussed Liam and the work he'd done before joining the unit—technologically oriented, of course. And the work he did now that was a natural follow-up.

He turned them around eventually, took Chase back to his enclosure with the other cover dogs and steered Rosa toward the cafeteria. "We're meeting the gang here for dinner right around now. You ready?"

"Sure." But the look she leveled on him was worried. "Are you?"

He knew what she was referring to. They would discuss his upcoming shift as they ate.

"Of course," he lied. He preceded Rosa into the small cafeteria and looked around. Sure enough, Patrick and the gang already occupied one of the tables. Other tables had men and women in camouflage uniforms sitting at them, too. The place was more than adequate for this relatively compact military base. It contained a salad bar at one end, as well as a nice-sized area where workers dished out some prepared food. There was also a beverage station and a grill. Nice place with an excellent smell, even for a shifter in human form.

Liam was prepared for this. He really was. He got a steak dinner, of course, while Rosa just picked up a salad. They sat down at the empty seats that had been saved for them.

And then they all began discussing, in low voices and generalities so non–Alpha Force people wouldn't know what they were talking about, what they would be doing later that night.

What *he* would be doing later that night.

He wished that their beverage bar served alcohol, but it was better that it didn't. That could affect how the elixir worked, of course.

And then, much too soon, dinner was over.

It was growing dark outside.

It was time.

Chapter 9

Rosa could tell after dinner that the guys, shifters or not, were gearing up for what would soon take place.

What would soon happen with Liam.

Everyone rose from around the table and picked up their dinnerware to take to the counter where used items would be dealt with by the staff. "So," Patrick said, "let's all head back to the building for now."

And then what? Rosa had some idea as she picked up her things. The Alpha Force members didn't pay much attention to her, but appeared to share glances filled with anticipation. And concern?

Looked that way to Rosa. Maybe that shouldn't worry her, since they all should be concerned because of their dedication to ensuring that everything worked out as well as they'd told her.

But it worried her nonetheless.

"Let me handle that." Liam, beside her, reached for

her plate. Somewhat startled, she let him take it and place it on top of his own, although she still held her iced tea glass.

"Thanks, but you don't need to," she said softly. He didn't need to do anything but…well, prepare, at least mentally.

But maybe doing something mundane and useful would help him with it.

"You're right." The smile he aimed at her appeared all Liam—cocky and happy and teasing. And yet there was something in his deep brown eyes that told her she was right.

He wasn't entirely himself. Not that she really knew him all that well after interacting with him for just a couple of days. But she'd been considering the concern of his fellow Alpha Force members.

It wasn't any surprise to her that he would be concerned, too. He should be—even more than all the others.

He was their experiment. Their potential scapegoat if things didn't go well—instead of Drew.

And she needed to stop thinking like that.

"So, I'm not sure where any of this is going to take place," she told Liam after they left their things on the counter. Then, side by side, they began walking through the still busy cafeteria and followed the others outside. "Patrick said we were going to the building, which I assume is the lab building, right?"

"Yes, but they'll be gathering up…what's needed. Our shifts around here…" He lowered his voice so she could hardly hear it, even though she figured that the other military people stationed here had to know at least something of what Alpha Force was about.

"…are generally held outside, in an area toward the north of the building."

"Got it," she said. They'd headed slightly in that direction to walk the cover dogs when they'd taken them out before. There was some lawn there, with woodlands abutting it. Maybe shifts were done best under the cover of trees.

And maybe that was a good thing, since surely if they thought things would go wrong they'd want to conduct their test inside, in the lab area, where they'd have access to chemicals and whatever.

Or was she just being too hopeful?

"So, I'm pretty excited about all this," Liam said. They were outside now, still following the others, this time along one of the narrow roadways toward the area of the base containing the lab and kennel building. "And I trust these guys. Things will go fine."

Rosa glanced toward him as they revved up their pace and saw he was striding quickly and determinedly, yet he once again aimed his smile at her. Sort of. Was he doing this to make her feel better—or himself?

No matter. He was a good guy. Brave. Intending to risk his own well-being not just because he was under orders, she was sure, but because he intended to help his friend and commanding officer.

She had an urge to reach over and grab his hand. In support and possibly comfort, not to show she had any feelings for him except as a fellow human being—and more—facing a potentially challenging situation.

But she swallowed that impulse. And soon they reached the building.

Liam stepped behind her as she followed the other

guys inside. "You can wait here," Jonas said to her. "We're just grabbing the necessary supplies, but we'll bring them outside for the shift."

Rosa wasn't sure whether they were telling her to butt out for this moment or just saving her the walk down, then up, the stairs. It didn't really matter. At least they hadn't ordered her to leave.

Then again, they were concerned they might need her.

She watched as Liam moved around her, nodded, then began talking to Denny as they hurried down the stairs after the others.

She fought the urge to follow, but since the current commanding officer had told her to wait, it made sense to listen to him.

What if she breezed down this hallway and stopped in to see the other cover dogs again while she waited? She didn't think Chase would accompany them to where Liam shifted. There shouldn't be any need for a cover dog when that shift would occur right here on the military base, and presumably where they'd go to accomplish it would not be near where non–Alpha Force members stationed here were likely to be.

All she would do, therefore, was potentially get Chase and the others stirred up, not a great idea.

Having nothing better to do, she pulled her phone from her pocket and began scrolling through email messages. There were a couple from the owners of veterinary patients, but when she opened them she saw that Melanie or one of the vet techs had already looked and responded. She'd just been copied on them, and for now her input wasn't needed.

Maybe she should—

"Here we are," called Liam's familiar deep voice.

The door to the downstairs lab had opened. Liam was the first to exit, followed by Denny, who held a large backpack in his arms. He shoved it over his shoulder.

Rosa had a good idea what that pack must contain. She knew that the Alpha Force elixir, at least in its prior formulations, required that the shifter drink some, then have an artificial light resembling a full moon directed on him or her.

Not that she'd ever seen that, but she had learned about it in discussions about how Drew had shifted but not changed back.

With the elixir, they used the light even when the moon was full. When the moon wasn't full, it was even more necessary.

But changing back? Some of the elixir's formulations allowed it despite the moon being full, but all the shifters could, and generally did, change back when the moon went down at dawn. And when the shift was done outside a full moon using the elixir, the shifter apparently could just elect when to change back.

Before.

The others—Patrick, Jonas and Denny, all still in their camo uniforms, as was Liam—had exited that doorway and Rosa now followed the group outside. Most of them also carried backpacks—more lights? Different elixirs?

Would she ever know?

And did it matter?

A car drove along one of the base's nearby roads, but fortunately didn't head in their direction. Rosa followed as the Alpha Force group headed over the adjacent lawn, then into the woodland beyond.

The night was dark now, although there were some lights here and there on the base, but no bright ones nearby. The cool air washed over Rosa, but her slight shiver wasn't because of the cold.

No, she was anticipating what was to come, and it worried her.

She remained with the group—and was unsurprised when they stopped in a fairly large clearing.

This had to be it.

Sure enough, the guys pulled the backpacks off their shoulders, lowering them to the ground.

"I think this is overkill," Patrick said to his subordinates, motioning to all those bags, "but we'll have some alternatives if anything doesn't work quite right."

Meaning if something went to hell during Liam's shift. Rosa didn't even want to think about that.

But she was glad they were prepared. She just hoped that, whatever they had, it would actually do what they wanted it to.

And then it was time.

The other team members flocked around Liam, sort of shielding him from her gaze, Rosa supposed. But she still managed to see in between them as Liam began taking off his clothes.

And aiming a glance, off and on, in her direction. He knew where she was—and that she was observing.

Yes, she was definitely observing. And getting aroused despite herself and the situation as muscular, gorgeous, sexy Liam was soon nude.

Heck, she was here as a doctor. A veterinarian. Her patients never wore clothes, although a lot of them

had fur. And at the moment, she was here in her professional capacity in case a shifted wolf happened to
need a vet.

She had to remain professional, no matter what she
saw.

No matter what happened.

And yet she managed to observe as Liam stood
there naked, stretching his body, flexing those amazing
muscles of his...and more. Making her insides react in
ways they absolutely shouldn't right now.

But scolding herself didn't help.

He accepted a vial of clear liquid from Patrick and
drank it. He seemed to shoot one more look toward her.
Then Denny lifted a large light from where it had been
in his backpack, turned it on and aimed it toward Liam.

She knew what to expect—kind of. But she still
couldn't help feeling amazed as his face lifted and its
features began elongating into a muzzle, as his body
grew smaller, furrier, more slender and shrank closer
to the ground.

And in a very short time, handsome, naked Liam
had turned, as anticipated, into a wolf.

His shifting was complete.

*Did he feel different than usual? No, despite know-
ing that the elixir he had swallowed was at least a
slightly modified formulation from the one he was used
to. It tasted the same. Under the light Denny had shone
on him, it acted the same.*

*And, fortunately, that meant he still retained his
human cognition while shifted, perhaps the largest
plus in using the elixir—in addition to having the ability to shift outside a full moon, of course.*

Now, he just sat, resting his tail on the ground in the glade among the trees, looking with wolf eyes from each of those around him to the next. Letting the discomfort of his shift ease away. Waiting to decide what to do next.

His gaze lit for the longest time on Rosa. She had watched him shift, and this was probably the first Alpha Force shift she had observed, despite possibly seeing some shifts during her childhood.

She had also seen him, in human form, completely naked before his shift began. He knew that, if he were still in human form, just thinking about having that lovely, sexy lady watching him would have caused the pertinent parts of his body to grow and ache and yearn for more.

But he was now in wolfen form. He looked away from Rosa and toward his current commanding officer, Captain Patrick Worley, to see if there were any orders pending.

What should he do next?

Attempting to shift back was the challenge he was to address, even knowing he was not supposed to have control over it now.

He wasn't about to try to shift back again this soon. A lot of the reason for this shift was to test the new formulation's resistance to any determination on his part to become human again on his own terms, at his own time. But he needed to let his body bask in this form first.

And let that pain and discomfort that went with the twists, turns, size reduction and change of a shift to ease, then end.

"Okay, Liam," Denny said. "How are you feeling?"

Liam looked at his aide and nodded his head, moving his canine ears to listen to the forest sounds as he did so.

He enjoyed being wolfen, hearing small creatures on the ground, in the trees, perhaps aware that there was now a large potential predator on the loose in their area.

But he wasn't about to hunt squirrels or birds or anything else right now. Not even people.

He had a lot more on his mind than pretending to act like the animal he now was. A wolf.

"Good. I'm glad you're okay." That was Patrick, who appeared to watch him the way a military officer observed cadets in his charge, making certain he was following orders.

The only order Liam was aware of for now was to shift on cue, as he had done. The next order he anticipated was to attempt to shift back—which was most likely to be unsuccessful, since that was the way his shift this night had been planned.

It would then be up to those here, his fellow Alpha Force members, to ensure he became human once more.

"Is there anything you would like me to do for you?"

He turned his head abruptly to regard the source of that question. Rosa. She had approached and now stood almost in front of him, closer than any of the other humans around, his fellow Alpha Force members.

Yes, *was the initial thought that came in response to her question.* Hold me. Be there for me. Make certain that I will be able to shift back soon, as promised. *He liked being wolfen, certainly, but remained fully* aware of what had happened with the leader of his pack, Drew Connell, and he did not want that happening to him.

Had he still been in human form, he would also have chosen to misinterpret Rosa's question as an attempt at seduction, one he would have gladly agreed to.

But now?

She remained a few steps away and he moved toward her, raising his head to keep staring into her eyes. Soon, he edged against her, feeling her warm legs against the fur on his body. Inhaling her sweet, human, womanly fragrance. Listening to the increased pulse of her breathing.

Was that because of her concern?

"I'm interpreting that to mean yes," she said, and he saw her look at the human men around her. "It won't hurt for me to give him a quick exam."

No one objected. He believed she would not have accepted that answer if they had.

For the next few minutes, she knelt on the ground beside him, staring into his eyes, his opened mouth, his ears. Touching his back, then his chest as she had him roll over.

He wished once more that he was in human form, to have her stroke him and caress him—and examine him—that way.

Oh, yes. He retained his human cognition.

Soon, she was done. She stood. "He appears to be in good canine health," she said. "I don't find anything wrong with him, from my veterinary perspective."

Those around her expressed their relief.

"How soon should we have him try to shift back?" That was his caring aide once more. Denny was also *the only one there who had no medical skills, plus he was talking to his military superior officers.*

"Let's move a little deeper into the woods," Jonas said. "No reason, other than to swallow up a little time."

"I assume that won't do anything to hinder his shift back," Rosa said.

"As we told you, we don't think his initial attempt will work, anyway. We modified the elixir we gave him to prevent his shift back from being as easy as usual so we could then try the other new formulation prepared for Drew on Liam first. This is just to prepare for it, not try it too soon."

"I get it."

And so Liam obeyed, enjoying the prowl into another part of the woods around them. He flexed his legs, his tail, his ears, considering how they would feel when he finally attempted to shift back.

Wondering how he would truly feel when, as anticipated, that vital act would be out of his control.

He allowed Jonas to lead the way, knowing that under other circumstances he would dash far from these humans, allow himself to use his swifter legs to get away, utilize his keener senses while shifted, as well. Hunt. More.

But not now.

Soon, Jonas stopped, as did the others. Liam turned to ensure that Rosa remained with them. She did, following the rest.

"Okay," Jonas said. "It's time. Liam, shift back to human form."

He sat on his haunches again. He closed his eyes. He sensed those parts of his body that needed to

*change, as he always did while shifting back. And
using his thoughts, instructed them to modify themselves into the way they needed to be now.*

There was no reaction.

*He looked toward Jonas, attempting to convey his
thoughts and his acceptance—temporary—for now.*

"No change?" Jonas asked.

*Liam shook his head slowly in the manner humans
considered to mean "no."*

"Try again," Patrick said.

*Liam stood, turned in a circle—and looked toward
where Rosa stood, watching him.*

"Are you okay?" she asked him.

*He nodded his head in human fashion to indicate
he was, not conveying his concern. His fear, despite
how he had anticipated this.*

*His gratitude that she asked—and appeared to
care.*

*But now...how long would they wait before allow-
ing him to truly shift back again—or trigger the attempt themselves?*

He had known this was coming.

All would be well. He hoped. Eventually.

But he hated that it was out of his control.

Chapter 10

Rosa stood back, outside the small circle of military men who surrounded the member of their team they were focused on. Watching him in the beams of several large flashlights they'd placed on the ground beneath the trees, aimed toward him.

Waiting.

She hated this.

Yet…not entirely. She also found it fascinating.

And frustrating.

And, well, hate was too strong a word. Or maybe not. Rosa didn't hate that Liam was a shapeshifter, only that there were questions remaining unanswered. Provocative questions.

When would he be able to change back into human form?

Would he be able to change back, under these circumstances? Or would he be like Drew Connell, no matter what the others said? If that was a possibility, how could she help?

She didn't really know much about shapeshifters except for potentially being able to treat them medically while they were in shifted form.

But helping them get that way, or out of it? She had no skills, no knowledge, of that.

All she knew was that she would hate it if Liam was unable to get back to being…Liam.

Now, she watched the expressions on that canine's face as he continued to sit on the ground in the middle of the humans observing him. Discussing him, as if he wasn't there—or couldn't understand.

But from his expressions, and reactions, as he watched their faces, listened to them, she knew that Liam the shifter had retained his human cognition the way she'd been informed that Alpha Force members who drank the elixir would.

Apparently other shifters did not.

"Okay," Jonas was saying, confirming what Patrick had stated. "You're right. Our modified version of the elixir worked the way we planned it. That's a good thing—but it's time to use the other, secondary formulation, the kind that we created to do the deal—get a stuck shifter to change back no matter what happened to him or her before."

"Right," Patrick said. He held his large backpack in his arms, as he had before. Now, though, he set it on the dirt in front of him, knelt down and started sifting through its contents.

"You got it?" Jonas asked. "If not, I brought some of that special concoction along, too."

"I've got it." Patrick pulled out a large vial whose

clear liquid contents sparkled in the artificial light. The container appeared full.

What did it contain?

Rosa didn't really need to know, although chemistry was an important part of her profession and she had always been reasonably good at it.

But she also recognized and acknowledged that there were plenty of things about the covert military unit Alpha Force that nonmembers weren't told. And despite her possibly being of assistance to them, she was definitely a nonmember.

Hopefully, after tonight, she wouldn't even have a reason to want to know those contents and how they blended together. If Liam—no, *when* Liam—changed back, it would demonstrate that the stuff worked. Plus it would also work on Drew.

"Okay, then." Denny had pulled his smaller sack off his back and now held it in front of him.

Good aide. Liam, in his current form, would have a difficult time lapping up liquid from a glass vial like the one holding the shift-back formula, or whatever they called it.

But Denny had removed a metal dog bowl from his bag and held it out in front of him. Patrick immediately pulled the plastic lid from the top of the vial and tilted it till some of the liquid poured into the bowl.

How much was needed? How much would Liam drink?

Hopefully, these experts knew how to handle this— even though this aspect of shifting apparently was new to them, too.

"Okay," Patrick said a few seconds later. "That should be enough. Put it down in front of him."

"Right." Denny bent and positioned the bowl on the ground where Liam could lower his muzzle and begin lapping.

"Anything we should tell him first?" Patrick looked toward Jonas, who must have been involved in this new formulation.

"Just drink," Jonas responded, looking at Liam and not Patrick. "We'll use the light on you, although it might not be necessary. In any event, make the assumption that after you drink it you can shift back the way you usually do—by choosing to, willing your body parts to go back into their human form. Got it?"

Rosa was glad to see Liam's immediate nod. *Work, please work*, she thought. Sure, she remained concerned, even if these more knowledgeable men felt convinced things were in order.

What if they were wrong?

Or what if they were just putting on an act for each other and for Liam, hopeful that all would go well... but not certain?

She watched as Denny once again removed the large light from his backpack where he had stowed it. He turned it on and aimed it at Liam.

Liam sat still for a moment, staring away from the light. Staring away from all of them, into the trees and, perhaps, beyond.

Was it working?

Damned if she knew.

But he started moving, twisting a bit, beginning to move his paws, his legs. He shook his head, aimed his gaze downward.

And then—and then his limbs started elongating. Slowly but definitely. His fur appeared hazy, seeming to be sucked inside him, again slowly. His ears moved sideways and started to change shape, even as his muzzle began retracting. He moaned.

"Is he okay?" Rosa heard herself whisper. This was astounding to watch, though she had seen a shift before. But she hated to see or hear an animal in any kind of pain, and Liam appeared to be hurting.

"Yes, this is normal," Denny replied softly. He remained standing right beside the wolf-man to whom he acted as aide. "He's changing back!" Denny sounded excited, perhaps a bit surprised. Maybe he hadn't really thought that what they had done here would be effective, would allow Liam to shift back.

But it did appear to be working, and Rosa glanced first at Patrick, then Jonas, to see their reactions, to determine if they, too, believed Liam was changing again as he should. Both were nodding as they watched.

But it looked so strange to Rosa. It looked so wonderful. Liam groaned some, first in a throaty wolfen growl, and then sounding like a man in pain.

Even as he continued to extend, to grow, to change, to somehow absorb his fur.

And then, in the dim but steady light, Rosa could see the man who was Liam—perfect, muscular, gorgeous... nude.

What the Alpha Forcers had done had apparently worked.

Exhausted.
Ecstatic.
Liam was both.
He continued to lie there on the ground, arms be-

neath his head, as Denny came over to cover his body with a sheet. First, though, Liam turned onto his back.

He knew Rosa was there, standing in the background, watching him. He liked that she was staring at his naked body, despite how limp he was all over after that intense but oh, so wonderful, shift.

His breathing was deep, labored—and all human, a good thing. He smiled, closed his eyes as he was shrouded in that sheet—and when he opened them he was looking straight into Rosa's face.

"Are you okay?" she asked. Somehow, she had imposed herself in front of the Alpha Force guys nearby to check on him. He appreciated it. He appreciated *her*.

Not that he would tell her or anyone else, at least not now. "I'm fine," he said, hearing his own voice rasp. He turned his head toward the others. "Can we go back to the lab now? I want to talk this over, find out what you all thought about this—and learn how quickly you'll be trying your new formula on Drew."

"Fine," Patrick said. "Tell us when you're ready to sit up, then stand. We'll help you back to the building."

Liam did feel somewhat like an open sack of flour, ready to collapse and flow back onto the ground as, with Denny's help, he began to stand.

But once he was on his feet, covered by the sheet, he felt like himself once more—himself after a usual shift back to human form, which meant he was achy and uncomfortable, but basically himself again. And given a little time, that discomfort would disappear.

"You want to get dressed now?" Denny asked him. His aide had helped him remove his clothes before and remained in charge of them for now.

"Sure," Liam said. That would give him a little more time here.

It would also give him a little more time to be naked in front of Rosa, as his body returned to normal. He hid his smile as Denny turned to retrieve his backpack, which contained the camo outfit Liam had been wearing.

As he stood straighter, squaring his shoulders, he glanced in Rosa's direction. She was watching him. Good. But he couldn't interpret her expression. Was that relief he saw? Maybe. She caught his gaze and smiled wanly. "Good to see you back, Lieutenant," she said.

Denny lowered the sheet then, holding out Liam's clothes with his other hand. He took his time accepting the items, slowly leaning over to don his briefs, then his pants, and finally his shirt.

All the time shooting glances toward Rosa, but not just her. He needed to get dressed—but he liked the idea that she continued to observe him. And the others were watching him, too, undoubtedly to make sure he was doing okay.

"Good job," Patrick finally said, when Liam was done.

They hadn't returned to the lab building when Liam was finished shifting back. Rosa found that interesting, since that had been the plan. But there apparently was no need right now.

What Liam apparently needed was rest. And so Denny left them for a while, then drove up in a car and helped Liam inside. "I'm taking him to his quarters in the BOQ," he explained to her.

The others apparently knew that. None apparently intended to accompany Liam and his aide.

Rosa wished she could——to make sure that Liam rested well, returned to normal. Didn't shift back or need a veterinarian.

Didn't need a hug, which she felt like giving him.

In support of him…and herself.

She kind of needed a hug after that. It had been an amazing experience to watch him shift—both ways.

To examine him in shifted form.

To see what he looked like when he returned to being a man. All man.

So maybe it was best that she stayed far away from his residence that night. She might be somehow turned on by seeing him that way, but clearly they would never do anything about it, particularly not tonight.

She walked back to the lab building with the others, since her car was parked near there. She talked with them about the experience she'd just had.

"Thanks for letting me watch," she said. "And I'm so glad Liam didn't really need my help as a veterinarian."

"We're all glad about that." Patrick looked down at her and smiled. She had noticed before that he was a nice-looking guy. He seemed a bit older than the others, which made sense. He was a senior officer, in charge for now. And he appeared to know what he was doing, as well as care about those who reported to him.

Something occurred to Rosa. "I'm sure you'll be talking to Melanie, right?"

"Yes," Patrick said. "We'll let her know tomorrow how things went, tell her we intend to use this new formulation to help Drew."

"You're sure it'll work for him, too?" she had to ask.

"We've every belief it will," said Jonas from her other side.

"Great. Is it okay if I tell her what I saw here with Liam? I'll let her know when I see her how well this went, although I won't make any promises to her. That's up to you." She sent a grin toward both guys, hoping it appeared real. She still had her misgivings about Drew.

But she really, really hoped the stuff worked as well for her boss's husband as it had for Liam.

"Yep," Patrick said. "It is. But sure, if you talk to her first you can tell her how things went today, and tell her I'll be in touch."

"At least we all have reason to feel optimistic."

"Yes," Jonas said, "we do."

And on her drive back home that evening Rosa felt more than optimistic. She felt happy.

But she wondered when she'd see Liam again, and under what circumstances.

She decided to stop at the clinic, partly to make sure all was well there, partly to talk to Melanie if she was present and partly just to check on Drew. She wouldn't say anything to him about what had gone on this evening, with Liam's shifts that first prevented him from changing back to human form, and then allowed him to choose. The wonderful result—Liam was once again in human form, as he'd wanted. As they'd all wanted.

But telling Drew was up to the Alpha Force people. She didn't want to provide Drew with any hope that could be dashed because of circumstances she didn't know about.

It was about nine o'clock when she parked on the

nearly empty street in front of the place and, after walking to the back door, used her key to go inside. Melanie was unlikely to be there that night, with her young kids at home, unless she happened to drop in quickly to see Drew.

As far as Rosa knew, there were no other animals besides Drew who were staying overnight and might need some additional attention before morning. Even so, she walked through the hospital and stopped at the room considered to be the infirmary, which contained crates where overnight patients were kept. It was empty. Good. She breathed deeply, glad she didn't have to handle any treatments that night.

She heard a whine from down the hallway, though— in the direction of the exam room where Drew was staying for now. She headed there. Was Noel Chuma hanging out there tonight? The aide hadn't been with them at the base for Liam's test shift, and Rosa had assumed he was still hanging out here with Drew.

But Noel wasn't in the room. Drew had clearly heard her walking around, since he was sitting up on the towels on his table, watching the door. "Hi, Drew," Rosa said in an upbeat tone. "How are you doing tonight?"

Not that she really expected him to answer, but he clearly understood what she said. He nodded his head slowly, but this time the sound he made was more like a loud, snorting sigh.

"I get it," she told him. She wished she could do something, say something, to make him feel better. But she again worried about giving him hopes that could turn out to be false. "Anything I can get for you? Anything I can do for you?" She confirmed there was a bowl filled with water on the floor that he could easily access, and she felt certain he'd been given his dinner earlier by Melanie. A burger? That was more likely than dog food.

Surprisingly, Drew stood up on his hind legs and braced his front paws on the wall of the exam room for support. He looked at her, nodding, then let go and danced in a canine circle.

"That looks like human actions to me," she said. "I'm delighted that you still know who you are." As Liam had, although his timing was far different from Drew's.

And Rosa, at the time, couldn't wait till Liam changed back again, too.

Drew uttered a low woof as he lowered himself back to the floor in a more canine position. He looked beyond her, moving his ears.

Did he hear something? Someone?

In a moment Rosa heard footsteps in the hallway. Drew must have heard them when the person was farther away.

No—persons, plural. A few seconds later the door opened. Noel came in first, then Melanie, carrying her son and holding her daughter's hand. Andy and Emily both wore pajamas and looked tired, as if they had just been awakened, but the adults appeared full of energy.

The grin on Melanie's face was huge, and Noel appeared happy, too. Rosa believed she knew why.

They must have talked to the Alpha Force folks, learned of their success with Liam that night.

But could they—would they—reveal to Drew what had happened?

She found out quickly. Melanie let go of Emily's hand and knelt down, carefully placing their son on the towels beside the wolfen creature there before giving him a big hug. "We've got some reason for optimism at last, honey. Just wait till you hear."

"Yeah, good news, sir," Noel said to his canine charge who was also his superior officer. "Are you going to tell him, Melanie?"

"Oh, yes." Melanie sat on the floor after picking up Andy again, and their young daughter joined her, on her lap. "Emily, you can tell your daddy that his friends did an experiment this evening, and it went well."

"Daddy, friends," began the child, but she was interrupted by Drew's bark, which somehow sounded ecstatic. He stood and nuzzled first Emily, then Melanie and Andy.

"You were there, weren't you?" Noel asked Rosa.

Busted. She nodded. "That's right, but I didn't think I could discuss it in front of Drew. I figured the Alpha Force guys would want to be the ones to let him know."

"Very appropriate." Melanie stood once more, holding their son and looking at Rosa. The sorrow and pallor Rosa had seen before on her boss's face had disappeared. "But Patrick phoned Noel and told him to go to my house to take a call there."

Then he'd changed his mind about waiting until morning, Rosa realized.

"I was so afraid at first…" Melanie didn't finish that sentence, but Rosa could guess what was on her mind. If Noel had been told to be out of Drew's presence for the call and had told Melanie that, she'd possibly anticipated bad news.

"Well, I don't know how these things are supposed to go," Rosa said, looking down into Drew's intense eyes. "But I saw Liam drink something, then shift into wolf form and not be able to shift back at first, then drink something else and change back." Oh, yeah. Into human form. Very human form.

"That's fantastic," Melanie said. "And since Patrick told Noel and me that in the phone call and didn't tell us not to let Drew know—well, that sounds like a good sign to me."

Rosa hoped that was true…

"Me, too," Noel said. "I gather that tomorrow night will be when they'll give it a try." At Drew's canine glare, Noel amended, "They'll do it. Everything will be fine tomorrow night."

Rosa definitely hoped so.

She didn't imagine she'd be there to watch, which was fine with her. If Drew needed some kind of veterinary attention before he shifted back, his wife would undoubtedly be there to help.

Liam would probably be there, too.

Once more, she wondered when she would see him next—for surely, sometime they'd be together for something relating to Alpha Force.

She couldn't help hoping that it would be soon.

Chapter 11

He was back at his apartment in the BOQ. Denny had left after driving him there and helping him inside.

Liam's energy was returning. His feelings of being human were all there.

It had worked! He had an urge to grab a bottle of beer from his fridge to celebrate, but knew better. Too soon after a shift wasn't any better than drinking before it, especially since some of the potions he'd imbibed undoubtedly remained inside him.

And so he decided to get his high another way.

Not at first, though. He got a bottle of water instead from his refrigerator and turned on his computer. For a while, he checked online. There weren't many new posts at his usual sites about shifters and damage they'd done under the recent full moon, and he was glad about that. Some did have added mentions of shifters more generally, and he assumed one of his false identities once more to add his own posts to make fun of them—pretending to be someone who was so excited about the idea of becoming a shifter he was willing to eat wolf poop to give it a try. Oh, that wouldn't do it? Gee, that's too bad.

And he quickly got some responses including LOLs—laugh out loud.

But he slowed down soon. It was nearly time to go to bed.

He had something he wanted to do first—the high he had considered before, sort of. This near eleven o'clock might be too late to call Rosa, but he did it anyway, sitting on top of his bed in his underwear. It was almost time to go to sleep, after all, and he was especially tired after this unusual evening.

As he picked up his phone, he noted he'd missed a call from Chuck. It was too late to call his brother back, especially since they opened the restaurant early in the morning. He'd pop in there tomorrow to see him.

Then he pressed in the number for Rosa.

"Hi, Liam?" she answered almost immediately. "Are you okay? Do you need any medical treatment or—"

"Not from you," he said. "I'm still in human form, or I wouldn't be talking to you this way. No, I just wanted to say good-night and thank you again for being there in case I did need some veterinary assistance before."

"Anytime," she said, and he heard a noise, with his intense canine hearing, that might have been a swallow, as if she'd just realized what she'd said. She'd sort of offered to always be there for him if he needed her while shifted.

Now maybe he could get her to make a similar offer while he was in human form…

No. She might accept the existence of shifters, but she probably had no interest in getting more involved with one.

Although she had seemed quite interested in seeing him naked while he was shifting—but that didn't mean anything other than the fact she was one sexy, non-shifting lady.

"I'm just calling to let you know I'll be at your clinic tomorrow morning to talk to Drew about how things went," he said.

"Melanie already did. She and Noel heard from Patrick, and they let Drew know about it, too."

"Well, I assume he'll want to hear it direct from this source, too. So maybe I'll see you tomorrow at your clinic."

"I'll certainly be there," she said, "so I'll see you tomorrow."

As they hung up, though, Liam ignored an urge to see her tonight. Really see her tonight.

As they both got naked…

Not going to happen tonight or any other night, he told himself, ignoring the beginning of a somewhat inappropriate, very human erection.

But the idea remained in his mind till he finally fell asleep.

Rosa had been reading in bed when Liam called, a detailed veterinary journal that usually wound up blurring her vision and relaxing her enough so she would eventually fall asleep. But after she heard from Liam she was wide-eyed once more.

She could no longer concentrate on the magazine, so she stopped trying. As she lay there with her eyes closed, what kept going through her head was a re-hashing of all that had happened around her that day.

Amazing stuff—watching a man shift into wolf form and back again.

Unnerving stuff—wondering if he would, in fact, be able to shift back.

And much too arousing stuff, seeing that sexy shifter nude in human form.

Still, she fell asleep eventually and woke up the next morning bright-eyed and ready to head to work.

Now if she only knew what time to expect Liam…

She arrived early and after putting on her white lab jacket went to check on Drew right away, as she had last night. Brendan was in the room with him, not Noel, and Rosa figured the Alpha Force aide might actually be back at his quarters getting some sleep.

"How's he doing?" she asked the young, thin vet tech in the standard blue scrubs. She watched Drew's reaction as he stretched on his bed of towels and looked at her. Was he irritated that she'd acted as if he wasn't in the room—or didn't understand her?

"He seems tired but okay," Brendan said from across the room, where he appeared to be reorganizing some bandages and other supplies in a metal cabinet. He responded in a way that also didn't acknowledge Drew's background.

The wolf-dog stood and moved toward Rosa. He sat and reached one paw out as if he wanted to shake, but as she reached down to oblige he batted her hand and growled.

"I get it," she said. "But if all goes as well as we

hope, you'll be...yourself later today." She didn't want to go into too much detail despite being sure that Brendan knew who and what Drew was. But since they didn't really talk about shifters around here, based on Melanie's preferences, Rosa chose to follow their employer's opinion and keep things discreet.

He nodded, then turned away.

The exam room door opened and Melanie came in. "Oh, good, you're here, Rosa. We need to talk about one of our patients."

Which was fine with Rosa, even suspecting that patient was Drew. "Okay," she said.

Melanie did her usual thing these days and knelt on the floor to hug her wolfen husband, which Rosa found both endearing and sad. When she stood again she faced Brendan. "Dina is at the clinic now, so since we've got a tech on duty I'd like you to stay in here for a while, okay?"

"Fine." Brendan patted his pants pocket and Rosa figured he was checking to see if his cell phone was there, since she doubted he'd hold any ongoing conversation, one-sided or otherwise, with Drew.

Rosa followed Melanie. Before they got to her office, the clinic's receptionist, Susie, entered the hall, followed by a large woman with a small and fuzzy Yorkie mix in her arms. "I'll show her into the exam room right there." As always, the senior greeter was dressed like the vet techs, but she had a choice as to what color lab jacket she wore. Today's was bright pink. She pointed her long fingers with nails matching her shirt toward a door across from them.

"Very good," Melanie said. "One of us will be there in just a minute." She smiled at the patient's owner, whose tense expression softened into what appeared to be relief.

Rosa wondered what was wrong with the little dog and hoped she would be the one to find out. Then she would do her damnedest to make sure the pup recovered from whatever it was fast.

Sure, she cared what was going on with Drew, but he appeared okay for now, and there was nothing she could do for him but make an attempt to keep him cheerful. Melanie would be better at doing that, although she needed to treat patients, too. Brendan seemed to have things together, so they could rely on him, at least for now. And maybe Noel would return after getting some sleep.

Before the rest of the Alpha Force people came to do as they'd done with Liam the night before...

Liam. He'd said he would be here this morning, but maybe he'd meant when the others came, late afternoon or evening.

She'd look forward to seeing him, of course, and convincing herself that he remained well—and in human form.

Whenever he got here.

They were in Melanie's office now, and her boss closed the door, motioning for Rosa to take one of the seats facing her desk. She did so, but was eager to leave so one of them could go examine their small dog patient outside.

"I guess there's nothing really new to discuss right now about Drew and what to expect." Melanie stood beside Rosa rather than sitting down. "We discussed it all last night—or I assume you didn't have any more to add about what you saw with Liam."

Only that he had a gorgeous naked human body, but she certainly wasn't going to mention that. She wished she could forget it…didn't she?

But she understood what Melanie really wanted—or thought she did. Rosa stood again and faced her boss. "I wish I could guarantee that Drew will easily slip back into his human incarnation tonight, Melanie. And I did see Liam struggle before he got that new Alpha Force drink, then succeed in changing back after he received the new formula they developed for this. I don't know much about it—and you're aware of that. I don't know what will happen tonight. But, hey, boss, at least there appears to be a good chance all will go well. We all certainly hope so."

Tears welled in Melanie's gleaming blue eyes. Rosa stepped forward and gave her a hug.

"Thanks." The word came out in a rasp, and Melanie hugged Rosa back. "Will you be here to watch this time?"

"If you want me to, and the Alpha Force folks let me."

"I do, and they will. Now—would you please go take care of our patient? I need to have a few minutes to myself right now, but I can assure you I'll be ready for our next patient."

"Sounds good." One more quick hug, and Rosa left the room.

It turned out that Nutsy, the little Yorkie mix, had been running around in his family's yard and started limping. His owner had swept him up into her arms and brought him right here after stretching his legs and touching the bottoms of his paws, but not finding anything to explain the limp.

Rosa, on the other hand, discovered the cause immediately after first gently squeezing those paws, then examining them using a flashlight. "Burrs," she said. "A couple of them between the pads on both paws on the right side. No wonder he was limping. That had to hurt."

It could have been discovered by his now relieved, hugely smiling senior owner, but it hadn't been. She'd have to pay for the visit, plus some antibiotic to ensure the areas didn't become infected, but she seemed thrilled that Rosa had rescued her little Nutsy.

Nutsy was just Rosa's first case that day. She gave shots and an annual exam to a cat who was a long-time patient. She provided another exam, this time to a six-month-old mixed breed puppy. She checked an older Great Dane with a heart murmur, and a much too young cocker spaniel with hepatitis.

Fortunately, they all left with happy owners and the likelihood of having happy lives for quite a while longer.

As Rosa entered the reception area after sending the cocker and her family on their way, she was surprised—well, not too surprised—to see Liam entering from the outside. It was now late morning.

"Well, hi, Doc," he said, then told Susie he was there to see their patient in the exam room. He didn't mention Drew's name in the crowded reception area—a good thing, since locals might know Melanie's husband's name but not his background.

"Fine," she said. "Go ahead back."

"Great. Doc, I've got a couple of questions. Could you come with me?" He aimed an innocent, large-eyed expression at Rosa that she didn't trust a bit.

But she wanted to know what was on his mind. Besides, there was only one patient waiting in the reception area, and Rosa knew Melanie was nearly done with her current patient. "Sure," she said, but nevertheless looked toward Susie. "Let me know, though, if I'm needed right away."

"Of course, Doc. But we're good for now."

And so Rosa found herself walking into the rear hallway with Liam. She was happy to see him—even though he was fully dressed, in his usual military camo uniform.

"So how's our patient?" he asked, when the door was closed behind them.

"In good health, as far as I can tell," Rosa told him, looking up into Liam's amused brown eyes, "though I have to admit I wouldn't necessarily recognize symptoms common to shifters that regular canines don't get."

"Oh, we're pretty much like regular canines when we look like them," he said.

"Except for your minds. And your abilities to shift back. And—"

"Okay, you have us pegged."

"I assume that was your first question," Rosa said. "Do you have any more?"

"That's the most important one."

The hallway seemed shorter than usual, since they reached the door to Drew's room quickly. Or maybe it was just that Rosa was enjoying being in Liam's company. He reached around her and opened the door into Drew's exam room.

The wolf-dog was sitting up, watching them enter. He'd obviously heard them. Noel was on the floor beside him with a bunch of bandage pads arranged in rows. Some had *X*s on them and others had *O*s. "We're playing a modified version of tic-tac-toe," he told the others. "Drew's using his nose and doing a pretty good job."

Rosa laughed, and Liam clapped. "Good job—and good way to pass the time till you can do it all again with your fingers," Liam said.

The wolf who was Drew barked softly, and all the others laughed.

"Okay, looks like you need a reward, sir." Liam looked at Drew. "It's nearly lunchtime, and I've got an urge to go visit my relatives and their restaurant. Care for a hamburger or two?"

Drew barked even louder, nodding his wolfen head.

"And I'm going to need help carrying food for everyone back here." Liam looked at Rosa. "Care to accompany me?"

"Why not?" she said, though she figured there were plenty of reasons not to. But unless a new, urgent patient came in or Melanie wanted her here, she would ignore all those reasons for now.

Good. Drew was doing well, and he would do even better tonight. Liam felt sure of it—as sure as he could be. Their initial triggering shifts for taking the new elixir formula had been different from what Liam was used to, of course, so no guarantees.

But after requesting a few minutes alone in the exam room with Drew and telling Rosa he'd meet her in the reception area shortly, Liam described for his mentor what he had gone through last night and assured him that he'd be among the Alpha Force members who'd be there for him that night.

It wouldn't hurt for Drew to be jazzed and optimistic.

"We'll celebrate in advance," Liam concluded, then told Drew he'd be back soon with his burger.

Drew nodded and shot him a wolfen smile. Then Liam left to find Rosa.

They were soon in his car driving to the Fastest Foods shop. "I almost brought Chase along today," he told Rosa, "but my cover dog was scheduled for some training with a few of the aides, who were going to pretend he and some of the others were actually us, shifted. It's good practice for our cover dogs to continue lessons so they act like regular canines even when they can tell via their senses that we aren't regular."

"Sounds interesting," Rosa said. "Maybe I should watch that kind of thing one of these days to ensure the wolf-dogs are treated at least as well as their human counterparts."

"As far as I'm concerned, you're welcome anytime." He paused to make a turn onto the street housing the restaurant—and couldn't help asking, "So what did you think of watching my shifts?"

"They looked pretty painful to me."

When he glanced at her, she was watching his face. There was a gleam in her eye that suggested she was remembering not only his discomfort, but what else he'd done during shifts—like, getting nude.

"Yeah, there's some discomfort involved, but it's worth it."

"I'd like to hear more about that," she said, as he

parked the car. "Why do you like it? Although I guess you really don't have a choice, even as a member of Alpha Force, right?"

"I've got more choices relating to my shifting thanks to my military unit, but no, the shifting just comes naturally under a full moon."

They were soon inside the restaurant. As always, it was busy. Liam looked around for his brother, wondering again why Chuck had called him last night. Well, he'd find out soon.

He got into the line along with Rosa, and found they had to raise their voices a bit to be heard in the crowd. Once more there were a bunch of people ahead of them. This time, he didn't see his family, but figured he'd run into them before they left.

The person who hurried toward them first was Valerie, popping out the kitchen door in her dark blue shirt and jeans with an apron on top, and stopping right beside them. "Welcome," she said, looking only at him. Liam had gotten the sense often that his sister-in-law's sister wanted more than a flirtation with him, but he didn't even want the flirting. Friendliness was fine, though.

"Thanks," he said. "Right, Rosa?"

She raised her dark brown eyebrows when she looked at him, but then turned toward Valerie. "Yes, thanks," she said.

At least Valerie was polite enough to look at her and smile—for maybe an instant.

"Looks nice and busy today," Liam continued.

"As always," Valerie said. "I'm really impressed with all Carleen and Chuck are doing here. I may even stay a while longer than I originally planned."

Liam wasn't thrilled to hear that, but it wasn't really his business. Although maybe he'd have to actually talk to Valerie one of these days and let her know he had no interest in her beyond being a distant relation of sorts. "Speaking of them, are they nearby?"

"Always. I think they're both in the backyard giving Louper a treat. I'll let them know you're here, if you'd like."

"That would be great." But almost before Liam had finished speaking those words he saw Chuck heading out the same door Valerie had come through. His brother made a beeline in their direction, and Liam couldn't help grinning. "Hi, bro," he called.

A moment later, they shared a man-hug. "Good to see you, bro," Chuck responded. "Everything okay?"

"Sure. And with you? I didn't see until too late that you'd called last night, and you didn't leave a message."

The people in front of them in line moved a bit forward. Liam glanced toward Rosa, who also moved ahead. Valerie was still there, too, but ignoring Rosa, who glanced at her, then shrugged.

"Well, yeah, I just wanted to talk to you a little about—well, stuff. Can you come back later, maybe dinnertime? We could talk then."

"No, sorry. I've got things going on tonight." Just as a teaser, Liam said, "And the reason I didn't get your call last night was…stuff." Chuck was being a good boy and not even hinting at the word *shifting* in his nice restaurant crowd. But they both knew what the other was talking about.

But a look of shock and—was it anger?—came over Chuck's face. "You did? Last night? Without telling me? That's not right."

Liam blinked. He looked away and met Rosa's gaze. She looked puzzled. And, almost beside her, Valerie, too, appeared confused.

Once again the line moved, and Liam watched as first Rosa and then he kept up with it. He said to Chuck, "It's very right. You know what—what's going on in my life. I can discuss some of it with you, but not all. And not here. And definitely not tonight. Maybe tomorrow."

"Yeah. Maybe. Well, you're almost at the head of the line. Carleen's taking orders. I need to go back and help her. Let's talk tomorrow. I'll give you a call—assuming you'll answer next time."

"Make it tomorrow, and I will."

Liam watched as both Chuck and Valerie headed back to the kitchen door.

"Everything okay?" Rosa asked.

"Sure," Liam asserted. Then he added, "Maybe."

"Oh, dear," said Rosa. "Anything I can do?"

"Not now, but—"

Somehow, smiling at each other, they both said at the same time, "Maybe."

Chapter 12

They'd given their order to the person behind the counter—Liam's sister-in-law, Carleen. Rosa had seen his interactions just now with his other family members and wondered why his brother seemed upset, unless, of course, she had misread his actions. She'd met the guy only yesterday.

But the way Liam watched him and Valerie as they went back to the kitchen area convinced Rosa that she was right. Liam's good-looking face was marred by what she interpreted as a possibly puzzled and even a bit angry expression.

Chuck wound up talking briefly to his wife behind the counter, then disappearing, probably to somewhere else in the kitchen. Rosa and Liam soon reached the head of the line and placed their orders with Carleen, for themselves and the others at the clinic, including

Drew. If Rosa was reading it correctly, the woman acted polite, but as if she and Liam were strangers.

Because of her brief conversation with Chuck?

Strange. But it really wasn't Rosa's business—except that she felt bad for Liam.

While they waited for their order, after splitting the bill in half as they'd agreed while driving here, Liam walked away from the order counter between the nearly filled tables. Rosa thought about joining him, but one of them needed to be nearby to pick up their food when their number was called. Looked as if that had to be her.

As she stood there, glancing now and then at the number on the receipt to ensure she recalled the right one—which, of course, she did—she couldn't help wondering what all these customers would do if they knew the owners of the place were shapeshifters.

Probably just laugh at the idea, as most people would. Not her, though—not since she was a kid and first heard of such things. Literally heard them, since she often was awakened during the nights of a full moon by howls. Still—

"Sorry it's taking so long."

Rosa felt a little startled not only about the comment, but by who'd made it: Valerie. She'd had the impression that Carleen's sister didn't like her, possibly because she'd come in here with Liam, and the woman—probably a shifter, too—kept attempting to flirt with him.

Rosa was glad, though, that Liam didn't seem interested. Not that she wanted him to be interested in her, either—except as a friend and veterinarian to the cover dogs and shifters.

Now she responded, "I'm glad, for your family's sake, that the place is busy. As it should be. Even though it's fast food, it's really good."

"Even for a...regular person?" Valerie lifted her eyelids beneath her silvery bangs in a way that suggested complete innocence, but Rosa knew exactly what she was alluding to.

"Absolutely." Rosa made herself grin. She definitely found this woman—or whatever—rather annoying, mostly because of what she said. Or so she assured herself. It couldn't be because she didn't like the idea of anyone flirting with Liam—anyone else, that is.

Not that she was flirting exactly...

"Glad to hear that. And of course most of our customers are regular people."

Rosa didn't like that Valerie had said "*our* customers." That implied that she was in business with her sister and brother-in-law. Although in some ways she was, since she clearly was working here while in town. Or at least appearing to help out. She was even wearing an apron like the others sometimes did, over her regular clothes.

"I figured," Rosa responded, just as one of the people behind the counter called another number. She glanced at the receipt again. It still wasn't their order.

"Look," Valerie said in a low voice, sidling up so close that Rosa felt a little uncomfortable. "I'd really love to talk to you one of these days about what it's like to be a veterinarian who works with—well, you know. Some of the animals associated with Ft. Lukman."

At least she was being somewhat discreet. There were, after all, real wolf-dogs hanging around there who were the cover dogs.

Rosa kept her voice soft, too, as she responded, "They're good, healthy canines for the most part, at least from what I can tell. And Melanie Connell, the head veterinarian at the Mary Glen Clinic, is the one who tends them the most."

"Except for now, I heard."

It wasn't surprising that someone associated closely with Liam would know what was going on with his commanding officer, and therefore, to some extent, Drew's family. Though Rosa understood that the Alpha Force people hadn't wanted that kind of information to be made public in any way. Still—

"Number 94," called a youthful male voice from behind the counter, and Rosa breathed a small sigh of relief. That was their number.

Liam must have recalled the number, as well, since he joined her quickly, despite the crowd noise that clearly didn't prevent him from hearing the call. Rosa wasn't certain where he'd been, though it couldn't have been far away. But after holding her ticket up and shooting a small smile toward Valerie, she was the one to move forward and collect the plastic bags of food.

"Glad it's ready," Valerie said, but the expression on her pretty face suggested frustration. She apparently wanted their conversation to continue.

"Me, too," Rosa said, meaning it. She was ready to go back to the clinic, both to provide lunch to the others who worked there and Drew and his aide, but also to get out of here—and end this potentially uncomfortable conversation with Valerie before it got very far.

But she wasn't surprised when Valerie didn't stop there. She edged up to Liam. "So glad you came in. Two days in a row. Is this becoming a habit? I'm sure that Chuck and Carleen are happy to see you…and I am, too."

Rosa had no doubt about the latter. But Chuck? He hadn't seemed happy to see Liam—or at least to talk to him.

"Oh, you'll see me back here, I'm sure," Liam said, "though it won't be to pick up lunch every day. And you can tell Chuck, since he clearly doesn't want to chat with me right now, that I will be in touch, and I'll answer some of his questions."

Which implied he wouldn't answer all his brother's questions, Rosa noted.

She wondered what those questions were—and if they'd led to the apparent disagreement she'd noticed before.

"I noticed that you and Chuck seemed to have some kind of disagreement," Rosa said from beside Liam as he began driving them back to the clinic.

He'd first taken her behind the restaurant and said hello over the fence to his family's dog, which resembled a wolf. Rosa said hi to Louper, too, then remarked she was glad to meet him this way and not professionally.

Now, Liam's car smelled really good once more, since the aroma of all those burgers, and a bit of chicken, too, wafted around them despite the food's enclosure in plastic bags. He had an urge to stop and grab one, rather than getting into the pending conversation with Rosa.

But she was right, and it would have been hard for her not to notice the way his brother stomped away from him almost as soon as they'd arrived.

"Yeah," Liam therefore answered, but added truthfully, "although I'm not exactly sure what it was about."

"Well, what did he say?"

Did it make sense to tell Rosa anything about it? Apparently, Chuck wasn't thrilled that Liam hadn't returned his phone call, especially because the reason was "stuff"—in other words, he was shifting outside the full moon, and hadn't let Chuck know in advance. But that certainly wasn't the first time, nor would it be the last.

So what was on his bro's mind?

"Actually," he finally said, "I'm not sure. For some strange reason, I wasn't able to return his phone call last night, and I figure that has something to do with it."

"Yes," Rosa laughed, "a very strange reason. And from your Alpha Force's perspective, and Melanie's and probably Drew's, a very helpful reason."

She got it, then. In fact, this smart, beautiful—and sexy—veterinarian seemed to get nearly everything, including the good and bad things about his shift last night.

Did she get that he had some interest in her beyond her healing capabilities? It would likely be better if she didn't, but he nevertheless hoped she did.

"Well, I'll talk to him about it soon," Liam said. "Or at least what I'm able to discuss with someone outside Alpha Force and not connected by necessity, the way you are." *And by your smarts and caring and all that,* but he wasn't going to mention it now. "I'm sure he'll be okay about it, especially if I'm able to report that all went well tonight and a difficult shift that didn't change back has been resolved."

Rosa didn't say anything for a minute. And then, from the corner of his eye, he could see her look at him. "You mentioned before that your brother and sister-in-law are part of an experiment that lets them drink elixir on some nights of the full moon. That lets them keep their human cognition then, right?"

"Right," he agreed, pulling onto the street where the veterinary clinic—and Melanie and Drew's house—were located. "It's definitely an experiment so far and only a few close family members can participate. Since Chuck and Carleen relocated here recently, they were a natural fit for trying it out, though they didn't necessarily have to be chosen. I'm glad they were, but I'm afraid that Chuck now is making assumptions about his ability to use the stuff, and if not, whether I should have the same restrictions he does."

"Well, I'm not a part of all that. But in a way I can understand why a regular shifter who knows about Alpha Force's capabilities might feel jealous."

"But he and Carleen should feel delighted to take part at all." Liam knew he shouldn't take it out on Rosa, not even a little, so he calmed his voice. "I know what you're saying, though. Maybe, if they hadn't bought the restaurant, so have nearly all their time taken up by it, one of them could join Alpha Force."

"But then only that one would be able to enjoy the ability to use the main elixir regularly, right? And even then, it would be limited to military orders and use and all that."

"You got it," he responded. "But they don't get it, and they don't get the opportunities to use the elixir as I do." He sighed. "Maybe it wasn't such a good idea for them to participate in this initial experiment after they joined me here."

"Maybe not," Rosa answered. "But they're here and so are you. I'm sure you'll figure out how to make sure things work best for them, for you and for Alpha Force."

Liam continued to consider Rosa's words as he parked and they went inside the clinic and shared lunch with Melanie, Drew, Noel and the rest of the veterinary hospital's staff.

"You ready for tonight?" he asked Drew, in the room that had become his, just before he prepared to leave.

Drew nodded his wolfen head. Of course he'd be ready.

Liam just hoped that everything went as well with Drew as it had with him.

Rosa felt somewhat sorry when Liam left, but not too sorry.

He'd checked with the powers-that-be at Alpha Force. And yes, they wanted her to be there that night during their attempt to bring Drew back from being shifted.

No, she told herself. She needed to be optimistic. It wasn't just an attempt.

They would bring Drew back, just as Liam had once again shifted into human form.

She'd said goodbye to Liam after lunch and confirmed she would come with Melanie to Ft. Lukman a little later.

"Do you think it's a good idea for her to be there?" she asked Liam at the back door before he left. "If things don't go as planned—"

"She's been affiliated with Alpha Force longer than either you or me." His deep brown eyes looked down on her understandingly. "I know she's expecting to be there, and I mentioned her to Patrick when I confirmed they want you there."

"Well, that's good, then."

"Very good, since if anything goes wrong while Drew's still in wolf form you'll be there to help. I doubt that Melanie would be able to stay detached enough to do it."

"Probably not," Rosa said. "So, we'll see you tonight."

The expression on his face appeared very welcoming, and very sexy. "Yeah," he said. "See you tonight."

She had an urge to reach out and hug him. Maybe even do the unthinkable and give him a kiss—just in support, nothing else.

But she did neither.

She had to remain professional.

Especially considering all that would go on that night.

Patrick, not Liam, drove the SUV that went to pick Drew and Melanie up late that afternoon, as well as Noel Chuma, who'd still been at the veterinary hospital.

Liam was told, though, that he could go pick up Rosa a little later. He was happy to do so. Very happy.

Was Rosa happy? He wasn't sure, although she clearly wanted to help out in the event something didn't progress as it should and Drew needed veterinary help. She had seemed to accept Liam's shifting without reservation, so she was unlikely to freak out about Drew's doing the same thing—assuming he did shift back, as they all hoped.

When he reached the clinic, Liam parked and tried to open the door of the waiting room, which generally was unlocked during business hours and beyond. But not today, and he understood that they'd closed early because the veterinarians would not be available. He pulled his phone from his pocket to call Rosa, but as he did the door opened and there she was, dressed in a casual shirt and slacks—no medical jacket. But she was carrying a medical bag. He, of course, remained in his military camos.

"Thanks for coming," she told him. "I was listening for you and heard you try the door."

"Hey," he said, "that's pretty good. Do you have the hearing of a shifter?"

Her face was the picture of lovely innocence as she said, "Sometimes I wish I did."

He laughed, then bent his arm and gestured with his other hand for her to grab it so he could guide her down the walkway to the sidewalk. He'd parked against the street's curb, as usual.

She hooked her arm in his and grinned. He liked having her that close for the short walk. He liked having her close to him anytime, he realized.

But after tonight, if all went well, he was unlikely to see much of her in the future. He might as well make the best of this short time.

"So how does everyone feel today?" Rosa asked, when they were both in the car and he pulled onto the street. "I mean at Alpha Force. I know how Melanie and Noel feel, and, to some extent, Drew, too."

"He's the most important in all this," Liam said. "How is he doing?"

"Just reading his actions and facial expressions, I had the impression of one very stressed canine." She hesitated. "How likely is this to work?"

"Very likely," Liam said, meaning it. "You already know it worked for me."

But he realized that didn't guarantee the same results for Drew. After all, he and others had shifted normally on the same night Drew ran into trouble, and no one knew what caused the difference.

They soon arrived at the gate to Ft. Lukman and followed the usual routine to provide credentials to the guards. "Things will be done somewhat differently today," Liam told his passenger. "It'll all take place in the lab."

"I wondered about that," Rosa said. "Drew is clearly already in wolf form, although I'm not sure that was the full reason why both your shifts were done out in the woods. But I thought that if something…er, if creating any changes to the formulation is necessary, or—"

"Or if something goes wrong." Liam parked the car in the lot near the Alpha Force building and looked over at her. "We're all concerned about that and, yes, I gathered that it'd be better to be near the lab in case they need to play with the elixir or with Drew, or anything else."

He reached beside him to open his door, but felt Rosa's hand on his other arm. He turned toward her and saw a look of concern—fear?—on her face. He grasped that hand as she said, "Liam, I— Things have to go well tonight. I don't have half the knowledge you do about any kind of shifting, let alone what Alpha

Force does. But I care about Melanie and Drew, and you and all the others who are being affected by what's going on with Drew. I want you to know that I do care."

"Thanks." He heard the rasp in his own voice. Then he couldn't help it. He stretched from his side of the car to Rosa's, bending over the console and reaching over to gently pull her head toward him.

And then he kissed her.

Briefly, yes, but for those few heated seconds, he felt as if his entire body had been captivated and engaged—and sexually stimulated.

"Wow," he said, as they mutually ended it.

"Yes, wow." Rosa's voice was low and raspy.

But she opened her car door and got out. And he did the same.

They had a highly important shift to observe.

The tension in the air was as tangible as if a veil of some kind had been lowered in the lab area. Rosa figured that if it was that obvious to her, the Alpha Force members, particularly the shifters with all their extra-acute senses, must be able to hear it and smell it and more.

But everyone sat in chairs set out at one side of the room—everyone but Drew, who sat on the floor in front of the rest. The seats had been brought from Drew's office, and Rosa assumed they all wanted to be closer to the counters and lab areas in case immediate modification to the elixir or something else scientific had to be accomplished.

Her mind returned often to that latest kiss from Liam, both reassuring and sexy. But the latter was totally inappropriate. She might like shapeshifters but it wasn't a good idea to be attracted to one, no matter how appealing Liam was while in human form. And she didn't feel entirely reassured, either.

Still…Patrick had left the lab area after greeting Liam and her. They appeared to be the last people expected. Everyone there talked quietly, allowing their conversations to include Drew, who sat in the center of them all, looking around with his wolfen eyes.

Appearing tense, or at least that was Rosa's official veterinary opinion.

"You okay?" Liam asked at her side. He'd been talking with Melanie and Noel. Melanie appeared anything but okay, so Rosa was glad she was at least talking to the other humans. Once again, she had left their children with a sitter. Rosa hoped that when Melanie returned home next, it would be with their dad, looking like himself.

"I'm fine," she responded firmly. She had to at least appear that way. But she was worried about what would happen if Drew didn't shift back.

Patrick returned to the room then. He immediately walked over to what appeared to be a large refrigerator and extracted a glass vial.

With great ceremony, he poured some of its liquid contents into a metal dog bowl, then turned to look down toward Drew.

"It's time," he said.

Chapter 13

Liam felt Rosa's eyes glance toward him. He swallowed the urge to reach toward her and take her hand in reassurance that all would go well.

First, he couldn't be certain of that.

Second, they were in a crowd who might misinterpret any indication that he gave a damn about how she felt. Or maybe it would be a correct interpretation. Either way, it was inappropriate.

For now, he just shot her a smile, then turned back to watch Drew eagerly lap up the formula in the bowl.

Would it work?

It had to.

The room was quiet as everyone watched, waited. Liam inhaled, his intense senses allowing him to catch a whiff of the specialized, important elixir. He recalled it, of course, from last night. Had it been modified at all since then? He didn't know.

He had felt his phone vibrate in his pocket soon after they had gotten in here and sat down. It vibrated again now.

He assumed it was Chuck calling, but he could be wrong. He would check later. He had already told his bro he'd be unavailable to talk that night, anyway.

He'd make time for Chuck tomorrow—and give him whatever update on the "stuff" happening tonight seemed appropriate and not under a high security alert.

One of these days he'd schedule a date with his brother to go someplace where they could talk and not be heard, where he could listen and respond to whatever was bothering Chuck.

Someday. Not now.

For the moment, he cast aside anything outside what was in his vision: Drew. Sitting on the floor as Patrick lowered the lights a bit.

Jonas Truro was acting as Drew's aide. The medical doctor who had been working with Patrick and others on the various formulas for the elixir now was the one to shine the bright light on Drew.

And now it was time to wait. To hope. To watch the shifter in wolfen form and hope that this time he would in fact shift—back to being Drew in human form.

To his surprise, Liam felt Rosa reach over to squeeze his hand where he'd rested it on his knee. Maybe it was okay now, since the lights around them had been dimmed and no one would be paying much attention to them, anyway. He turned his hand over and squeezed hers back.

They both needed some reassurance—even though everything that might or might not happen now was far from being anywhere in their control.

Still, he shot Rosa a quick, comforting glance, saw her smile slightly and turn back to watching Drew.

He did the same thing.

Drew moved his legs. Did that mean anything other than discomfort, frustration?

Yes! His rear legs began to firm up, elongate, grow larger. His front legs then started changing as well, back into the form of arms. At the same time, his body began taking his wolfen fur back inside. He grew larger, his head changing its form into one that was human. All of him was becoming human.

It was working!

Around him, Liam heard gasps of happiness, words of support, sounds of delight. Rosa squeezed his hand even more as she moved closer to his side, calling out Drew's name encouragingly. Liam did the same, catching her glance yet again, sharing happy smiles before again looking down toward the floor where Drew, naked except for a beach towel placed on him by Jonas, writhed, grimaced—and grinned.

Liam looked toward Melanie then. Her voice was perhaps the loudest, shrillest, happiest, and tears of joy ran down her face.

"Go, Drew," someone called—Noel? It turned into a group chant. "Go, Drew."

"Go, Drew."

That towel changed shape around him. Drew changed shape beneath it. And after a few minutes, the chanting still going on, Drew grabbed the towel with his now completely human hands, clutched it around himself as he stood and looked around, smiling broadly.

He was a tall man with hair that resembled his

wolfen fur—dark, highlighted by silver. He appeared somewhat unsteady, yet he continued to stand, to smile, then to gesture with his hand that wasn't grasping the towel.

"Hi, everyone," he called. "I'm back!"

The celebration was beyond anything Rosa had ever seen before. Better than a family happy to retrieve an ill pet whose health had been restored at the veterinary hospital—or at least most families. Better than a major birthday party. Better than a wedding celebration, or milestone anniversary festivity.

Well, maybe her mind was exaggerating a lot, but everyone had gone upstairs to the main floor of the building, let the cover dogs out of their enclosures and entered an area Rosa hadn't seen before, a paved, high-ceilinged inside courtyard not far from the kennel.

She wasn't sure where the music came from, but it resounded throughout the room. It was upbeat, definitely danceable. Everyone watched and cheered and clapped as Drew took Melanie into his very human arms and led her around the improvised dance floor.

Two people, in love, dancing joyously. Lovely, Rosa thought. And appropriate. Even for a military unit? Well, why not?

At their feet, the wolflike dogs roamed the room, accepting pats from the other people there and acting as if they, too, were happy.

For the moment, Rosa was the only other woman there besides Melanie. She half hoped Liam would ask her to dance—but it was Patrick who requested that she join him.

Of course she did, as part of the ceremony. Besides,

she'd heard he was married. But his wife, Mariah, was a well-known wildlife photographer, and Rosa gathered that she was off on some kind of research assignment. As far as Rosa knew she wasn't a member of Alpha Force, either, so she probably wouldn't have been there that day even if she was in town.

The song ended. "Thank you, m'lady," Patrick said to her, bowing at the waist.

What else could she do but curtsy? "And thank you, sir," she said.

"Hey, everyone," Liam called. He stood near the entry door, and Denny, beside him, held up a can of beer, with a case on the floor beside him.

Apparently, that was what Liam's aide had been up to, under the assumption that all would go well that night. He'd brought back drinks for the group to share, probably in a toast.

"Come on over here and grab a beer," Liam continued. "We're celebrating."

And in human form, Rosa thought. No chance of any of them shifting that night, at least not as far as she understood the process. She didn't know if drinking alcohol was ever good for shifters. She certainly wouldn't want to treat an inebriated dog.

But the celebration was clearly ongoing. As a result, she followed the others and picked up a can from the case. It felt cold, and she looked forward to drinking it.

"Let me propose a toast," Liam called, confirming what Rosa had anticipated. "To Drew, our amazing commanding officer, who's undoubtedly ready to command us once again."

"Hear, hear," everyone responded, lifting their cans in unison. In moments, they all had taken a swig of their beer—all except Drew, if Rosa was correct. He just held the can up and grinned widely, then waved it in the direction of Patrick, Jonas, Liam, Rosa and, finally and happily, Melanie.

He had, of course, drunk something else of great potency not long ago, so he was being smart, Rosa thought.

The crowd didn't stay together long, though. "I need to get this guy home for a good night's sleep," Melanie called out. "In his own bed, for the first time in a few nights." She wiggled her dark brown eyebrows in a suggestive manner that caused everyone to laugh.

Rosa figured, though, that the idea of a good night's sleep worked, but she doubted that Drew would be ready to take on any other enjoyable challenges in his bed that night. Not that she'd ever know.

Liam took hold of Chase's collar. "I'm taking my buddy home with me tonight," he pronounced. "How about the rest of you?"

The other Alpha Force members with cover dogs also took control of their own canine doubles— including Drew. He bent to hug Grunge, who had been among the others that evening. Melanie was the one to take control of Grunge, though. "Hey, guys, it's time for us to go home and see the kids," she told both shifter and dog.

Which made Rosa smile. She recalled then, though, that she had ridden here with Liam, and his BOQ unit was right here, at the other side of the base, from what she understood. "Would you mind dropping me off at my place?" she asked Melanie.

"No need." Liam was beside her now. "They need to head on home. I'll be glad to be your chauffeur again."

"Oh. Thanks." Though that might not be the most efficient thing, Rosa agreed that she didn't want to interrupt the married couple's attempts to get back into their routines now that Drew was himself again.

The entire group then dissipated. Rosa walked with Liam, Chase at his other side, as they headed to his car.

"That was amazing," she told him. "I anticipated that things would go well, of course, after all that went on with you last night. But since I'd been helping to keep an eye on Drew for the past couple of days I'm even more impressed that he's back in human form again. And that I got to see him shift. Shifting is—well, I don't know what to call it other than amazing."

"Yeah, it is. It's also a thrill for those of us who do it. Fun. Uncomfortable, sure, but well worth it."

"I'll bet it is." They'd reached Liam's car in the parking lot near the building, and Rosa got in while he leashed Chase in the back seat. When Liam got into the driver's seat, Rosa found herself asking, "Did you ever wonder what it would be like not to be a shifter? I mean, that's clearly so much a part of your life, what would you do if you lost the ability to shift?"

"Well, in our society, I'd rather get stuck in human than wolf form," Liam replied. "Especially after our little experiment, when I couldn't shift back as usual. I rather like being who and what I am, though. Shifters aren't fully unique, but we're definitely different from what's considered normal by most people. Good different. Really good different."

He hadn't started driving yet, and now he looked over at her, grinning. The expression on his handsome face did look smug, as Rosa anticipated. But there was more. The way he looked at her suggested heat and sexiness, as if one reason he was glad to be in human form at the moment was because of what he could do with his hard, muscular—and damnably sensual—body.

Which made Rosa wonder what it would be like to make love to him, and the very idea—not for the first time—ignited her insides and moistened her in her most vital area.

Their eyes met and Rosa saw heat and desire in Liam's gaze, too, which only turned her on all the more.

But no. That was wrong. Inappropriate, no matter how good it might feel.

She forced herself to yawn, covering her mouth as she looked out the windshield. "Boy, this has been quite a day, hasn't it? I'm looking forward to going home and heading to bed."

Uh-oh. Dumb way to put it, since that only seemed more suggestive.

But maybe it was all in her own head, since Liam started the car and said, "Yeah, I'm tired, too. How about you, Chase?" He glanced in the rearview mirror, and his dog barked softly. "Right. Time to go get some sleep soon, boy." And then he drove out of the parking lot.

Okay, he had to be imagining things. But he thought he'd seen heat and even desire in Rosa's gaze. Where had that come from?

Yeah, his own desire for her, he figured. Driving her home was a good idea. They needed to leave each other's company, the sooner the better.

Unless… No. He needed to think rationally. Act rational. Get his mind off his yearning to strip the clothes off her curvaceous and tempting body.

He was just feeling like celebrating even more after the Alpha Force success of this day—and yesterday with him. That was all.

He had to calm down, though.

It dawned on him then that he was heading in the direction of the veterinary hospital, but he wasn't sure where Rosa lived. Because they had previously discussed how things would go today, Rosa had taken a car service ride to the clinic that morning, after being told she would be driven to the base, and then home that night.

They were on the same wavelength, though—as they seemed often to be. "I figure you're driving us toward the clinic, and I do live near there," Rosa said, "so going this way is just fine. We're just about to cross over Mary Glen Road. But instead of turning left onto Choptank Lane, where the clinic is, make a right. I live on Porter Street."

"I was about to ask," he said, nodding. "I'm not familiar with Porter, so you'll also need to direct me when we get there."

"My place is a duplex, only about a block away from where we turn onto Porter."

With her instructions, they arrived at the place she designated in about five minutes. The street appeared entirely residential. Cars were parked along it, as well as in many of the driveways. Streetlights lined it, and most of the homes appeared to be single or two-family structures. Rosa's place was one of three duplexes in a row. It was two stories high, attractive, with a redbrick facade decorated by a large white front door and white window frames.

"Nice," Liam said.

"I like it. In fact, if things go as I think they will, I'm going to offer to buy the whole building. My land-lady lives in the other unit, but she's been talking about moving. If so, I'll rent her place out."

"Great idea."

And it sounded like Rosa had every intention of staying here in Mary Glen. That was good. At this point, Liam had every intention of remaining in Alpha Force.

Not that he wanted her to stay in his life or anything. But it didn't hurt to have another skilled veterinarian besides Melanie in the area—

Who was he trying to kid? Himself?

He liked the idea of having Rosa in his vicinity. Too much.

Then again, he was in the military. He wouldn't re-main at Ft. Lukman all the time, even though his main responsibility was using technology for the unit's good and therefore hanging out in his designated office. But having Rosa somewhere in the area was irrelevant to who and what he was. It had to be.

Still, he might as well enjoy her company for now.

He parked in front of her house, and she opened her door. Chase stirred a little in the back seat. Did he need a bit of exercise, or a walk for another reason?

He was at least a good excuse. Liam got out of the car, too, unsecured Chase from the back and put his leash on. "Care to go for a short walk with us?" he called to Rosa, who was watching them.

"Sure." She had been carrying the medical bag she

had brought along earlier, and now hurried to place it on the stoop by her door. Then she joined them on the sidewalk below what appeared, in the muted light, to be a neatly trimmed lawn.

Liam walked slowly, watching as Chase sniffed the grass and pavement. Rosa stayed with them.

"He's a good dog," she said softly, "no matter what his background or responsibilities are working with you."

"Yes," Liam responded. "He is." Chase also appeared ready to go back inside. Time for them to head back to Ft. Lukman. But Liam didn't feel in any hurry. Still—should he ask Rosa if he could have a drink of water? Tell her he wanted to discuss more about what happened that evening with her, in private?

Those could both lead to spending a little more time with her. Bad idea or not, he wanted to do so.

Before he said anything, though, she once again demonstrated their thoughts were somehow synchronized. "Would you like to come in with me for a little while—you and Chase? I could use another drink, and you seem sober enough to join me and still drive home safely. And maybe we could go over again what it really feels like to do…what you do, and Drew. It might help me in case I ever need to provide any veterinary treatment to the Alpha Force crew."

"Sounds good to me," Liam said. "And, yes, I'm sober. Maybe too sober. I'd love another drink, but I promise not to overdo it. I need to make it back to the base tonight in one piece, with Chase safe, too. And now that what happened tonight actually happened, I need to get up early tomorrow to dig back into my real work."

"All the more reason to have a drink together." Rosa had stopped walking, and in the light from the nearest streetlamp Liam could see that the expression on her face as she looked at him was somewhat sad. "We probably won't be seeing much of one another now that things are resolved."

"Maybe not," Liam said, "but since they were resolved favorably I'd be happy to toast it all again."

Chapter 14

Okay. Maybe Rosa wouldn't be seeing as much of Liam from now on, and maybe that was a good thing. It would mean there weren't any cover dogs—or shifted people—around Alpha Force who needed veterinary attention.

As she led Liam and Chase into her front hallway, she considered thanking him and telling him to leave. A few more minutes in his presence might only make her feel worse.

Although…maybe, if they talked over their drinks, she'd come up with a way to keep him nearby, at least for the immediate future.

"My kitchen is over here." She gestured beyond the open living room to their left toward the door just beyond it. "I'm much better at uncorking a bottle of wine or grabbing a beer bottle from the fridge than I am at mixing an honest-to-goodness drink, so I hope that's okay with you."

"Beer pretty much always works for me," he said, and she led Liam and his sweet wolf-dog down the hall.

Fortunately, Liam liked the ale she happened to enjoy and keep around. Rosa also put a bowl of water on the linoleum floor for Chase, then watched for a long minute as he began lapping it up. She felt enthralled and somewhat sad to see the dog refresh himself in her kitchen. Though Rosa didn't currently have any pets of her own, she of course adored animals. Why else would she have become a vet?

She had recently lost her only pet, a cat who'd lived a nice, long life and then left it peacefully. She missed having Rally around, but it had hurt so much to lose him that she had been waiting to rescue another.

When she finally looked up and took a sip of beer from the bottle she held, she saw that Liam was watching her instead of his dog. She felt a little embarrassed. Was her sadness obvious—or was he watching her for another reason?

"Let's go into the living room," she said. Not that sitting at her small kitchen table would be a bad thing, but they'd probably be more comfortable on her couch. Although maybe allowing Liam to get comfortable wasn't a good thing. Even so, she gestured to him and led him back down the hall in the direction from which they'd come. She didn't have potato chips or other snacks to share, but maybe that was okay. Maybe he would just drink his beer quickly and leave.

She sat on one side of her rather ordinary light green couch, and he sat at the other. She had end tables on both sides, so there were places for each of them to rest their beer when they weren't drinking.

She decided to start their conversation on a neutral note—though it wouldn't be something most people would discuss. "So what's next with Alpha Force? I know your group is secret and there are things you can't talk about, but do you have any missions or whatever coming up?"

"You're right that it's secret, and I probably couldn't answer you if I happened to know something, but I don't. Best I can say is that some of our teammates aren't at Ft. Lukman right now, so I assume they're either on some kind of mission or engaging in practice maneuvers."

Liam's expression appeared wry—why did that wryness look so appealing?—and he lifted his bottle to his lips. His very sexy lips…

If Rosa had considered his presence here a possibly bad idea before, now she felt sure of it.

Or maybe it was a really good idea.

"Okay, then what can you tell me about Alpha Force and shifting that ordinary citizens like me are allowed to know about?"

"It's preferred that ordinary citizens not know anything," he responded, "except in very limited circumstances, like somehow getting involved in one of our operations, or being related to an Alpha Force member, or taking over veterinary care of one of us while shifted, that kind of thing."

"I definitely know part of that. And you know I'm fully aware of the existence of shapeshifters. What can you tell me about shifters that I probably don't already know?"

He laughed. Then he grew more serious. "Want to know why I'm really here tonight, Rosa?"

Her insides suddenly caught fire—with hope, she realized, not necessarily because of what he was about to say. "Yes, I would."

"I wanted to have another opportunity to get together with you after all our meetings and whatnot this week. I figure we're both going back to our normal lives now, which is a good thing because it means that Drew will also hopefully get back to normal. But I've liked our discussions and… Well, you know."

She did know. But she wanted to tease him—especially since he happened to be describing exactly how she felt.

"No," she lied, "I don't know."

"Then let me remind you." Liam's beer bottle was suddenly on the table beside him, and he had moved his butt—his firm, sexy butt—closer to her on the sofa. Really close. He took her beer and put it down on the other table. And then Rosa was in his arms.

His kiss this time was the most erotic she had experienced with him, not just the generally friendly, though suggestive, lip contacts he had given her before. Somehow, he repositioned her so her back lay on the sofa, her head on its arm, with both his hands behind her—one gripping her behind.

His mouth was hot, and his tongue imposing in a delightfully sexy way. What could she do but kiss him in return?

His hands soon moved forward, first to touch her breasts, and then down to grasp her most sensual areas outside the slacks she was wearing—giving her a hint of what it would be like for him to really touch her there.

"Oh, Liam," she whispered against his mouth. They were supposed to be talking, weren't they? But this was much more fun. And then, impulsively, giving no thought to what she was saying—or was she blurting out exactly what she was thinking?—she said, "Let's go to my bedroom."

In reply, he gently rolled off her, and for a moment she missed the bodily contact. But he grabbed her hand, as if he was going to lead her, but instead said, "Take me there."

Which she did, out of the living room and to the end of the hall toward the stairway to the unit's second floor. She walked slowly up the stairs, still clasping his hand with one of hers and the railing with the other to keep herself from falling, thanks to her weakened knees, the way she kept turning to look deeply into Liam's dark, luminous, infinite brown eyes.

She heard the sound of Chase's paws as the dog followed them up the stairs, which were carpeted only in the middle. Soon they reached the second floor, which held two bedrooms and a bathroom. The master bedroom's door was around the landing, toward the front of the house, and Rosa led Liam there.

She hadn't had a relationship that encouraged her to bring a guy home since she'd started working here in Mary Glen. Now, after she turned on the lights, she looked at the room from the perspective of how seductive it was.

Not very, perhaps, with the mirrored dresser at one end and another chest of drawers at the far side of the closet door.

But the queen-size bed was in the center. Pillows were stacked at the end against the headboard, and the blue-and-green-patterned comforter covered the rest.

Sexy? Maybe not—but that bed absolutely looked inviting to her now in a way it never had before.

She glanced at Liam beside her. His eyes weren't on the bed, but on her. Eyes that spoke of desire. Eyes that appeared to strip her of her clothing as they slowly ranged down her.

But he didn't grab her or begin removing those clothes. Instead, he said softly, raggedly, "I want you, Rosa. You seem to want me, too. You know what I am, so before we do anything I want to make sure you—"

She grabbed him, pulling his head down so his mouth was on hers again. At the same time, she reached behind him and began tugging his camo shirt from his uniform pants.

Want him? Hell, yeah.

He maneuvered so he was soon unbuttoning her shirt. He pulled it off before she got his off, and in moments he took her breasts into his hands, massaging them roughly, but not uncomfortably, before removing her bra.

Her breathing turned ragged, her body heat became totally centered in her most sensitive areas—and soon, somehow, they both were naked and on top of her bed.

His hands were everywhere, on her nipples, below, all places on—and in—her that made her desire more than his fingers inside her.

At the same time, she took his hard, long erection into one of her hands, teasing it with her fingers, rubbing it up and down as it somehow seemed to grow even harder, more elongated.

"Rosa…are you ready?" His voice was even raspier now. Sexier.

"Oh, yes," she said, though she realized she might be making a big mistake. She had no protection here, or anywhere, since engaging in sex hadn't been part of who she was for the longest time.

She moaned as Liam suddenly pulled away, wondering for an instant if this was all a joke on his part—a very heated, sensual, unfunny joke. But as she watched in the dim light from the hallway, he moved off the bed and reached for his pants, which were on the floor beside Chase.

His dog moved his large, wolfen head from the area rug and looked at Liam as if taunting his master. Oh, yes, Rosa's imagination was on overdrive. Chase was an actual wolf-dog who didn't have human thoughts, yet she was ascribing mental acuity to him as if he was a shifter.

But she didn't think about the dog for long. She was relieved, happy—and admiring—when Liam extracted a small package from his pocket. He had brought a condom.

Good, smart, well-equipped guy, in more ways than one. His personal equipment outshone any Rosa had ever seen, in reality or fiction.

In moments, he'd sheathed himself and lain back down beside her. He began stroking her gently, as if she needed to be restored to sexual desire. At the same time, she rubbed his sheathed arousal.

And then he pulled himself up by his arms on the bed as if about to do a pushup—but instead held his body up by one arm while he used his other hand to aim his amazing sexual organ toward her own aching area.

The lovemaking act was every bit as incredible as Rosa had anticipated. She reached climax nearly immediately, as Liam apparently did, too.

Both breathing irregularly, they lay side by side for a short while, holding hands, laughing, discussing what they had just accomplished.

And teasing one another. Rosa was delighted, and not at all surprised, when they did it again. And again.

She was also amused—and delighted—to realize that Liam was prepared for each act.

He stayed the night. She was glad.

And when she woke in the morning, hearing Chase moving on the floor, she hoped that all they had done that night was an introduction, not an ending, to their being together despite not needing to work on an Alpha Force issue together any longer.

Rosa wasn't exactly the domestic sort, but she still managed to make Liam and herself some breakfast— nothing fancy, though. Toast with butter and marmalade, coffee and an orange.

"Thanks," he said, as he sat at her kitchen table peeling the orange. "This is a great, sweet ending to a great, sweet time."

She had to laugh. "That's almost poetic."

"Yeah, it is, isn't it?"

They had both taken Chase for a short walk first, after showering and touching one another again and— well, taking more time than Rosa had anticipated to start their day.

But when they finished eating, she locked her home

behind both of them as Liam fastened Chase into the back seat of his car. Her car was in the garage, since she'd left it there purposely yesterday and relied on a local ride-share service.

And so there was no more need, for Drew's sake or Alpha Force's or any wolf-dog's, for them to stay in each other's presence any longer, at least not right now.

She stood near Liam's car and ignored the fact that neighbors could be watching when he took her into his arms and gave her one final kiss. "Hey," he said. "Looks like we'll need to plan to get together just for fun one of these days, right?"

"Right," Rosa replied, then initiated the kiss she figured would be their final, at least for a while, since Liam seemed interested in seeing her again. "Keep in touch." And then she walked away as Liam drove off.

And ignored the moistness in her eyes. It was better this way. Sure, the guy was damn sexy, but he was a shifter. A healthy shifter. One she had no reason to see anymore—except for fun? Or maybe just if one of the Alpha Force dogs needed some vet care.

Well, she would just have to see if he meant that he wanted to get together again. But he'd have to call her, since she wouldn't be calling him.

Care for him? Yes. But have an ongoing relationship with a shifter? And what if something happened and he became like Drew and didn't shift back right away?

Could she live with that? Did she want to find out?

She just wasn't certain.

A few minutes later, she was in her car driving the short distance to the clinic. It was difficult for her to drive.

For one thing, she felt exhausted. After all, she hadn't gotten much sleep. And she still remained aware of every inch of her body, which had been touched so sensually, so often, by Liam. Her usual white scrubs almost felt too constricting.

And those kisses this morning, despite being enjoyable, hadn't been too heated out in the sunlight of the early day. Even though she doubted she wanted anything long term with him, she missed Liam's erotic touches already.

Besides, this was the beginning of a new day of sorts. She was on her way to work, to do her job, to take good care of animals that needed veterinary care. Including a couple of spayings she'd been warned about by Susie, since the receptionist also kept the schedule.

Drew wouldn't be at the clinic. If he felt well enough, he'd probably have headed right away to Ft. Lukman to take charge again. And if he didn't, he'd stay home and rest in human form now.

Either way, Melanie would be thrilled. As she should be.

Would she want Rosa to take over more patients while she celebrated? Before, she had wanted to spend all her time as a veterinarian, possibly to keep her mind off how her husband was doing. Now, she might want to spend more of her time with him—although if he was at the military base that wouldn't work.

And their kids? Rosa figured little Emily and Andy would be delighted to see their daddy as much as they could now.

Rosa reached the clinic and parked her car. She entered, as always, via the back door, then went to wash her hands at the sanitary sink before letting Susie know she was here.

Melanie was in the back room washing her hands,

as well. "Good morning," Rosa said. "And how are you today?"

Her boss's grin lit up her entire face. "A whole lot better than I've been for a while, that's for sure."

"I figured."

"Which is a good thing, since we're going to have a busy day. We'd scheduled a couple of dog spayings today before…well, before we got sidetracked."

"I know. Do you want me to take care of both?"

"No, let's each do one. Brendan can work with you, and Dina with me."

And so Rosa's day began. Both spayings were to take place that morning, and along with those patients were a few annual physicals, inoculations, a skin issue on a cat, an injury on a dog's paw.

A standard day at Mary Glen Veterinary Clinic—without a shapeshifter wolf in one of the exam rooms.

And no reason to believe that Rosa would hear from Liam any more that day.

Chapter 15

"So, any more social media posts about violent or murderous shapeshifters that we need to deal with?" asked Denny.

Liam had been sitting at the computer in his private tech office for an hour and felt a little stiff as he turned to look at his aide, who stood in the doorway.

"Nothing new posted within the last twelve hours," Liam said. "I've stopped having a good time making fun of all the dumb allegations, for now, at least, as well as the ones about shifters in general that make sense. I'm focusing on trying to find the sources of the original ones that contained all those false accusations."

"Any luck?" Denny came in and bounced into a seat beside Liam, scowling at the computer screen. The young Alpha Force helper, in his camos like the rest of them, appeared to have a lot more energy than Liam that day.

But it wasn't the seven-year difference in their ages that did it. No, Liam had engaged in lots of exercise and little sleep the night before—a very good thing.

Except it wasn't too helpful with his work here.

Neither was his regret that new posts had pretty much tapered off—nor his expectation that there would be more.

"Not so far," he said to Denny. "I gather that whoever did it might have some of the same skills that I do, the kind I taught you. They managed to create identities that make no sense if you dig into them, and the sources so far aren't clear. At least some of them are related, though."

"Yeah, like the ones who signed with the names of Greek or Roman gods. Well, knowing you, you'll figure it out." Denny popped up again, a grin raising the slight beard on his face. "I'll leave you alone for now, but I'll look forward to your showing me in more detail how you approached it. You're one damn great techie teacher!"

"Thanks. And now that you've complimented me like that, what can I do but comply and teach you more?"

"That's the Alpha Force spirit," Denny chortled, then left the room.

Liam hadn't wanted a distraction like that, but now he was glad it had occurred. He didn't feel like he was getting anywhere that day, and he was really frustrated.

But at least he was back on the job he was supposed to do, not just researching how a shifter could be denied the ability to shift back.

Still, even now that Drew was back almost to normal—they'd had a short meeting earlier where their commanding officer showed off how he looked and how his mind was working—Liam wondered how it had happened in the first place.

Not that it was in his job description to find that out, as it was the doctors like Patrick who'd figured out how to bring Drew back.

But even so… Instead of returning to his research on who'd really made those social media posts, he did some additional research of another kind: shapeshifter sorts of websites and all, those few that appeared to take it seriously, to check at locations he hadn't looked at before whether anyone suggested problems with shifting in either direction.

He had already discovered a site or two that sounded somewhat realistic, but even if they talked about things like different light emanations from a full moon or other triggers to shift or not to shift, nothing seemed potentially applicable to what Liam was looking for.

But he fully intended to make sense out of it somehow. Alpha Force had not only had its existence plastered somewhat over social media, but its members had been made to look like killers when they were shifted.

Sure, he'd laughed at the whole idea online on a number of sites, made jokes out of it, and got more people to agree with his foolishness than to seem to buy into the idea.

But it still wasn't good for Alpha Force.

He wanted to help his military unit now—and in the future. To envision, and help to bring about, everything the members could do to help their country. Change the world.

But to do that, they had to remain covert.

Which was difficult. Somewhat impossible. Yet

Liam intended to do all he could technologically and otherwise to accomplish that.

"Hey." Another voice called to him from the doorway. One most recognizable, and most welcome, especially now.

Drew's.

Liam turned. "Well, hi, boss. How ya doing?"

"A whole lot better now, partially thanks to you. You're probably the only other one around here who knows what it's like not to be able to shift back on schedule, though your circumstances were a lot different—despite being somewhat intentionally alike."

In his human form, Drew still resembled himself as a shifted wolf—at least a bit. He was slightly taller than Liam, and his dark hair was highlighted with silver—the way he'd looked at the veterinary clinic. Like Grunge, he had gold-colored eyes. His eyebrows were dark.

"Very true." Liam paused. "Do the guys have any idea yet why you didn't shift back naturally, let alone long after the moon wasn't full anymore? Something wrong with the original elixir?"

"Still checking into it. But—well, it doesn't hurt for you to know. The suspicion now is that somehow the elixir I drank wasn't the same as the one the rest of you had, or I was otherwise treated differently. But so far there's no evidence as to what it was or how it happened."

Liam looked into his commanding officer's face. "I've been checking the possibilities online, too, but nothing has stood out enough for me to even mention it."

"Well, keep at it." Drew walked up to Liam, slapped

his back lightly and looked over his shoulder at the computer screen. "Anyway, thanks for all you did. I've asked Melanie to thank Rosa for participating in attempts to cure me, too. You can second that for me when you see her next."

Liam took a deep breath, then looked into Drew's face. His CO was grinning broadly.

"Not sure when that'll be," Liam said honestly. "Or if I'll see her again, since I'm not the one who takes ill cover dogs to the veterinary clinic or anything."

"Well, I maintained some of my human cognition, and I gathered that you two had something going on, or might someday. And speaking from my own experience, there's nothing wrong with getting involved with non-shifters if they happen to be veterinarians who believe in shapeshifting."

Liam laughed. "Maybe not." But then he grew serious. "I do like her. But not all women, or women veterinarians, are like the really great one you found." Although Liam had a sense that Rosa was even better. Still… "I'm just not sure about getting involved with anyone, shifter or not. There's just too much going on around here."

"I get it," Drew said. "Anyway, it's all your call. She's a nice lady, and you're right. I happen to have a particular affinity for veterinarians."

Drew then asked about what Liam had been up to, what he had found, and they discussed the online social media stuff dealing with shifters, some of it possibly correct and some of it clearly wrong.

And in a while, Drew thanked Liam again and left. "Time for you to do some more of your unique research," he said. "Let me know if you find anything

interesting. Oh, and forget what I said about Rosa—
unless you decide not to." He laughed, then left.

Liam figured he wasn't going to forget anything
about Rosa. Not any time in the foreseeable future.

At least he had no reason to believe she could have
been involved in what happened to Drew.

Although with her background knowing about shifters, her ability to access Drew and the rest of Alpha
Force thanks to Melanie...

No. Surely it couldn't have been her, even if she had
the knowledge and skills to mess with the elixir. He
saw no motive for her to do such a thing. She seemed
to like shifters. A lot.

Unless she was a damn good actress and had some
reason he didn't know about to harm them. Maybe
she'd even become a veterinarian to gouge at them
more easily.

But why?

No. Couldn't be.

Yet if he was still going to seek answers, since the
idea had now crossed his mind, it wouldn't hurt to
see her under the pretense of dating...just to be sure.

And after last night—well, she would probably not
be surprised if he happened to ask her out for dinner.
Maybe even tonight.

Really?

Heck, yes.

Rosa sat at her desk in her small office, finishing
up some records on the computer. She needed to finish fast, yet still do her usual thorough job of noting
details, as well as questions, regarding the patients she
had seen that day. She first reviewed her prior notes

on the spayings, then began adding her most recent exams and treatments.

That's when she'd felt her phone vibrate in her pocket, and pulled it out.

Liam. His text message? Join him for dinner. Where?

No trouble guessing that: at his family's fast food place.

Well, that allowed him to kill two birds with one stone, though Rosa the animal lover always grimaced when she thought of that expression.

Even so… Rosa pushed the buttons to call Liam, smiling as she stared at the computer page in front of her where she'd been describing how she had treated that dog with burrs in his paw. The dog might still be limping a little now with that paw treated and bandaged, but should be fine soon.

"Hi, Rosa." The deep voice at the other end of the phone sounded pleased. And sexy. But then it always had sounded sexy to her, even before that aspect of their knowing each other had come true.

"Hi, Liam. Got your text. I'd love to have dinner with you tonight."

She considered suggesting someplace other than Fastest Foods. But she liked what they served, and she figured Liam always enjoyed the excuse to see his relatives again.

Well, for tonight—again—that was fine. But their dinner conversation would include some suggestions of other, nicer restaurants in town. She would be glad to pay her share, if that was the issue, or even treat him.

Assuming they continued to see each other…

"Wonderful. I'll pick you up at the clinic at—what? Six o'clock?"

"Sounds good. See you then."

That was only about an hour away.

And of course Liam was right on time. He called her on his phone from the clinic reception area, where he was waiting for her. "Susie is watching me. I don't see any ill animals out here, so I assume you can come now, right?"

"Right," Rosa said. "On my way."

She figured Susie was about to close the office, since Melanie had already left, saying goodbye first and letting Rosa know she was on her way home—to relieve her afternoon babysitter. Besides, though Rosa had hardly thought about it, today was Sunday and their workload was supposedly lighter—though that always depended on how many patients were brought in. Rosa was supposed to get a couple days off a week, but rarely took advantage. Melanie almost never took time off.

Right now, Rosa wondered when Drew would be home from the military base, if he wasn't already. As far as she could tell everything seemed normal, finally, with the Connell family.

Which made her feel very happy.

She shut down her computer and headed down the hall to the reception area. And sure enough, there Liam was.

He stood by the desk as if he'd been chatting with Susie. The room was empty except for them, a good sign that the clinic would be closed soon till early tomorrow. Unless, of course, an emergency called in.

"I'm ready to go," Rosa announced, looking first at Liam, then toward the receptionist. "Unless you say otherwise, of course."

"Hey, Doc, you're in charge here, not me," Susie said with a laugh. Then, looking from Rosa to Liam and back again, she said, "And I'd imagine you're going to have a good evening whether or not I wish it for you, but... Have a good evening."

Laughing, Rosa wished her the same, then strode up to Liam's side. He was one good-looking tall, muscular guy, and tonight he was wearing a nice beige shirt over dark slacks—no sign of his military affiliation right then, unless she counted his short hair. "You have a good evening, too," Rosa told him.

"I'm planning on it." He held out his arm, and Rosa grasped it.

"See you Wednesday," she called to Susie as they exited through the outside door. Susie's days off this week were Monday and Tuesday.

Rosa had grabbed Liam's arm as part of the show, but didn't release it till they got to his car.

Chase was fastened in the back seat, and Rosa finally let go of Liam to open the rear door to give the dog a greeting pat. By then, Liam had opened the passenger door, and Rosa approached to get inside.

First, though, Liam pulled her close and gave her a quick but sexy kiss. Then he said, "That's just to ensure I'll have a good evening, like you told me."

In response, Rosa got close to him again and they shared another kiss. "My turn to ensure I'll have a good evening," she said, and then got into the car.

Yet on the drive there, she wondered how good her evening would be. Maybe it was her own mistake, since she'd asked Liam how his work as chief technology officer was going.

He had pulled onto one of the main streets on the

way to the restaurant. The sky wasn't completely dark, so she could see the look he leveled on her then. "Not as good as I'd like it to be," he said.

"Really? Why not?"

"Maybe you can help," he countered. "Admit to me if you were one of the people who posted online about all the shapeshifters during the night of the full moon and all the horrendous misdeeds they accomplished."

He had to be joking, but his expression remained blank. He was focused forward while driving so she wasn't able to meet his glance as she responded as if he'd meant it, "You know I'd never do such a thing. I like and respect shifters. You've seen that."

"Just kidding," he said, though he didn't sound that way.

And Rosa kept quiet for the next part of their drive.

Chapter 16

Was it frustration that led to Liam's bad mood—frustration at not completely solving the puzzle that was his job, finding the identities of those who had posted those vile social media comments about shifters a few days ago?

He knew it hadn't been Rosa. He'd already given her a few moments of blame in his mind for causing Drew's difficult shift. And now this. Dumb. And wrong.

Heck, he had what he wanted for the moment: Rosa's company. His job, his responsibilities, his concerns—whatever the reason he was worried, it could all be put on hold.

"Hey, you know what?" he said.

"What?" Rosa's tone, unsurprisingly, sounded wary, and she didn't look at him. Which made him feel miserable. Having that beautiful lady look him in the eye—

when he wasn't driving, at least—and smile at him, give him one of her sexy stares…well, despite his not-so-great state of mind, the idea aroused him now where the sun didn't shine.

"I could use your help," he replied. "One of the things I'm trying to do on the computer, in addition to figuring out who posted some really nasty and incorrect stuff about shifters, is to make it all into a joke. We'll be at the restaurant soon, but for now would you help me come up with some new ways to make fun of shapeshifters—so I can stick them up on the web and make people laugh at the whole concept?"

Rosa was the one to laugh. "In other words, you want this ordinary human being who just happens to know that shifters exist to help you convince others that it's all just a big joke?"

She was looking at him now. He had pulled onto the street where Fastest Foods was located and slowed down. "Exactly," he replied. "For example, one of the posts on a major social media site said something like the person heard so many howls under the full moon that he grabbed his phone to use as a camera. Sure enough, when he got there he claimed to have seen a bunch of wolves that, catching his smell, began to stalk him. He snapped a picture before running away, but when he looked there weren't any photos. He was convinced of what he'd seen, but mad they'd gotten away without his being able to prove they were werewolves. I figure it should be easy to make fun of him, since he can't substantiate what he saw. I've got some ideas, but what would you say?"

This was actually a situation he'd run into frequently after responding to people who'd claimed to have seen shifters, but hadn't captured any pictures.

Sure enough, Rosa came up with almost exactly what he'd replied sometimes—dumb, corny, yet cute enough to make fun of the supposed shifter-viewer. "Easy," she said. "Just reply 'Were' and when they follow up reply something like 'Were? Where! Where are the weres?'"

Liam laughed. They'd unfortunately reached the restaurant parking lot and its long line at the drive-through. He considered driving around the block to give them more time to create answers to the posts he could describe to her, but figured this wasn't a good time for that.

But it would give them something else to talk about in private, in the future, when fellow diners wouldn't be eavesdropping.

"Hey, I think you'd be good at my job, too," Liam said. "One of these days I'll make a list of some of the idiotic posts that claim there are werewolves around, and get your input before I respond to them." Except for the ones that claimed shifters had hurt regular people around here—possibly shifters connected to the military. Those he didn't want to talk to her about.

Those he would deal with himself.

After pulling into one of the few vacant spots in the crowded lot Liam opened his car door and wasn't surprised when Rosa did the same. In fact, she was the first to open the back door to unhook Chase from his safety constraint.

Rosa was a veterinarian. A woman in charge. Someone who could take care of herself.

Just another reason he couldn't help feeling attracted

to her—which he had to tamp down before it slugged him even harder in the gut.

Rosa might be a woman in charge—but she wasn't Melanie Connell, not only knowledgeable that shifters existed, but willing to hook up with one permanently.

Although the sex he had shared with Rosa...

"Hey, Chase," Rosa said, as Liam got close to them on the smooth asphalt and held out his hand for his cover dog's leash. "Wouldn't you rather walk inside with me tonight?"

She reached down to pat the wolf-dog's head, and Chase leaned into her touch, clearly happy for the attention.

Which made Liam wish for a little attention, too.

"Okay," he said. "You've got him for now. But remember, boy, you're my cover dog, not hers." Liam had kept his voice low despite not seeing anyone with them in the lot. When he looked at Rosa, she grinned at him, then turned to lead Chase inside the back door of the restaurant.

As always, the aroma of cooked meats permeated the air. A good thing. And as he'd expected, the place was packed. He considered suggesting to Rosa that they go someplace else. In fact, one of these days he would ask her on a real date, where they could dine well without running into his family.

Although at the moment, eating here was the best way for him to find the time to see Chuck and Carleen.

"Hi, guys!" They were greeted nearly immediately— by Valerie. "Come on in. Are you eating here? I'll find you a table right away."

"Thanks," Rosa said, then glanced back at him. "I take it you do want to stay."

He nodded. "As long as it won't hurt the place's business."

"Anything but, since you've got your dog here, too," Valerie said. "Customers like dogs. Too bad Louper's at home today." She winked at him then.

The woman wouldn't quit, would she? But Liam hadn't ever faced off with her and made it clear he didn't really want to flirt with her.

And he certainly didn't with Rosa around.

Rosa had clearly seen the wink, since although she appeared to be scanning the full restaurant for a table, her body seemed to freeze for an instant. Chase, sitting beside her, stood as if he sensed her tension.

Maybe Valerie's actions were a good thing for triggering Rosa's interest in him, Liam thought. But did he really want her interest?

And if so, did he want it this way?

"Hey, bro." It was another feminine voice speaking from off to their side, this time Carleen's. "Glad to see you. Hi, Rosa, and Chase, too."

Hearing his name, Chase looked up. Rosa looked sideways and said, "Hi, Carleen. Good to see you."

Did she mean it? Rosa was a nice, polite lady, so he wasn't sure about her feelings regarding his family. But she never objected to coming to Fastest Foods and she undoubtedly knew she'd see them there, so she must be okay with it.

They soon got in line and despite the number of people ahead of them received their food—a hamburger for him and a salad for Rosa—fairly quickly. They'd left Chase in the corner at the table Valerie had found for them among the crowd of noisy patrons, and were soon sitting there eating.

But not alone, as it turned out. "Can we join you?" Carleen asked. She held a tray containing a couple sandwiches. Liam assumed he would see his brother behind her, but instead of Chuck she was accompanied by Valerie.

He looked toward Rosa, across from him, for her opinion and she nodded. "Sure," he said. And then, as they sat down, he asked, "So where's Chuck?"

"In the kitchen," Carleen said. "Where else? He's helping our main cook, since one of our assistants called in sick. I'll go spell him there soon as we're through."

"Great," Liam said.

Valerie started a conversation then about Rosa's veterinary practice, asking the number of dogs she worked with versus the number of cats, what other kinds of pets came to the clinic and that kind of thing. It seemed like a pleasant conversation. At least Rosa appeared happy to respond.

At a lull, Carleen asked, "How long have you been here in Mary Glen?"

"About a year," she responded.

"How did you happen to end up here?"

Rosa shot a somewhat pleading, somewhat exasperated look toward Liam as if asking for his help. He knew the story, but also knew she didn't want to talk about it, even to shifters—especially in public.

"From what I gather," he said, "Dr. Melanie Harding Connell was in need of a new vet to help her and Rosa just happened to fit her criteria." There. That was true, but it was general enough not to make any waves.

"That's right." Rosa sounded relieved.

The table nearest him emptied then, and it didn't

take long before there were other customers seated there. The group of twentysomething men and women who were about to leave stopped near their table, though, as if to say goodbye.

One guy, with a shaved head and short dark beard, waved in the direction of Carleen and Valerie, who sat next to one another. He was followed by the other two guys, who were dressed similarly to him, and the girls who wore casual yet flowing dresses in shades of pink. "See ya soon," the first guy said. "You know we'll be back."

"Hope so," Carleen said.

"When are you getting those summer seasonal sandwich combos that you've been promoting?" one of the girls asked. She was taller than the other two, with short, blunt dark hair.

"It's still May," Carleen said. "We're starting them in June."

"Got it," the girl said. "We'll definitely be back before then, won't we, Horatio?" she asked one of the men.

"Of course."

They turned to leave at last. As they did, the girl said to one of the other guys as they maneuvered away, "But can you wait till June for that summer fruit salad combo with a double burger that they're promoting now, Orion?"

Orion? A Greek god's name? One of the names in some of the worst posts about what shifters had done under the last full moon—a writer whose real identity Liam had been trying to track down.

"Excuse me," he said, standing to follow them. He took Chase's leash, partly as an excuse to go outside, and partly in case he needed assistance from a current canine if his target recognized what Liam was after and didn't want to cooperate. Chase might be a cover dog, but he was also protective and would attack if anyone attempted to harm Liam.

He saw Rosa's puzzled glance but had no time to explain now—and probably wouldn't want to explain later, at least not as long as they were here.

But by the time Chance and he weaved their way out of the restaurant, all he saw was the suspicious group of people entering an unmarked SUV, probably a shared ride they'd called.

He noted the license number just in case, but figured that wouldn't help identify any of them, let alone Orion.

Damn.

Rosa could tell by Liam's furious expression and the way he hurried after those people that they'd said something to really trigger something inside him. But what?

She remained at the table with Carleen and Valerie, who had stared after him and then returned to eating, pretending nothing was wrong. This was pretty much the first time Rosa had been in their presence when Liam wasn't there. She had no problem being with them. She'd have been friendly and pleasant even if they hadn't been Liam's family members.

Although maybe it would have been less stressful if there hadn't been a connection—especially the possible attraction between Liam and her.

"So tell me something about your upcoming seasonal meals," Rosa said to Carleen, so they'd have something to talk about. Carleen's smile looked a bit relieved, as if she, too, had been searching for a way to start a conversation. For the next few minutes she described how their new dishes were still fast food, but would have sides like fruit and salads that were a bit healthier.

Not necessarily things that shapeshifters like them were likely to enjoy, at least not when they were in wolf form, Rosa thought. But she didn't mention that even teasingly—especially here, where they were still surrounded by a crowd of probably regular people, like her.

Valerie ate her burger and drank water with it, but only picked at her french fries. Liam had told Rosa that his family members, including his sister-in-law and her relatives, were also shifters. Rosa was curious about how the non–Alpha Force members did under a full moon around here, but clearly couldn't ask that, either. She of course knew that Chuck and Carleen, as Liam's close relatives, had been part of that experiment the military unit was trying with their special elixir. Another topic not to get into, despite her curiosity.

To everyone in town, including these people, she was merely a veterinarian at the local clinic working with animals who needed medical attention.

And she wasn't supposed to talk about how, sometimes, some of her patients were of human background.

It didn't take long to exhaust the topic of the new meals. Rosa mentally searched for something else to discuss that wouldn't lead to anything secret or controversial.

Where was Liam? When would he get back here?

As it turned out, his brother got to the table first. "Hi, ladies. I assume it's okay if I join you." Without waiting for an answer, he sat down on the chair Liam had previously occupied. Fortunately, there were a few other empty chairs around, so Liam could commandeer one on his return. Assuming he did return soon.

Rosa certainly hoped he would.

Chuck carried a burger—what else?—and a glass of water on a small plastic tray. Once again, Rosa noticed the similarity in the brothers' appearances, although Chuck, slightly older, wasn't quite as good-looking as Liam.

Rosa worried that, in her mind at least, no man, whether a relative or not, seemed as good-looking as Liam. Well, it was okay to be attracted to him, as long as she kept reminding herself that their relationship was based more on their respective backgrounds and careers than on any independent attraction. Fun, yes. Long-lasting? Unlikely.

"So," Chuck said after he was seated. "I saw Liam sitting here before. Where is he?"

"Oh, he got up a little while ago," Valerie said. "Looked like he had something on his mind."

"Like the restroom," Carleen said with a grin. Rosa wasn't about to contradict her, since that could lead to a discussion she didn't want to have. She knew what had triggered Liam's departure—those people. What she didn't know was why.

For the next few minutes, Chuck talked about how good business had been that day.

"You always look busy when I come here," Rosa said.

"Which is a good thing," responded Valerie.

Before they got any further, Liam finally returned, Chase leashed and maneuvering behind him among the crowded tables. Liam clearly saw the situation and brought a vacant chair with him.

"Hi, bro," he said, sitting down. Chase lay on the floor beside him.

"Hi back, bro." Chuck scooted the open paper wrappings that contained Liam's food toward him—half of a burger and some onion rings.

Rosa wondered if Liam would mention why he'd left for a while, and he did. Sort of.

"So, Carleen," he said, "those folks who stopped here to talk about your new menu. Sounded like you know them."

"I know them as frequent customers," she agreed. "But that's all. Why? Do you know them? Is there something...about them?"

Rosa wasn't sure if Carleen was asking if they were shifters, too, or something else. She was interested in the answer.

"I just heard recently about a guy named Orion. Interesting fellow, and if that was the same one, I wanted to talk to him. Do you happen to know where he works? Where he lives?"

"No, like Carleen said, they're customers," Chuck said. "All of them, and some others, too, who are sometimes with them. Don't know if they work together or live in the same area or what, but they seem like one big crowd."

"Got it," Liam said. "Well—tell you what. Rosa and I will be heading out of here when we're done eating, but I'd like to follow up with those guys, especially Orion. Would one of you call me next time they come in?"

"Sure," Valerie responded. "But what should we tell them?"

"Not a thing," said Liam. "I'll just head here if I can and make contact with them. Since why I'd like to say hi is a little obscure and I might just forget about doing it, there's no need for you to mention it to them."

"Okay…" Carleen said, drawing the word out as if she was confused. Rosa figured they all were.

She wanted to get Liam off alone to get an explanation. Assuming he'd give one to her, since he hadn't to the others, and they were closer to him than she was.

He changed the subject then, and soon they were laughing over some stories Chuck related about a few customers—not those—who had tried to wheedle their ways into jobs at Fastest Foods. But their klutziness with their own bags and trays of stuff made it clear they wouldn't be able to handle the work here.

In just a few minutes, though, Chuck finished his last bite of sandwich and rose. "I've got to get back to the kitchen. Carleen, you, too."

"And me," Valerie said. "I've got some cleaning to do."

They all said their farewells to Liam and Rosa. Rosa was glad. She'd thought it might take some maneuvering and even begging a bit to get this evening ended. She wanted to go home and rest—and ponder all that had happened today. Not as much as on some days recently, but she was tired nonetheless.

Although if Liam decided to come to her place to tell her what all that had been about before, she would be glad to give him a good-night drink.

And if it led to more… Well, that was hoping for too much.

Plus if he really thought she could be making absurd comments online—well, she certainly hoped he was just considering everyone and didn't really believe it could be her.

A short while later they were in his car. He had to drive her back to the clinic to get her vehicle. And maybe that would be the end of the evening.

But Rosa hoped not. And so once they were settled with Chase in Liam's vehicle and he'd begun to drive out of the parking lot, she said, "I know there's something going on, and I want to hear about it. I'll even bribe you to let me know. Follow me to my house after we get my car, and I'll give you an after-dinner drink." And hopefully confirm that he didn't really mistrust her.

He pulled up at a stop sign under a streetlight and glanced over at her. "A drink sounds good. Spending some time talking—and maybe more? That sounds even better."

How could she refuse?

Chapter 17

A short while later, Liam and Chase were with Rosa in her living room. She had, as promised, poured drinks for Liam and herself, a nicely aged brandy from a well-known manufacturer that she particularly liked.

They first tapped glasses as Liam toasted shifters and people who helped shifters. That made Rosa laugh, but the intense and sexy expression on his face caused her to grow more serious.

"So," she said, to change the subject that was now percolating not only in her head, but in the rest of her body. "Tell me why you chased those people out of Fastest Foods."

"I didn't chase them out of there. As I said, I wanted to catch up to them. Talk to them."

"About what? I gathered your family doesn't know them well, only as sometime customers. What's going on?"

Liam took a deep sip from his glass, then put it down on the end table beside him. He turned back toward Rosa.

"Okay," he said, "I'll tell you—because I know you can be discreet. You know the reality about the existence of shifters, and you keep it to yourself except when talking to your boss and others with direct connections to Alpha Force. Or that's the way I see it. Right?"

"Yes, that's right." She swallowed a hint of hurt at his feeling he needed to ask for her confirmation. He knew her that well, at least, didn't he?

She felt a little better as he continued, indicating he must trust her, after all. He started telling her more of what he apparently didn't want anyone else to know.

It was about his job—his real job with Alpha Force as its chief technology officer. And about what she knew he'd been doing: researching online social media posts about shifters and shifting, particularly related to the last full moon—had it been only a few nights ago?

"Those posts that all but accused Alpha Force shifters of doing some real damage, particularly against people in the vicinity of Ft. Lukman—I've found a bunch, and so has Denny. Like I described to you—and you helped me with—we've made fun of them online to help make people who don't know the reality of shifting think it's all a big joke. No way of guaranteeing that, of course, but some of the comments we get in return make it appear that a good percentage of those who aren't sure at least enjoy the jokes—and hopefully consider them more of the reality than what's actually true."

"I get it." Rosa took a sip of her smooth, intoxicating brandy. "I've seen that kind of thing online, too, and have since I was a kid and started learning about shifters. Some people just like to talk about them, although most seem not to accept their reality." The fact that Liam had suggested she might be doing that now had hurt, but at least he'd retracted it.

"Which is generally a good thing on our behalf. And fortunately, a lot of the posts seem to be about books and movies, all fiction, that portray shifters the way their creators want them to appear. But a few seem real—and those that claimed that shifters injured people this last time mostly sound genuine, but they're not. Those who posted them sound frightened, though, and afraid what will happen during the next full moon and after."

Rosa pondered that for a few seconds. "But you're sure no shifter around here did hurt anyone, right?"

"I checked with all Alpha Force members, and Denny and I both looked online for the claims of what was done and the identities of those who were allegedly harmed—and it all seemed false. I also looked for the identities of the people who posted those claims... and one was named Orion."

Rosa felt her eyes widen. "Ah. That's why you chased those folks, including the guy called Orion. And it also makes sense that you'll keep trying to find him." She paused and took another sip while looking into Liam's deep brown eyes. They looked angry. And at the same time, she got a sense that he felt pleased that she now understood. "Isn't Orion a Greek god? A hunter?"

"Yeah, which also worries me. Some of the other people who posted that stuff also had mythological names. Don't know if it's the same person or a group, or they're just imitating one another, but whoever they are, they've made it nearly impossible to track down their origins—and I'm usually damn good at doing that." This time, Liam nearly finished what was left of his brandy in one gulp. "And by the way, one person who was out there a lot was named Diana. That could be her real name. It's a somewhat popular name. But—"

"Wasn't Diana the Roman goddess of the hunt?" Rosa pondered that. She hadn't spent much time studying mythology as a kid, but she'd always been interested in myths involving animals, so she'd learned at least something about it.

"That's right," Liam said. "And guess what? Diana's also the Roman goddess of the moon. Appropriate, don't you think?"

"Definitely." Rosa considered offering him more brandy, but if he was driving back to the base she didn't want to encourage him to do something dangerous, like getting drunk.

"Anyway, that's your answer. I want to talk to Orion, or at least the guy who was called that by his friends at the restaurant. He might have nothing to do with this situation. His name might actually be Orion, though I've never met an Orion before."

"Me, neither, though I've always enjoyed viewing the Orion constellation on clear nights when it's around."

"Ditto." Liam smiled at her. This time his smile seemed genuine. Amused. Caring?

She could be reading a lot into it.

A lot that she wanted to see there.

"Tell you what," he said.

"What?"

"Let's take Chase out for a short walk. That way he won't bother us."

"He never bothers me," Rosa responded, though she had an idea where Liam was leading her.

"Not me, either. But I want him to sleep later while we're…" He stood and held his hand out to Rosa. She put her glass down and grasped his warm, firm, sexy fingers.

He pulled her close, and the kiss they shared then made it very clear to Rosa where they were going that night.

And it would be a very good thing if Chase was nice and empty and sleepy, so he wouldn't bother them till they were ready to get up in the morning.

Liam stayed overnight. A good thing. A really good thing.

And over the next couple of weeks he managed to spend even more time with Rosa, sometimes volunteering to take cover dogs into the vet clinic for checkups, sometimes just asking Rosa out on a date—and not always at his family's fast-food joint. She invited him to her place often for dinner, too, which he liked. A lot.

Enough to not worry about whether he was seeing her too much. Enough to feel certain that the little hiccups of accusation his mind had aimed toward her now and then were totally false. If—when—they stopped seeing each other so much, or at all, he'd simply have to deal with that. And since neither of them wanted to call what they had any kind of relationship except for having fun…well, that was fine for now.

Meanwhile, he also popped in at Fastest Foods

sometimes on his own. No one had called him to say that Orion or anyone in that group had stopped back in, but just in case…

For though he still found posts to make fun of that mentioned shifters, he remained unable to track down in cyberspace the true identities of those who'd posted the nasty allegations against shifters, especially those supposedly in the military. Frustrating. Very frustrating for someone with his vast online skills.

Each time he went to the restaurant, he spent at least a few minutes talking to Chuck. At first his brother seemed to have calmed down after being upset with Liam, but not explaining why.

As time went on, Chuck seemed more snappish again, and Liam finally took him aside and confronted him about it.

"You know what it's about." Chuck glared at him, not a particularly good thing, since they stood facing each other in a corner of the kitchen—and sharp-edged knives used to carve veggies and fruit for the June menu were on the counter.

Not that Liam really figured his brother, who so resembled him physically, was angry enough about whatever to attack him. But he still wanted to know Chuck's supposed rationale, to be sure.

"Pretend I don't, and tell me," Liam said, crossing his arms and leaning against the wall.

Chuck drew closer, so close that his mouth nearly touched Liam's ear. "Shifting," he whispered. "Are Carleen and I going to get to—you know."

Ah. Liam did know. He'd definitely suspected that was the reason, but Chuck knew Liam had no say over whether the experiment continued and he'd be able to allow his brother and sister-in-law to get a dose of the elixir under the next full moon.

The upcoming full moon. It was getting closer.

And Alpha Force intended to be better prepared for it. In fact, Liam was scheduled to engage in a practice shift tomorrow evening.

But would Chuck and Carleen be happy when they next changed naturally under that full moon because they'd gotten a dose of the elixir and kept their human cognition?

Liam could make no promises.

"I don't know," he responded. "I'm not sure where the experiment stands right now. Everyone seemed okay with how things worked out last time, but that could mean they don't need to experiment again for a while. Or it might mean you and a couple of others at other locations could be permanent elixir-drinkers. I'll check, though I don't know if any decision has been made yet."

Their conversation ended then because Carleen and Valerie joined them. "Hey, brother," Carleen said. "I've got your lunch on the tray over there. I'm going to eat now, too, and intend to join you at one of our wonderful tables. You okay with that?"

Liam was definitely okay with that. In fact, he appreciated that his kind sister-in-law must have recognized what was going on and decided to stop it.

And when he sat at the table, it wasn't just Carleen who joined him, but Chuck and Valerie, too. They had a nice, friendly conversation as if they were just regular family members without anything else on their minds.

Liam got up to refresh his water glass, needing a moment to breathe despite how well things were going.

When he returned, a woman was standing there talking to the others. She was a pretty lady with short blond hair and narrow red lips, and looked vaguely familiar.

Was she one of those who'd been with Orion?

Apparently so, since Chuck said, "I just asked Johnna here if she knew where some of the others she ate with the other day happened to be now."

"Chuck said you wanted to talk to Horatio or Orion, right?" she asked.

Not wanting to appear too eager, Liam just nodded.

"Haven't seen either of them for a week or so, but next time I do I'll try to bring them in."

"Great," Liam said, and hoped that would actually occur.

But he wouldn't hold his breath.

If the decision whether Chuck and Carleen could use the elixir again had been made, no one was informing Liam yet.

He'd spent last night at Rosa's—again. He'd told her about his frustration that day at meeting Johnna but still not learning more about Orion.

He had also told her he was about to imbibe some more of the elixir and shift outside the full moon—tonight.

"You're sure you'll be okay?" she had asked while they were lying in bed, resting after a really great bout of no-holds-barred sex, his favorite, especially now that he was engaging in it with Rosa.

Too bad he couldn't convince himself he could go there every night forever.

He couldn't convince himself of that because Rosa still seemed remote at times, concerned…and unsure whether she really wanted to be doing this with a shifter, although she never said so aloud.

But that made Liam doubt himself and his strong internal goal of someday having regular people accept shifters as they were. That couldn't happen if even someone like wonderful, dedicated veterinarian Rosa, who knew and worked with shifters, didn't necessarily want to have a long-term personal relationship with one.

"Of course I'll be okay," he'd asserted, hoping he was right.

"I assume Melanie won't be there. Could I hang out on the base just in case you…you need some veterinary assistance?"

That was sweet of her. Although, in some ways, it was just part of who she was. Part of her job.

The veterinarian that she was would care for any animal in need, no matter how he'd gotten in animal form.

Which was all the more reason for Liam to not get any further involved with her. She might care for shifters in either form—but still not completely accept them as equals.

And now he was back at Ft. Lukman, down in Drew's office on the lab floor, where Drew was telling Denny and him and the others who'd be with them that evening about the formulation of elixir Liam would be taking.

"It's just the latest regular formulation," Drew said, leaning forward with his arms folded on his desk. "Although, since it's the same formulation I took on the night of the last full moon, we're testing it again—on you. You're okay with that?"

"I was okay with testing the stuff that wouldn't let me shift back, so why not the latest good stuff that let everyone but you shift back during the last full moon?" Liam grinned at his boss, although inside he kind of wondered if he was being told the truth.

Well, he did trust Drew. And his fellow Alpha Forcers. And what good would it do any of them to lie to him?

But he was, after all, one of their latest recruits, so he could be subject to more stressful and questionable stuff than most of the others…

"Why not the good stuff indeed?" Drew rose and, maneuvering around his desk, approached Liam. "And I still appreciate your agreeing to be our test shifter the last time, to try to make sure I was given the right stuff to make me normal."

"Oh, you're always normal, boss," Liam said, as he stood and they grasped hands. "Besides, I'm nearly always ready for a shift. Looking forward to tonight's. You going to be there keeping an eye on me?"

"Sure," he said. "And since Melanie has to stay home with the kids, I'm hoping your buddy Rosa will be there to ensure all goes well when you're shifted."

"I'm hoping that, too." And when the meeting was over and Liam called Rosa, he confirmed that she definitely would be present.

Which somehow made him feel more relieved about tonight's shift.

Rosa was with them again, in the woods at the far side of Ft. Lukman. The sky was dark, the air cool.

"You good to go?" Denny asked Liam. Those two Alpha Force members stood side by side beneath a canopy of dark trees, while others from their military unit hung out nearby, talking.

Rosa was closest to Liam and Denny, yet not part of either group.

This was beginning to feel familiar to her, though. Too familiar?

Not hardly. It was only the second time she had been here for any shift. But the shifter, once more, was Liam.

Would this one be like last time, when his Alpha Force teammates had purposely made it hard for him to shift back? Supposedly not...but what if they hadn't told him the entire purpose for this exercise?

Last time, she had been curious. Interested. Caring, yet not emotionally involved except for wanting to ensure the animal Liam became remained healthy.

This time—well, they had a relationship of sorts now. A fun one filled with companionship and sex. And yes, she had sort of admitted to herself that she would fall in love with him if she let herself.

Assuming she wasn't already.

No. This definitely wasn't the time to puzzle over that. Too many things to think about. Too many issues and problems and—

"You ready, sir?" Denny spoke to Liam, his tone somewhat satiric. He held a glass vial of some clear liquid—obviously that all-important elixir. And beside Denny on the ground was the large battery-operated light that Rosa understood was supposed to resemble and act somewhat like a full moon.

"Yes, Sergeant," Liam responded, his own voice also sounding somewhat mocking. "Hand it over, my trusted aide."

The other Alpha Force members who were there—Drew, Patrick, Jonas and Noel—had stopped talking and now looked at Liam and Denny. "It's time," Drew acknowledged. "Go ahead."

Nodding, Liam took the vial from Denny and drank the liquid within. When finished, he began removing his clothes—glancing at Rosa with a smile that looked teasing as he got down to his underwear.

And then he removed that, too.

One quick look at her, and then all his attention seemed, appropriately, to focus on Denny. Denny lit the lantern and aimed it at the nude, attentive man beside him.

In moments, Rosa watched as Liam went down on his knees, his limbs began moving and shrinking, his body started to grow its wolfen hair.

His shift had begun.

Chapter 18

It had been short. It had been sweet.

And now Liam was already back in human form.

That had been the intent for this shift. A test to ensure that the elixir was still a good formulation and still did its duty. That all was well with Alpha Force, although there would be a bigger test for all of them in a few nights, under the next full moon.

And fortunately, it did appear that all was well.

Beneath the canopy of trees, Denny had helped him put his clothes back on. Liam was tired, but nothing unusual about that.

Next, Drew and the others who were medical doctors conducted a quick physical exam and pronounced him well and in good condition.

He'd made sure not to look at Rosa till he was dressed once more. And when he did, she was on her cell phone, not watching him.

Although he had glanced at her as he had shifted back and noticed her attention was fully on him. And now she seemed slightly furtive, as if she was purposely pretending not to notice him for now.

But he suspected that wasn't true.

If he hadn't been so tired, and if his body hadn't had at least some residual of the elixir's formula within it, he might even have suggested they engage in a late drink to toast what had happily occurred.

Instead, though, his commanding officer approached her. "Thanks, Rosa, for being here. But I have to say I was glad your services weren't needed."

She shoved her phone into her jeans pocket and gave a smile that Liam wished had been directed at him. "I'm glad, too. I assumed all went as well as it appeared to, right?"

"Right," Drew said, moving in Liam's direction. He motioned for Rosa to join him, which she did. "I'll be telling Melanie soon not only how well things went, but how much I appreciated your being here just in case."

The crowd began to disperse then. Denny was directed to take Liam back to his quarters, while Drew motioned for the others to join him as he walked Rosa to her car.

But the night wasn't completely over. Once Liam was back at his place and getting ready to go to bed, he called Rosa.

"Thanks again for being there," he told her.

"I'll be there again during the full moon," she replied.

"Great. And hopefully we'll get together before then."

"I'd like that," Rosa said, making Liam grin and parts of him rise to attention.

"Dinner tomorrow night…to discuss all this?" he suggested.

"Good idea," she said, and when they hung up Liam was definitely hopeful that they would do more than eat and talk.

Rosa had felt so good at Liam's test shift. Who knew that she would wind up caring so much about a shape-shifter?

Well, it was partly her job. Speaking of which, she was at work now, about a week after that shift. She was in one of the exam rooms—the one that had been occupied by Drew when he had been staying there, in fact. But today she was waiting for Brendan to bring in an aging rottweiler with kidney issues that just needed a follow-up exam after the meds she had put him on.

She had spent several evenings—and nights—with Liam since then, including his staying overnight at her place the night after his test shift. She had talked to him often in between, too.

Time had passed quickly. The moon would be full tonight.

And she had plans to go to the military base just to watch and be there and offer veterinary help if any of the shifters needed it while in wolf form.

Her phone began vibrating in her pocket. Since her latest patient hadn't yet come in, she pulled it out.

Liam. Her heart began racing. Was he okay? Was all in order for the major shifting that would go on that night?

And why was she so worried?

"Hope I'm not calling at a bad time," Liam said when she answered, which made her feel better.

"I wouldn't answer if I couldn't talk, but I can't talk for long."

"Quick question. Can you join me for dinner at Fastest Foods tonight before—"

The exam room door opened and Brendan brought in Graf, the rottweiler.

"I'll look forward to it," Rosa said. "Gotta run now." And then she hung up—smiling and looking forward to that evening, or at least the beginning of it.

Liam, sitting back on his chair in his office at Ft. Lukman, patted Chase on the floor beside him, stared at his computer screen and shook his head.

He had second thoughts after his phone call with Rosa. Not about getting together with her for dinner. Oh, no, he really wanted to see her, even spend a little time with her, since it had been a couple days since their busy schedules had allowed them to do more than talk on the phone.

Unfortunately, he still hadn't solved his problem regarding the identification of whoever had made those totally false claims against what was probably supposed to be Alpha Force, after the night of the last full moon.

And he had spent a lot of time on it, ramping up the amount and intensity over the past week—since another full moon was coming that night. Definitely frustrating.

Even so, the second thoughts he was experiencing involved where Rosa and he would meet tonight. He'd enjoyed dining at other Mary Glen locations with her.

But, his preference for that evening or not, Fastest Foods was, in fact, the appropriate place for them to go. He would see Chuck and Carleen, make sure they were ready for their shift that night.

And yes, fortunately, they would once again be using the elixir, and Sergeant Kristine Parran would be their aide for their shift. He hadn't even had to step in and argue on their behalf, although he would have tried it if necessary. No, fortunately, Drew had let him know that the decision had been made. He couldn't say how long their experiment would last, but Liam's brother and sister-in-law would at least get to use the elixir this one additional time.

And he'd kind of hinted that it was partly to thank Liam for his test shifts over the past month, including the one that had helped Alpha Force figure out how best to try bringing Drew back to human form.

Liam's phone rang and he pulled it from his pocket. It was Drew. "I've been thinking that we ought to all meet in the cafeteria for an early dinner tonight," he said. "Celebrate in advance what'll go on later. Our unit has always seemed to enjoy doing that, and I've already checked with Patrick and a couple of other members. You up for it?"

"I'm up for a get-together," Liam confirmed, "but how about doing it at Fastest Foods so Chuck and Carleen can join us, too? They're participating tonight the Alpha Force way, after all." And that way he wouldn't have to change any plans with Rosa, although he'd let her know they'd be dining with a bunch of people who'd also be anticipating what would occur that night. "I'll call and tell them to reserve a corner of the room for us."

"Sounds good," Drew said. "I'll let the others know."

The evening before their shift would be a lot dif-

ferent from the way he'd planned, Liam realized as he
hung up. That was okay, he told himself. He would still
be with Rosa, though they wouldn't be eating alone.

Well, they wouldn't have been alone anyway, dining at Fastest Foods and checking in with his brother
and sister-in-law.

And there should be plenty of occasions after this
when just the two of them could dine—and more—
together.

Though Rosa had known she'd be joining Liam at
the restaurant that evening, so there would likely be a
bunch of people around them as they ate, she hadn't
initially known that that bunch of restaurant customers would include a fair-sized group of Alpha Force
members as well as friends—like her.

But Liam had warned her, and the early evening
seemed to have turned into a bit of a party. A party of
anticipation, where everyone seemed happy and optimistic. She hoped they were right.

Now, she sat at one of the small wooden tables that
had been saved for the group on one side of the always
crowded dining room, with white folded cards saying
Reserved. The Alpha Force members who attended
were in casual civilian clothes, and so was she.

Melanie was also there with Drew, and they'd
brought their adorable children, Emily and her little
brother, Andy. Jonas, who Rosa knew was Drew's aide
and would help him with his shift that night, sat with
them.

Emily, who had dark hair with shimmers of silver
in it that resembled her daddy's, had a kiddie-sized
burger on a paper plate in front of her and every once

in a while picked it up in both hands and took a bite. Her brother, who had similar looking hair, seemed to love french fries.

As far as Rosa knew, it wasn't usual for little kids to have shimmery hair like that. She still wondered if Emily or her brother resembled their father in other ways—like shifting—but she hadn't learned that yet.

Drew and Melanie hadn't brought Grunge, Drew's cover dog. Nor had Liam brought Chase, and Rosa saw no other dogs present, either. All shifters, including Patrick, and Drew's cousin Jason, were there with their aides.

Rosa figured that if any of them were seen while shifted, in a situation where an explanation for non-shifters would be needed, their aides would retrieve whichever wolf-dog was required, after the shift back. Maybe that was true of Louper, too, but the Corlands' dog wasn't there that evening, either.

"So everything's in order for later," Denny said, from Liam's other side at their table. Rosa was well aware that Liam's aide would be the one to hand him his elixir and monitor his shift, as well as his shift back.

They sat at a larger table—in fact, two tables that had been pushed together. With them were Chuck and Carleen, and another chair had been saved for Valerie.

Rosa had been nibbling on a salad. She would be present when the shifts all occurred, supposedly together, and she could only hope that she would remain calm. Seeing one person shift—Liam—and both he and Drew shift back individually, had drawn a lot of emotions from her. Seeing an entire group?

Heck, she could handle it. She had to—particularly

because she couldn't know whether her veterinary services would be needed.

Okay. Not that she was that hungry, but she had been only picking at her salad, and mostly eavesdropping on everyone else at the table without saying much.

"I need an iced tea," she declared, unsure if anyone was paying any attention to her.

But Liam turned and leaned toward her. "I suspect you need a break from all this," he said softly, "at least a short one. Go grab that iced tea." He smiled.

She couldn't help smiling back as she stood. She had an urge to give him a big hug—and not only because he seemed to understand her current mood. But that would only be appropriate now if they were alone—and they were far from alone.

"Can I get anybody anything?" she called. A couple of the aides—Denny and Kristine—asked for a large order of fries that they promised to share, and Rosa felt just a little relieved that she had another reason to go to the order counter.

Fortunately, there was no line and she was able to grab her small order quickly. Valerie was behind the counter, which surprised Rosa a little. She had even been there earlier, putting the orders together for the Alpha Force group and others. But she'd be shifting that night, too, right? Shouldn't she be resting or something?

Rosa had the opportunity to ask her, very softly, as Valerie joined her to walk to the table, "Are you okay? I mean, I'm aware that you're going to have an...exhausting evening, right?"

Valerie did resemble her sister, with her silvery hair

and dark brown eyes. Would they look alike while shifted?

Would Carleen's ability to drink the elixir make a difference in her appearance?

"That's for sure," Valerie responded, also in a soft voice. "But I'm used to it. I'll be fine."

But Rosa was curious. "I know that Chuck and Carleen will have…well, help. Will anyone be helping you?"

Valerie laughed, though it didn't sound entirely humorous. "Nope. I'm here on my own. Being Carleen's sister doesn't really connect me to that Alpha Force, so I still do things the old-fashioned way. I always know what's coming, of course, and around here I just lock myself in my room at Carleen and Chuck's house, where I'm staying. Of course, I have to lock their dog out to make sure we don't get into a dogfight when… you know."

They had reached the table, but before Rosa sat down she had to ask, "I know they're getting—I mean, things will be a little different for them, like it was last time. You're okay with doing things the 'old-fashioned way'?"

"Oh, I'm fine with it." Valerie's dark eyes shone as she glanced at Rosa. "Like I said, I'm used to it. Sure, I'm curious…but it's not like I have any choice, anyway. But come see me afterward. I'd like to hear your version of what they go through. I'd imagine that in most ways it's no easier than what I'll do."

Rosa smiled sympathetically at her, recalling how uncomfortable Liam's shift appeared. And maybe in some ways it would be better not to take the elixir that would allow her to keep human cognition. That way maybe the pain and discomfort of shifting wouldn't be as memorable.

But how would she know?

"Sure," Rosa said. "I'd like to hear your version afterward." They both sat down at the table with Liam and the rest of his family.

But almost immediately, the people Liam had followed from the restaurant the other day appeared, walking by them—and the one known as Orion even bumped their table.

"Hey." Liam rose and faced the guy. "Don't you say 'excuse me' in person when you mess up? I know you don't online."

Orion was short but muscular, and he drew himself up almost to Liam's height to face him. "What are you talking about?"

"Aren't you Orion? And don't you like to post lies on social media?"

"Yes to the first. But I don't lie on social media. I post a lot of pictures, play a lot of games, but that's all. And you? Why are you giving me a hard time?"

"Because someone calling himself Orion is giving me a hard time online. And—"

"And forget it. I don't have to talk to you. And you can be sure I won't be communicating with you on the internet."

With that, Orion, and the guy Rosa thought was called Horatio, stormed off toward the counter to order food.

"If it wasn't starting to get late I'd follow the guy," Liam said. "But at least I know he turns up here now and then. And if you can get some contact information for me one of these days…" He looked from Chuck to Carleen. "I'd appreciate it."

"We'll try," Chuck said. "But we don't see him that often, and…"

"I get it," Liam said. He looked frustrated, but Rosa certainly understood why he couldn't do much now.

The light outside had started to grow dimmer.

Rosa soon finished her salad and iced tea, while the others also finished their dinners, including the fries she had brought back.

Then it was time for the group to leave. Many of them had things to do that night that they wouldn't want anyone else around here to see…

Chuck and Carleen excused themselves to talk to their employees, who'd be closing up the restaurant early, in about an hour.

Rosa rode in Liam's car, which was driven by Denny. She got out with Liam and headed for the familiar clearing, as did the other shifters and some of their aides, who'd also parked nearby. Some of the aides headed for the lab building, though, where Rosa understood they would retrieve the elixir and lights.

Rosa waited at Liam's side. So did Chuck and Carleen, both of whom seemed jazzed. "It's so great to really be part of this group tonight," Chuck said quietly. "If only we could get a commitment of some kind that this won't be the last time, either."

"You know," Liam began, "I can't—"

"Right," Carleen interrupted. "You can't." She shot an almost accusatory glare toward Liam in the waning daylight, and Rosa wanted to kick both of them.

She knew enough to realize that Liam had been attempting to help them remain part of this experiment, but they should feel thrilled to get any use of the elixir, not pushy about the future. And Liam had made it clear that the decision was not his.

Too bad they didn't share Valerie's attitude that the old-fashioned way was a good thing.

Soon all the aides had joined them. Jonas was with Drew, and Melanie had taken the kids home. She hoped to have a sitter come for part of the evening, but in any event Rosa was at least currently in charge of any veterinary needs.

It was growing darker. Liam and Drew, Patrick and Jason all seemed restless, pacing around the clearing near each other.

And then the aides returned with their equipment. Soon the shifters, including Liam's brother and sister-in-law, all drank some of the elixir from their respective vials. Rosa watched from the edge of the clearing, hoping it all went well—and in some ways eager to see Liam naked again, even for only a short time and for this difficult reason.

The lights were soon aimed at the shifters, even as the sky grew darker and the full moon appeared at the horizon.

Liam was naked now—and as Rosa watched, his shift began.

His shift had gone well.

He had felt Rosa's eyes on him as he'd removed his clothes, making as much of a show of it as he could, considering his limbs were already changing, fur beginning to erupt from his skin.

He also watched his brother and his wife change,

after imbibing the elixir. Their shifts seemed to go well, too.

After they were all in wolfen form, Liam motioned with his head for his relations to join him as he ran through the woods, rejoicing in his changed form, the fleetness of a wolf at his disposal. The earth was covered with leaves and tree branches. The smell of the trees and other plants filled the air. But of more interest, he scented small rodents on and under the ground, birds sleeping in trees—and people around, mostly those stationed at Ft. Lukman. Even though non–Alpha Force members were cautioned, without any formal explanation, to remain in their quarters on nights such as this, not everyone obeyed.

But Alpha Force shifters would not harm them. Not with the human cognition they maintained after drinking the elixir.

With his relations, he continued through the forest, sometimes in a somewhat straight line, sometimes circling areas of particular interest where other fauna had a presence—rabbits and raccoons and more. But he had no intention of attacking any of them—not with his human cognition.

Time passed. He kept note of how the moon was progressing, especially when that bright, full orb began to approach the horizon, where it would soon disappear.

Again using his head to gesture, he waved for his family to follow him. They soon reached the clearing, as had that night's other shifters.

Although he did not need to, particularly after drinking the elixir, Liam sat and closed his eyes and told his body to begin its shift back into human form.

Strange. Nothing happened.

It felt like the time when he'd been given that special elixir to prevent him from shifting back, to test the formulation developed to assist Drew in regaining his human form.

Liam opened his eyes and saw the others, unlike him, rolling on the ground.

Shifting back.

"You okay, Liam?" That was his aide, Denny, now at his side.

He nodded, determined to become human once more.

But once more, his shift did not begin.

"Is he all right?" That was Rosa, who had joined them, talking to Denny.

"I don't know. He's not shifting."

And Liam could see that all the other shifters had again achieved human form. All of them but him.

Yet again he did as he always had since joining Alpha Force—closed his eyes and willed himself to shift back. Even without the elixir to rely on, this shift would simply have occurred after a full moon, with nothing further to do on his part.

Still nothing. Not even a semblance of a shift.

He opened his eyes, sitting on the ground, head raised toward the heavens beyond the trees, and issued a loud and mournful howl.

Chapter 19

"Oh, no!" Rosa cried. "What's going on? Liam?" She began running toward him on the uneven, leaf-covered ground in her athletic shoes, unsure what she could do, if anything. But something definitely looked wrong.

She had been standing at the edge of the clearing, watching in the early light of dawn as the wolves returned and began shifting back to human form.

All but Liam.

She reached him quickly. Denny was already kneeling at his side, talking into his erect canine ears. Jonas kept looking toward them, but was busy acting as Drew's aide. The Alpha Force superior officer, though back in human form and starting to get dressed with Jonas's help, looked tired.

Rosa immediately knelt beside Denny. "Do you know what's going on? Did he accidentally get the wrong kind of elixir? Is there anything I can do for him medically?"

"Don't know answers to any of that." Rosa could tell that Denny was attempting to act amused and calm, undoubtedly to keep Liam that way, too. "Hey, dude," he said to Liam, "anything hurt? Or is there some other reason you'd like Dr. Jontay, here, to examine you? Touch you?" He raised his brows suggestively, and Rosa smiled almost involuntarily. But keeping things light was certainly preferable to all of them showing how upset they were.

Liam barked then, nodded and looked at Rosa. She made herself laugh. Maybe the only good thing about this was that he at least had apparently kept his human cognition.

But what were they going to do? Was he going to remain in wolf form for the rest of today? Longer?

A fully dressed Drew came over to them then. "Not again," he said, shaking his head as he stared at Liam. "Well, at least this time we have a solution. Let's go back to the labs."

The entire group, now in human form and wearing clothes, picked up backpacks and lights and began walking in the direction of the main Alpha Force building.

They talked to one another, and to Liam, in cheerful and even joking tones, clearly wanting to keep his spirits up.

Rosa wished she could join them and joke and feel better, but she didn't know what the Alpha Force members were really thinking. No despair was evident. No frustration or anger that they were in the same situation as before, after the last full moon, when their superior officer had failed to change back.

Were they truly happy or relieved that it was only Liam this time? But they all seemed like nice people—when they were in human form. No, she truly believed they were just putting on an act for his benefit.

Apparently, no one even thought about including her in their banter, and she was just as glad.

Liam's family members, Chuck and Carleen, walking with them, were clearly upset. There was no way they could get completely out of Liam's hearing, Rosa figured, but after greeting him and pretending to joke with him, they headed toward the far side of the group. Their aide, Kristine, stayed with them. Not having a shifter's hearing, Rosa didn't know what they were saying, but their demeanor as they talked with her appeared angry.

Who or what were they blaming for Liam's condition? Or were they simply upset enough about the situation that they were venting?

They soon reached the building, and Drew told a couple of the aides to go take the cover dogs out for a walk, then feed them. He immediately directed Denny to take Liam downstairs to the laboratories.

Then he faced Chuck and Carleen in the hallway outside the kennel area.

"I know you have questions, and so do we. But we need to take Liam downstairs to a private area to work with him and bring him back to human form. First— were you okay with the elixir you drank? I gather from Kristine that you maintained your human cognition."

"That's right," Chuck said. "Good stuff. It worked well for us, and we really hope we can join you again."

"Assuming that elixir isn't what affected Liam—well, you know," Carleen said.

"Right," Drew said. "We know—and understand. I gather that Kristine has your contact information, right?"

Chuck nodded.

"Good. I'll have her keep in touch with you about Liam. But for now...well, the sooner you leave, the sooner we can start working with him."

Rosa had been standing off to the side during the conversation and winced at the fury she thought she saw on Chuck's face. But Liam's brother just nodded, took his wife's hand and led her down the hall to the exit. Presumably, they had driven here last night after their last conversation with their employees at the restaurant.

And now Drew looked toward her. Was he going to tell her to leave, too?

Just the opposite. "Can you join us, Rosa? We hope we won't need any veterinary assistance, but just in case..."

"Yes," she said. "I'll join you."

Denny had used a key card to open the door. Patrick held back and asked Rosa to walk with him as they went down to the lab floor. As they followed the others down the steps, he said, "We're hopeful that the formulation Liam helped with during the shift when he couldn't immediately change back, the formulation that finally allowed him, and later Drew, to do so—well, there's no reason we know of that it shouldn't work for Liam now."

No reason they knew of. But they didn't really

know, did they, what had caused Drew to remain in wolf form before under the full moon, or Liam now?

Even so, she smiled as they reached the bottom of the stairs, and said, "That's great. I'll look forward to congratulating him once he's in Liam form again."

Patrick shot her a much briefer smile, then hurried to catch up with the others.

Rosa followed them into the main, vast laboratory. She remained near the door, just watching. Liam was on the floor near the main counter, in the middle of where the cabinets lined the walls. He stood up on his hind legs against that counter and looked from one human to the next, as if attempting to communicate his command that they fix this situation for him. Fast. And Rosa was all for that.

The next few minutes seemed a bit chaotic to her, but she gathered that the medical doctors among them were retrieving the required liquids from the refrigerator, checking their consistency and getting them ready for use. The others were setting things up, grabbing the light they would use after Liam drank the stuff. Soon, they all appeared to have accomplished their assigned tasks.

"Come over here, Liam," Drew called. He gestured for Liam to follow him into a glass-walled room that contained a sofa and some upholstered chairs—a lounge of some kind.

Maybe they thought a comfortable area would be preferable for all to go as it should.

Liam followed Drew, and Denny joined them. Only the three of them went into that room. Rosa joined the others as they settled behind the glass walls, watching.

Denny first removed a seal from the top of the vial

he held, then poured the clear liquid it contained into a dog bowl on the floor. Liam immediately drank it.

Next, Denny turned on the light that resembled the full moon, which was fairly bright here, downstairs, below the main floor of the building. Rosa heard no sound from anyone around her as they all watched.

And waited. As nothing happened.

Liam did not change back.

Damn.

He recalled how things had seemed when his commanding officer failed to shift back after the last full moon, and was eventually treated with the special form of elixir that Liam himself had helped to test.

And how both of them, in their respective time, had shifted back right away, thanks to that new formulation.

He knew that had to be what he'd been given now.

What had gone wrong?

And could it be fixed?

It had to be. But when?

Rosa knew she was not in a position to insist on anything, and yet after a while, when everyone's frustration was evident, she demanded an opportunity to examine Liam.

After all, the only other medical people here were human doctors.

They waited a bit longer, though, clearly hoping things would change. That Liam would shift. But he didn't.

And so Denny left the lounge room and Drew motioned for Rosa to come in.

She wasn't exactly sure how to conduct this kind of exam, but was determined to do it nonetheless. She would use all her veterinary skills to see if there was anything different, anything clearly wrong, with this wolf-dog who happened to be Liam.

She felt his entire body, one area at a time, moving his limbs, his ears, his tail, the skin along his back and elsewhere, and observing those areas as she grasped them. She opened his mouth and checked his teeth, his throat.

Everything appeared in order for a healthy dog of his size.

That was a good thing, of course. And Rosa hadn't really believed she would be able to figure out what the problem was just by examining him.

No, she hadn't believed it. But she had hoped.

She walked away from Liam for now, after seeing his eyes on hers, his head bowed as if he was depressed. Not surprising.

Moments later, she joined the group of those in charge back out in the lab area, Drew and Patrick and Jonas, as they talked very quietly about what had, and hadn't, happened.

The fact that they kept their voices low and stood in a different room didn't mean that Liam couldn't hear them. Rosa knew that, and clearly they did, too.

They didn't express any anger or frustration or any other emotion they must be feeling, the way Rosa did. They might even feel more, since Liam was their colleague, and Drew had found himself in the same situation not long ago.

But the gist of what they said concluded that members of their unit would remain here in the lab area that day with Liam, alternating who stayed when. They would occasionally shine the light on him, just in case there was a delay in when this shifting formulation worked. Those with medical and chemistry backgrounds would work once more on that formulation.

If he didn't change back by tomorrow morning, they would go through all this again.

And Rosa? Of course they didn't mention her. But she finally stepped up to them, let them know she intended to stay here as well, although she would have to clear it with Melanie and would also need to go to her home for a change of clothes.

"That's fine with us," Drew told her. "Thanks." There was a touch of relief in his expression, so Rosa figured he was concerned about Liam's health under the circumstances.

And so, first thing, she went to the far side of the lab area, leaned on a counter with her back toward the others and called Melanie, explaining what had happened.

"Oh, no!" her boss exclaimed. Of course her emotions would be involved, too. She had also gone through this. "Stay as long as you need to."

"Thanks."

Rosa didn't head home for a few hours, wanting to spend the time with Liam to make sure that he remained okay. Eventually, though, she did go home to shower and change clothes—then returned. Still no improvement.

She lay down on the sofa in the lounge area for a nap, and was amused somewhat when she awoke to find Liam in there with her, lying on the floor parallel to her.

Not changed back.

Alpha Force members kept coming in and leaving. Rosa talked briefly to one or another of them, but no one described what they were doing to change—or not change—the shifting-back formulation.

They did shine the light on Liam now and then, but nothing happened.

They brought in meals for Liam and her, and she nibbled at them though she didn't feel particularly hungry.

And that night she hardly slept at all. Would anything good happen the next morning?

She stayed out of the way when, just after sunrise, the main Alpha Forcers returned—Drew and Patrick and Jonas, along with Denny.

Once more, they had Liam go through the procedure they had tried the previous morning.

Rosa felt tears rise in her eyes as, after he'd drunk whatever formulation they gave him, the wolf-dog who was Liam sat on the lounge area floor as the light was shined on him once more. What would happen if he stayed this way forever?

Could he bear it? Could she?

But… Yes! Liam moaned and lay down, his limbs beginning to lengthen, his fur retracting into his body.

It didn't take long, and yet it felt like forever.

Soon, Liam was writhing on the floor, all human once more. All nude human, and Rosa found herself laughing and crying in relief.

Liam spent the rest of the morning being examined and interrogated by his Alpha Force superiors.

At least Rosa had stayed for a short while after he

had shifted back to his human form. Once he was dressed and could breathe normally again, he had even gotten her to join him for coffee in Drew's office, while the others remained in the lab.

"I'm so glad you're okay," she'd said, eyeing him over the cup she held to her lips.

Those lovely lips of hers. Now that he was human again, he noticed them once more. And the rest of her.

But she had shot him down nearly immediately.

"I'm glad, too," he said. "Thanks for hanging out here."

"Oh, I was just doing my job." She took another sip of coffee. "You seemed to be fine in wolf form, but I was ready to try to help if you weren't."

Just doing her job. Sure, that was the truth—and yet he'd hoped she'd also hung around because she was concerned about him.

Cared about him.

Heck, that had been his own emotions, juggled along by his somewhat frightening inability to change back even after taking that other form of elixir developed for just that purpose for Drew.

She stayed only a little while longer.

But she did hearten him a bit by saying, as Chase and he walked her to her car, "I hope we get together again soon." And then, after unlocking her door, she turned back to him and gave him a kiss. A quick one, and yet it made him feel at least a little better.

He'd nearly asked if they could get together that night. But he still felt tired.

And his superiors had already said they wanted to conduct an examination. Plus he still had his regular work to do as the chief technology guy for the unit, although Denny had told him he'd started checking social media after this latest full moon.

Sure enough, his aide had pointed out some of the posts about shapeshifters and their reality, and their alleged aggression while shifted, attacking regular people in this area. And that some of those supposed attackers allegedly belonged to a secret military force.

As a result, Liam had spent what was left of his energy getting online, assuming some of his false personas and making fun of all those nasty posts. A couple had come from someone named Orion, but the addresses and locations didn't jibe with what the guy who'd shown up again at the restaurant and finally given him some info had provided. Nor did it appear real when Liam conducted his own investigation of the source.

Could he rule out the guy he'd met? No, but he couldn't be sure that Orion was involved, either.

When he finished, he was exhausted. With Chase, he walked back to his quarters early that evening, grabbed a sandwich with fixings from his fridge—and was pleased when Rosa called.

"How are you doing?" she asked.

"Well enough," he replied.

"Good. Stay that way." Her tone sounded like a command, but then she said, "I was worried about you before, you know."

"I know. Thanks." But neither of them suggested that they get together again sometime soon—or even sometime in the future.

Therefore, he had spent that night alone…with his thoughts.

Chapter 20

A week had passed since the night of the last full moon—and Liam's failure to shift back as he was supposed to.

But fortunately, he had eventually shifted back. And Rosa had not seen him since then.

This morning she sat in her small office at the veterinary clinic, checking out the file on one of her upcoming patients of the day, Boom—a much beloved rescue dog whose family had adopted him a little while ago. He was a middle-sized dog, apparently part Irish setter and part golden retriever, who'd previously been abused—and now had a wonderful life, from what Rosa had seen.

He'd first been brought to the clinic around the time Rosa had started working there, about a year ago, by his new family, the Orcharts. This was his annual checkup.

And everything seemed to be going great with him—pending the results of his blood test, which Rosa was having sent out to the regular lab.

But just drawing the blood reminded her...

"So what do you think, Dr. Jontay?" asked Millie Orchart, the wife of Bill and mother of the boy and girl who were like Boom's siblings.

"I think sweet Boom has a wonderful family," Rosa responded. "And as to his health? I've found nothing to worry about. Of course, we need to wait for his blood test results, but I'm fairly sure he's fine. This is one lucky and sweet rescue dog."

"We think so," Bill said, as Rosa lifted Boom down from the examination table. The two kids ran to the dog and hugged him.

Soon the entire family left, with Rosa staying behind in the room, smiling after them. But only for a short while.

In a minute, she was sure she would be summoned to one of the other exam rooms, as she should be.

This was her life. Who she was. And yet...

She pulled her phone from her pocket. Time to call Liam. Again. They'd at least spoken daily since they had last seen each other. He sounded busy, and she definitely was.

And yet...why not at least get together some evening for dinner? Like tonight?

"Hi, Rosa," he said into her ear, answering his phone right away. That soft smile she had aimed at Boom and his family now grew much larger as she pictured Liam's handsome face—and that body of his without clothes as he shifted back...

"Hi, Liam. How have you been?"

"Up till now, just fine since you last saw me. Did you hear what's going on, or do you have ESP?"

Her heart froze, and she stared at a spot on the metal sink at the side of the room. "What do you mean?"

"I'm going to be shifting again tonight, just as a test."

Shifting, on this night a bit over a week since the full moon. An Alpha Force shift. A test. After what Liam had just gone through.

"Oh, and in case you're wondering," he continued, "Drew has asked Melanie to be here in case I need any help. If all goes well, we plan to continue with test shifts every couple of days with all the shifters around here, not just me, so maybe you'll be asked to help out, too."

Or not. Melanie hadn't mentioned it to her. Things around here seemed to be much as they had before the full moon when Drew hadn't changed back and Rosa had had to step in to help. She'd known about the shifters under the full moon and otherwise, but hadn't truly been involved then.

And suspected she wouldn't be involved more now.

"That's fine," she said. "I hope it all goes well." She realized her tone sounded falsely bright, and ended the call by saying, "Just wanted to see if we could get together for dinner sometime soon, but I need to get to my next patient now. Maybe after this test shift of yours. See ya, Liam." And then she hung up.

Liam felt miserable, even as he decided he had to feel good. He looked forward to this next shift, determined that it work out well with whatever elixir he was given to drink.

But now, moving in his office chair, he looked at his computer screen, one reason he had been avoiding Rosa. He had spent a lot of time online, still trying to figure out the real source of the various lies against shifters and particularly Alpha Force. Nothing conclusive so far except the name Orion now and then, as well as other Greek or Roman god names.

He had remained in touch with the guy he knew as Orion from around here—who'd conveniently been out of town.

Since Liam had been able to figure out the guy's location by hacking into the GPS on his phone, he'd seen that Orion truly had been elsewhere, in New York City, for the past week or so. Sure, he could have sent his phone with someone else—but maybe not.

In any event, more of those nasty accusations against unnamed Alpha Force had been posted. Names including Orion had been used again. And Liam still hadn't nailed down the actual identities and locations of those who posted them, but neither had he eliminated that Orion as the perpetrator.

Orion was back in town now, and they were planning to meet at Fastest Foods tomorrow night to chat.

So that meant Liam couldn't meet up with Rosa then. And for the last few days and nights he had been pretty well glued to his computer.

"I'll get away from you tonight, at least," he said, glaring at the screen in front of him. "Tomorrow night, too."

Yet if he'd really wanted to get together with Rosa, he'd have found an hour or two. He knew that. But he'd realized, when he couldn't shift back this last time, that he cared for her too much.

Why would the woman want to be involved long-term with someone like him, with his existence so different from hers? Who sometimes couldn't even shift back into human form?

He understood that, and knew he had to stay away from her as much as possible now or hurt even more when they parted for good.

But he also recognized that seeing her, however briefly, was worth the pain.

His phone rang again and he snatched it from the desk beside his computer screen. Was Rosa calling again?

But his hopeful grin disappeared when he saw who the caller was: Patrick. "Come on over to Drew's office," he said. "We need to talk about tonight."

Liam's manufactured shift last night had gone well. Rosa knew that.

But she didn't hear the news from him.

It was the day after she'd talked to him. She had spoken briefly with Melanie after that in her office, expressing her interest and a hint of her concern.

Not that Melanie was surprised. "Drew expressly asked me to be there for the shift this time," she had said, the tilt to her head and a somewhat sad smile conveying what appeared to be sympathy. "But from what I've heard, this will be the first of several shift tests they'll be conducting before the next full moon, and you and I will both be involved, with alternating ones."

"That's kind of what Liam said," Rosa agreed. She didn't bother asking why she wasn't the one last night. Drew was in charge of his gang, and Melanie was in charge here. End of story.

But she had hurried into Melanie's office first thing this morning, on hearing her boss was there. Melanie had motioned for her to sit down, and gazed at Rosa over her desk. Rosa saw no signs of stress there, which was a good thing—and what Melanie said only supported that impression.

All had gone well. Melanie had given Liam a brief veterinary exam while he was in wolf form. Then Liam had shifted back on schedule, when he had been directed to, with no problems.

"So the first of these new experiments went fine," Melanie finished. "Hopefully, the rest will, too, and they'll act as a harbinger of successful shifts under the next full moon."

"Hopefully so," Rosa agreed. She meant it. Even if she now had no relationship with Liam outside of being an occasional vet for him and his colleagues while shifted, she wished him well.

She also wished she understood why he seemed to have backed off. Or maybe he truly was under stress with his important military job, and just couldn't find time to see her…

Sure.

Still, she left Melanie's office feeling glad that Liam was okay, even if they weren't seeing each other.

Since no one was in the hall escorting an animal to one of the exam rooms, Rosa headed to the reception area to check on what appointments were scheduled that day.

The room was small but pleasant—and empty, except for the compact desk at one side where Susie sat, staring at her computer screen as she sipped coffee from a mug. But none of the six metal-and-red-plastic chairs was occupied, and all the balls and other toys there to amuse dogs while they were waiting still sat in the large wicker basket on the floor.

"So where are today's patients?" Rosa asked, and Susie looked toward her and smiled.

"We've got a busy schedule later," she said, "but right now we have just one dog scheduled, for an exam in five minutes—Grunge. He's just coming for a checkup."

That was Drew's cover dog, Rosa knew, and he mostly hung out at Melanie and Drew's house next door during the nights. But he joined the other Alpha Force dogs at the base on most weekdays.

She assumed that Drew himself, or maybe his aide, Jonas, would bring Grunge in—and was somewhat shocked when, before she left the reception area, Liam walked through the front door with Grunge on a leash behind him.

"Oh. Hi, Liam. And Grunge. Good to see you both." Rosa realized that sounded lame. What she wanted to do—sort of—was dash into Liam's arms and give him a big, sexy kiss.

But not here. Not in front of Susie.

And really? Not at all. Not the way he'd been avoiding her. Or at least had seemed to. Though maybe he really had been as busy as he'd claimed.

"Hi, Rosa." His deep voice, plus the way he looked at her—ruefully, apologetically, sexily—stirred her even more.

Or was she imagining, hoping for, all that?

She watched him for a few more seconds before shaking herself mentally. "So, how's Grunge doing?

Is there anything I should know before conducting his exam?"

"He seems fine, or so Drew told me. It's just time for him to get his annual exam, Drew said."

So why were you the one to bring Grunge? But Rosa didn't ask that. Didn't say anything at all, except, "Great. Let's take him into an exam room."

"Number three," Susie said, after looking again at her computer.

"Okay." Rosa led Liam and Grunge down the hall. "So how's Chase doing?" she asked, as they entered the third examination room.

"Fine. He'll be due for a regular exam, too, one of these days."

"Let's get Grunge up there." Rosa gestured toward the tall metal table.

Liam lifted the wolf-dog, and Rosa helped by grabbing him behind his front legs to guide where he would be deposited. While doing so, she accidentally touched Liam's warm, bare skin. He was wearing his usual military camos, but the long sleeves had been rolled up.

That jolted her a bit, but she determined not to let it show.

Only—well, maybe it had jolted Liam a bit, too, since the moment after they both carefully let go of Grunge, Rosa found herself in Liam's arms.

The kiss they shared was exactly as she had wanted it to be—hot and hard and sexually exciting, particularly since their bodies melded together.

It was a nice, long kiss, too—but eventually Rosa ended it. She was here on duty. A veterinarian with a dog patient to examine.

And this was a highly inappropriate place for a kiss.

"Well," she said, stepping back. "It's good to see you, too. Now, let's take a look at Grunge."

She turned her back on Liam and began a very thorough and professional examination of Grunge.

In a short while, she was able to say with assurance, "He seems to be doing just fine. No problems that I can see, although I'll want to draw some blood and have it checked."

Since Grunge was a regular canine, despite being part of Alpha Force, she would be able to have the sample sent to their laboratory, as she had yesterday with Boom and others.

She stepped into the hall and saw Brendan. Good. She asked him to come in and hold the large animal to make sure he didn't bite when he felt the needle. Which he didn't.

And that ended the exam. Brendan left the room first with the blood sample, and Rosa was alone once more with Liam and Grunge.

"So," she said to Liam, "good to see you." *And to kiss and touch you.*

"You, too, Rosa." The way he said her name only made it all worse—soft and, again, sexy and…did she really sense a hint of longing? No, that had to be her imagination.

If he really wanted to be with her, why hadn't he called her, let alone set up a time for them to get together?

But he continued, "I've missed you. And—well, I'll be eating at Fastest Foods tonight around seven. Will you join me then?"

Yes, yes, she wanted to shout. But instead said, "I think so. In fact, count on it unless you hear otherwise from me. My schedule around here has been a bit crazy these days." Which it had, though her evenings had mostly been free, except for two nights ago when she'd been handling an emergency.

"Got it," he said. "I'll look forward to seeing you there…I hope."

Then, with Grunge, he preceded Rosa out the examination room door.

Before he left the vet clinic, Liam told Rosa that he had a meeting set up with Orion at the restaurant that night. He saw her expression grow chilly.

Maybe it had been a bad idea. Maybe he should have asked her out on a genuine date, with just the two of them, on another night. His invitation had, after all, been somewhat impulsive.

He did want to see her.

But he had to talk to Orion, and this was the first opportunity he'd had since the guy returned from his trip.

Now he drove to Rosa's house to pick her up, since she'd called earlier to confirm she would join him. She had then gone home after her day at the clinic. This did feel like a date, at least somewhat. And that was good.

Oh, yes. When she greeted him at her front door, she was clad in a really pretty pink dress with a skirt that revealed a lot of leg. Plus she'd traded her usual casual athletic shoes for dressy black ones with narrow heels.

Definitely date attire. Good thing that he, too, had dressed up a bit—not in his usual camo wear, but a nice blue button shirt over navy slacks and loafers.

"Glad you could join me," he said, once they were

in the car. He'd left Chase at his quarters on base, so the back seat was empty.

"Me, too. And—well, I know it's not my business, but why are you meeting with that Orion?"

"Because, though I've made some progress narrowing things down in my online search regarding posts about shapeshifters—and you know I can't tell you more than that—I think he may have some answers."

A while later, Liam was certain of it. His family, including Valerie, had joined Rosa and him at the table where they'd taken their usual burgers and sides. That gave Liam a good opportunity to grab his cola and join Orion when the guy strode into the restaurant and got his own food order. Now they sat in a different corner.

"So what did you want to accuse me of this time?" Orion said, taking a big bite of his burger as he shot a cynical glance toward Liam.

"As I've said before, I'm trying to find the real source of some posts that were written by someone named Orion. Now, from what I've learned about you, your real name is Ellis Martoni and Orion is your middle name. And you use that name more than Ellis, including online. And—"

"Enough," Orion said. "You're right. I gather you've got some pretty good online research skills. Well, so do I, though I'm actually a CPA working for an accounting firm."

Liam already knew that about him, too.

Orion leaned toward him. The guy was beefy, with short hair and a long face, plus glaring green eyes. "I also play a lot of online video games, and that's when I mostly use my Orion persona. Anyway, I've done my own research and found what I figure you did—that there are a lot of posts on various sites that are really pretty stupid because they seem to think shapeshifters, werewolves and such, are real. And a whole bunch of them were supposedly posted by someone named Orion. So that's why you came after me. But why do you give a damn about them?"

"Like I told you before, I'm a member of the US military and some of my superior officers think the references in some of those posts to a supposed military unit of shapeshifters needs to have the source tracked down and stopped. Stupid stuff, but it's a matter of policy, so I have to do it."

That was somewhat true—as true as he could admit. But he certainly couldn't refer to the fact that shapeshifters themselves were true.

"Okay. Got it. And just so we're square on this, first, I didn't do those posts. Second, though I don't know who did, I used some of my own resources and came up with some online sites that are really good at hiding sources and making it look like stuff was put out there from all over the world. Secret sites, of course. But here." He slid an envelope he'd pulled from his pocket toward Liam. "I wrote down some websites you can look at, along with passwords I made up for this situation. Check 'em out. You'll see that a lot of the supposed sources are actually local—but they're not me or the company I work for. Maybe they'll help you. But don't bother me with this again."

"Thanks," Liam said simply. He would check into this, of course. It didn't sound like something he hadn't done himself. But there were an infinite number of websites out there in cyberspace, so maybe this guy's information would help.

He hadn't narrowed it all down to local people posting, either, though Liam had always figured that those who made claims about shapeshifters around here, and seemed to stick those posts online from faraway countries, had to be playing some pretty skillful games. In any case, it was high time he figured out exactly who those people were.

This Orion guy could still be one of them, but Liam would at least look into what he'd given him.

The man rose, picking up the wrappers from the sandwich and fries he'd finished, along with his soda cup.

"You're welcome," he said to Liam, as he started walking away. "Now, leave me alone."

Maybe so, Liam thought.

And maybe not.

Chapter 21

Rosa had been having quite an interesting conversation with Liam's family—Chuck, Carleen and even Valerie.

They'd secured a table in a corner, as it was their privilege, as owners of the place, to do.

Apparently they had enough staff on duty that all of them could take the time off to eat dinners together, and talk to her.

She'd picked up her food and they'd joined her. Keeping their voices low, they began to grill Rosa about shapeshifter things within her knowledge—like, how did she conduct veterinary examinations of those in shifted form.

They knew she had examined Liam when he had failed to shift back. What had he been like then? Had she been there when he had actually managed to shift back? Had the stuff he had drunk, that elixir, helped or hurt?

Ah. That was a good reason to get the topic off Liam, at least for a short while. Rosa was well aware by now that Chuck and Carleen had, as part of that experiment being conducted, gotten to drink the elixir both during the most recent full moon and the one before that.

When, both times, someone had failed to shift back... Drew and Liam. But apparently Chuck and Carleen had both shifted again, right on time, back to human form.

"We did just fine," Carleen told her, when she asked how things had gone. "It was really fun both times—getting to maintain our human cognition while shifted. Most shifters don't, you know."

"That's what I've been told."

Rosa hazarded a glance toward Valerie, who simply changed like other shifters under a full moon—in this case, into a wolf with only a canine's cognition. Valerie was watching her sister and brother-in-law as she ate her own burger, and didn't even glance at Rosa.

And then came what Rosa figured was their goal in spending time with her.

Carleen, who was sitting at her right side, leaned toward her, a cup of coffee in her hand. "We gather that you have contact, at least sometimes, with the people in charge at Liam's military unit. We know he doesn't have the authority to make their elixir available to us during every full moon, let alone at other times. And you surely don't, either. But—well, they must think a lot of you to have you be their sometimes veterinarian, which is important to them. If you could put in a good word for us, we'd really appreciate it. Maybe they could conduct more experiments, for example, with other shifters outside their unit."

"We heard that Liam did get to shift again this week when the moon wasn't full," Chuck added. "He can't say a lot about what he does with the military, but he mentioned that. We're not part of his Alpha Force, of course, but they are recognizing somewhat that we're his family. Maybe you could mention—"

"Maybe Rosa could mention what?" Liam was suddenly there, standing right behind Carleen. He dropped down onto the chair across the table from Rosa and glared at his brother and sister-in-law. "Look, we've gone through this before." He kept his voice down, but there was still a note of anger in it. "My ears are always open when my superior officers talk about expanding their experiment, and I've made it clear you want to continue being part of it, if possible, and I'm happy with the idea. But I have no control, and Rosa certainly has none, so—"

"I'm sure they understand," Valerie interrupted. The expression on her face, which looked so much like her sister's, was sympathetic. "At least they've had the opportunity to try that elixir, and hopefully will again. I'm jealous, of course." She smiled almost sadly. "I'll be leaving Mary Glen soon, so I'm not asking to be included in that experiment, anyway. But if there was only some way to ensure that they could continue, well—Liam, you know how much it means to them."

"I do," he said. "And I'll keep doing what I can to help them continue. But you need to understand my lack of authority, and certainly Rosa's."

"But they apparently do think a lot of Rosa, right?"

Valerie asked. "You've mentioned that the other veterinarian at that clinic, the one who's that officer's wife, is highly respected not just because of being married to the guy, but because of all she does to help them while shifted. And now that Rosa does that, too—well, surely they respect her and like her, right?"

"Definitely," Liam said, looking at Rosa. She had to smile, even though she recognized that, as far as Alpha Force was concerned, she was a sometimes asset but otherwise a nobody. "But look. If you want the possibility of another opportunity to use the elixir—" he looked from his brother to his sister-in-law, then back again "—you need to just go along with things as they work out. Neither of you is military, but in a way you need to follow orders and listen to what you're told. If they continue liking and respecting you, you have a better chance of getting what you're asking for. Understand?"

"Yes," Chuck said, looking Carleen in the eye. "We understand." He turned to Liam. "And we appreciate your being on our side, speaking up for us when you can. We'll listen to you, bro. We promise."

"One thing you should know, though," Liam said, then stopped. Rosa looked at him when he didn't continue right away. He was looking down at the sandwich he held, as if communicating with it in some way.

"What's that?" Chuck prompted, his tone curt, as if he expected Liam to say something bad.

Rosa expected it, too, since he hadn't finished what he'd begun.

"Once again," he finally said, "I don't have control over any of this—and you of all people, Chuck, know how nasty I can get when I don't have control." The lopsided grin he shot toward his brother didn't change the scowl on Chuck's face.

"Yeah," Chuck said. "I've experienced that now and then." At least his response was somewhat light, despite the clear frustration he was feeling.

"The thing is, with my not changing back on time, and my commanding officer not changing back right away during the prior full moon, the unit's attention will be focused on that. My understanding right now is that other experiments, such as the one with you, will likely be put on hold till they figure that out."

"And there's nothing you can do about that?" Carleen asked, also clearly upset. "None of your technological expertise or whatever can resolve that situation?"

Rosa saw Valerie reach over and grasp her sister's hand on the table sympathetically.

"If I could understand it, fix it at all," Liam said, "I would have by now."

Their conversation was pretty much over. Rosa joined in for the final words, unfunny jokes and clearly unhappy goodbyes.

Goodbyes. Standing, collecting her trash to dispose of, she anticipated just heading home on her own. After saying goodbye.

Well, good-night, at least. She intended to talk to Liam again tomorrow, as she'd been doing.

But that was all.

Liam was friendly enough to all of them, of course, particularly his relatives. But he clearly was through talking and listening and explaining his position—and what he could talk about regarding Alpha Force. It seemed clear, after all. He might care for his family, but all he could do was explain the position he had to take as a member of his military unit. Not only did he have to refrain from making promises, but it seemed as if he also had to wrest away most vestiges of hope they might have for continuing their experiment, at least for now.

Even if Rosa wanted to, she couldn't cheer them up. Any hope they might have certainly couldn't be encouraged by her.

She knew Liam well enough to recognize he wasn't particularly happy about having to shrug off his brother and sister-in-law's wishes and pleas, but he was a military man as well as a family member and shapeshifter.

He was doing what he had to.

She decided to let him know that she, at least, understood, as they both headed out of the restaurant. He walked ahead of her through the usual noisy crowd. She wondered what he, with his extraordinary senses, thought about the conversations around them, the usual aroma of cooking meat and more that even she could smell.

They'd talked about that before, and she figured he still simply accepted it, even if his mood wasn't as happy as it sometimes was.

She followed him out the door and onto the empty sidewalk. Cars drove by on the downtown Mary Glen street, and they both turned right toward the parking lot.

"I'm sorry you can't give your family better news," she told him, now at his side.

"I'll bet you are." He looked down at her, his blank expression, his irritated tone, not altering the gorgeousness of his sexy, all-masculine face. "Do you want to kick me in the butt, too, for not being able to accommodate them, to tell them they can drink the elixir and shift my way whenever they want?"

"I of all people understand that sometimes things we really want to do are out of our control. In your case, that means that your relatives, right about now, aren't happy with you. In my case, if things are out of control, that sometimes means I can't save the life of a sweet pet who deserves to live. Not the same thing, but both can hurt."

That expression softened, and he looked human again—sympathetically, caringly human, at least for this moment. "I'm sorry. I'm being pretty selfish, aren't I?"

"Maybe," she said with a smile, as she looked him in the eyes. "But I figure you're just being self-protective. You're kind of in the middle of your work and your family, and at the moment they're both giving you a hard time."

"Boy, do you understand." Instead of smiling back, he bent down and took Rosa in his arms.

She hadn't paid attention before, but now wondered if they were the only people in the parking lot.

Well, who cared? She stood up on her toes, flung her arms tightly around Liam's back and pulled him close.

Their kiss was outstanding. Maybe even more so than many others they'd shared. Maybe not. But it certainly roused Rosa. Made her want more. More kisses? Sure. But really…*more*.

She pulled away after a minute and looked up at him. "You know," she rasped, "I like this restaurant, but one thing I don't like about it is that it doesn't serve alcohol. Care to take me home now and come inside for a drink?" *And more?*

Maybe he read in her eyes what she wasn't saying.

Maybe he simply wanted a drink himself.

Either way, his response was just as she'd hoped. "Let's go," he said.

Liam wound up spending the rest of that night at Rosa's. Drinking beer—yes. And doing more. Much, much more that stimulated him to wish for even more than what they did overnight.

Hot, incredibly arousing sex hadn't been his initial goal of the evening when he'd asked her to join him for dinner.

Not that he hadn't considered the possibility.

But as he drove back to Ft. Lukman the next morning he couldn't help thinking even more about it.

He appreciated Rosa understanding about how he had to essentially slap his closest relative, his beloved bro, Chuck, in the face, telling him that he still had no control over Chuck's or Carleen's use of the elixir.

Liam hated that, but it was the way things were, and at least Rosa got it and sympathized.

He had been trying to stay away from her on a personal basis, since there really could be no long-term relationship between them, not like Drew and Melanie.

They both wanted more.

And yet…

Well, he would just take each day as it came.

That became his ongoing mantra for the next couple weeks. He kept busy with his online stuff, but still came up with only a few answers to who had posted critical allegations against shifters after the last full moon—not all the answers by any means. Although his commanding officers were understanding and encouraging, claiming they were happy he'd been able to accomplish as much as he had, he was beginning to feel like a failure.

Him. Liam, who'd always considered himself one talented guy in online skills, and had received substantial recognition for it, including this job in the military. It almost felt as if someone as skilled was purposely attempting to outwit him. And had, so far.

But not forever. He would figure it out. Definitely. He'd promised himself…and Alpha Force.

At least his state of mind was helped by his talking to Rosa every day, sometimes more than once. He saw her several times in her veterinary capacity, on days Melanie was unavailable, when Alpha Force members worked outside a full moon to continue testing the elixir and shifting back—even though the two issues they'd experienced had been only during full moons.

So far.

He visited her at her home a few times, too. Not every night, but often enough to make him feel addicted, wanting more, knowing that, in the long run, it might wind up being bad for him.

Especially when, now and then, he hinted at the possibility that they were developing a relationship, and she turned it into a joke.

Which, despite how it hurt, he understood. She might understand that shifters existed, and be willing to help them medically. But she was a regular person with a life to live, outside of what most humans considered "woo-woo" and weird.

And now it was approaching the night of the next

full moon. Rosa called to invite him to join her for dinner, preferably somewhere other than at Fastest Foods, but that would be okay, too. They'd eaten at a few other restaurants in Mary Glen besides his family's, and that might have been the better choice that night when he accepted her invitation.

And yet…well, he did have some news to convey to his family, and it wasn't good. At least not entirely.

But it wasn't all bad, either.

And having Rosa around for comfort when he related it sounded damn good.

Back at his family's restaurant.

Maybe Rosa should have insisted on someplace else this time. Sure, eating the food they served was fun, even if it wasn't always the healthiest stuff.

Worse was the atmosphere when Liam argued with his brother and sister-in-law, or wound up teasing them, thanks to what Alpha Force made him do.

But…hey, this night actually wasn't so bad, after all.

Once again Rosa sat at the same table as Liam, Chuck, Carleen and Valerie, in a corner where they could keep their voices down.

And when they all had their meals in front of them, Chuck turned to Liam.

"So what is it you wanted to tell us tonight, bro?"

From what Rosa saw, Chuck seemed to cringe, as if he expected to be kicked in the teeth by Liam's news.

Instead, though—well, it might not have been exactly what Chuck and Carleen wanted to hear, but it could have been a lot worse.

"Here's what I understand," Liam began. "The experiment that includes you has been put on hold, as I thought it was."

Carleen started to rise. "We understand," she said, although her tone was chilly. "Thanks for letting us know."

Valerie stood, too, putting her arm around her sister's shoulders. "It's okay," she said. "Shifting the old-fashioned way is just fine. I can vouch for it."

"Sit down, please," Liam said. "I'm not finished."

And then he informed his relatives that, as long as none of the shifters failed to shift back on the morning after the next full moon, the experiment would restart the following month.

Rosa felt tears of happiness in her eyes as Liam was hugged and thanked by his relatives.

But how were they sure there'd be no problems shifting back this time?

Chapter 22

Rosa talked to Liam on the phone the next couple evenings. She was pleased that he did all the calling. They made plans to get together at least one more time for dinner—and maybe more—before the next full moon occurred, which now was only four days away.

Rosa had been asked to make herself available to help out in case any of the shifters needed veterinary care while in canine form. Of course, she'd planned on it, anyway.

In fact—well, it was midmorning now, and Melanie had asked Rosa to pop into her office for just a few minutes between patients. Rosa was on her way there.

She knocked and waited for Melanie's "Come in." She soon was sitting across the desk from her boss and friend, whose pretty face looked concerned.

"What's wrong?" Rosa asked right away.

"What do you think?" countered Melanie. "We've already talked about our duties during the upcoming full moon. Has Drew contacted you about it?"

"Yes," Rosa said. "Of course I let him know I'll be available. I didn't bring that up with you because I figured you knew it was a foregone conclusion."

Melanie's expression softened. "Yes. And it just gives me another reason to feel sure I hired the right assistant vet."

"Well, of course." Rosa attempted to sound insulted, but instead she laughed. "Okay, boss. Let's both hope that none of the shifters, especially those we like best, have any problem shifting back this time."

"Definitely," Melanie agreed, and then she led the conversation into a discussion of a few of their veterinary patients with particularly challenging medical issues, and who would do what to help them.

Susie knocked on the door and let them know that a couple more patients had come in, as scheduled, which ended their conversation.

The rest of the day zipped by, thanks to Rosa's treating a cat that had been vomiting because of dehydration, and a dog she diagnosed as being pregnant—fortunately a purebred Westie whose owner showed the breed and had planned for a new litter. Then there were a couple other canine patients who needed an exam or shots, and soon the regular day was over. Rosa was free for the night except if notified of an emergency.

Which, unfortunately, was exactly what happened. And the source particularly worried her.

The call came in on her cell phone, not the office line. "Rosa? It's Valerie. Sorry to bother you, but I really need help. No, Louper needs your help."

Valerie sounded panicked, and she kept on talking, not entirely making sense.

"Hold on," Rosa said. "Slowly. Please tell me what's wrong with Louper."

There was a moment of silence, perhaps while Valerie got her mind under better control. Then she said, "We're at home. He was playing with a ball. He carried it to the top of the basement steps and began shaking it, then seemed to drop it down them intentionally. He started to follow it and… Oh, Rosa, he fell down the stairs! He's just lying there. He's breathing, though heavily, and I'm afraid he broke some bones. Can you come check him out?"

"Of course," Rosa said with no hesitation. Too bad it was too late for her to get assistance from one of the vet techs, and Melanie had probably already left to go home to her kids.

Well, Rosa would go check Louper out. Hopefully, it would be safe to move him, and if she needed help carrying him to the car to bring him here to the clinic, she'd call someone.

Liam.

"Give me your address," she told Valerie, realizing she had never visited Liam's family's home. "I'll be there as soon as I can."

The front of the clinic was already locked for the night, and Rosa made sure to lock the back door behind her as she raced into the parking lot, her bag of medical equipment in her hand. She had a general idea of where the Corlands lived, thanks to getting the address, but she programmed it into her phone's GPS anyway. She definitely didn't want any delays in her arrival there.

What kinds of injuries had poor Louper suffered?

Broken bones? Which ones? Concussion? External wounds? A combination of those and possibly internal injuries, too?

She would find out soon.

She drove through downtown Mary Glen and in the general direction of Ft. Lukman, but turned off at a major intersection into a nice residential area. She didn't know much about architecture, but believed most of the houses were forms of Craftsman styles, with two stories, wide porches, mostly stone with wood trim. The Corlands' house resembled many of the rest. Rosa quickly parked her car in front of it and jumped out.

She ran up the walkway to the porch, hurried up the steps and quickly knocked on the wooden front door.

It opened nearly immediately, as if Valerie had been waiting there for her. Was that a bad sign regarding Louper's condition?

"I'm so glad you're here," Valerie said, closing the door behind Rosa. "Come in."

Rosa was startled when Louper came running up, long tail wagging, to greet her.

The dog looked fine, perfectly healthy.

Rosa turned toward Valerie. "What—" she began, and stopped.

Valerie was aiming a gun at her.

"Let's go into the living room, shall we, Rosa?" It wasn't really a question. The expression on Valerie's face looked evil, menacing, as if she was waiting for Rosa to make a misstep so she'd have reason to shoot her.

What the heck? Rosa hadn't seen anything like this coming.

And Carleen's sister seemed so mentally unhinged at the moment that she didn't need an excuse to shoot.

Rosa felt certain she wouldn't get out of this alive.

But only for a moment. She had to figure this out, figure Valerie out—and definitely figure out a way to end this as safely as possible.

She proceeded to walk in the direction Valerie pointed with her free hand, through the entry area and into a room off to the side that was filled with matching dark wood furniture with taut bright red upholstery.

Bright red. Blood might not show up on it...

"Okay, Valerie," Rosa said, as she took a seat on the sofa Valerie pointed at, and Louper came over to get petted. "What is this about?"

"You'll find out soon enough." Valerie shooed Louper out of the room and closed the door. Good. At least the dog wouldn't actually get hurt. Then Valerie dragged one of the two chairs to face Rosa and sat on it, gun still pointed at her. She pulled her phone from her pocket with her left hand, glanced at it as she used her thumb to push a button, then, after a few seconds, said, "Hi, Liam."

Rosa gasped but said nothing.

Valerie continued. "I assume you're done working for the day, right? Back at your quarters?" She smiled and held the phone out.

She must have put it on speaker, since Rosa heard Liam say, "...eating here tonight, not at the restaurant. But I'll get there one of these days again, probably before the full moon."

"Full moon," Valerie continued. "Funny you should mention that. It's partly why I called. You see, I want you to bring me some of your super-duper elixir before then—like, right now—so I can keep my human mind and all, this time."

A pause, then Liam said, "I assumed you understood why that's not possible."

Rosa's mind was working—hard. If she said something to Liam, would Valerie shoot her? But why was she allowing Rosa to listen in?

"Oh, but it's got to be, even though I'm not a near enough relative and your damned experiment is on hold, anyway. You see, I've got Rosa with me, and unless you bring me a good supply of that elixir right now, at least a year's worth, and one of those lights, poor Rosa isn't going to be around much longer." She looked toward Rosa and said, "Are you, Ms. Veterinarian?"

What should she do? What should she say?

Calmly, she said, "Liam, I'm with Valerie at your brother's house, and she has a gun. I know there isn't much you—"

"Damn you, Valerie!" Liam shouted. "Don't you dare hurt Rosa. I'll go talk to the officers here and see what I can do. I'll call you back soon."

"Real soon," Valerie said with a huge grin. "You know, I've heard people talk about their trigger fingers getting itchy. Just assume mine is. I'll be eager to hear from you." And she pushed the button to hang up.

So would Valerie pull the trigger now? She could get rid of Rosa and just wait for Liam to come with the elixir—and Rosa had little doubt that Liam would come with something, at least, to try to convince Valerie to calm down, give up.

If Rosa wanted to stay alive, she needed to keep Valerie occupied in a way that still gave her power. And she did want to stay alive.

"I'm sure you know, Valerie," she began calmly, although she heard a waver in her voice, "Liam and I are friends. But though we see each other socially some that doesn't mean we're particularly close."

Which was fairly true and a damn shame, Rosa thought. Maybe, if she survived, she would try to move their relationship up a level, or several.

"But—well, I'd really like to understand why you're doing this." Maybe because she considered it unfair that her sister, who happened to be married to a man related to an Alpha Force member, had been allowed to sample the elixir, at least a bit. It had crossed Rosa's mind before that it might not be completely fair, but Valerie had seemed to accept it.

"Because I want some of that damn elixir," Valerie spat. She started shaking as she remained sitting there. "Do you know how long I tried to develop something like that myself? I'll tell you how long. Most of my life." Her glare seemed to stab Rosa as she continued. "You probably think I've spent my life as a restaurant server. Well, hell, though I like doing that and admire good servers, until I moved here temporarily I was a scientist. By design. I'm a shifter, and so's my family. I also like being a shifter—but it's got its drawbacks, like being all wolf when I've changed, and having no say about when I change."

Valerie proceeded to describe to Rosa her interactions with other shifters attempting to achieve the same kinds of results—more control. Scientific experiments. Not-so-scientific stabs at anything she heard about or thought of. She'd put together some pretty good formulas that she'd hoped would allow her to change when she wanted, keep at least a little of her human cognition when she did—but nothing really worked.

She was particularly excited when she learned that her brother-in-law's brother was being recruited into the military—especially when she heard the rumors that the group recruiting him was a very special unit of shapeshifters...with powers. She'd assumed that if all that was true, family would be included, too.

And was horrified to learn that wasn't the case.

She kept on trying to create something herself. Made it clear to Chuck and Carleen—without allowing herself to nag—that she'd be interested in what was already out there, too.

Interested? Hell, she craved it. Deserved it.

Would do anything for it. Planned to analyze the elixir and make a lot more for herself.

"And that's not all," she said, once again waving the gun.

Rosa shuddered again. Would Liam be able to help...somehow? She was sure he couldn't, wouldn't, surrender any of the elixir.

And maybe, to prevent this clearly mad shapeshifter from getting anything that could increase her powers, Rosa should figure out a way to attack her, stop her—even if the result was that she was stopped permanently, too.

Liam had contacted Drew first after hearing from Valerie.

Not, of course, to beg him to hand over a bunch of elixir to that insane indirect relative of his. But, oh yes, it did involve the elixir.

Could he be sure Valerie wouldn't harm Rosa? Of

course not. And he didn't think the best way to handle this would be to let Carleen and Chuck know. They wouldn't be able to convince Carleen's sister to become sane suddenly and back off. He knew they were working late at the restaurant tonight, a good thing—hosting some kind of party.

Hopefully, they wouldn't be around to get involved.

And his getting in touch with Drew was for a purpose that just might work to get Valerie under their control before she hurt anyone.

Before she hurt Rosa...

Now he sat in Drew's office. Fortunately, his commanding officer had still been at the base, and it hadn't been hard for Liam to get him to meet with him.

Not when he briefly explained what was going on.

"Damn. Well, I've got some ideas how to handle this." Drew leaned against his desk, watching Liam with his golden, intense eyes. "But I suspect you do, too."

"I do," Liam agreed. "I'm glad to hear yours, too, as long as we both do this quickly. But here's what I've got in mind."

He explained what had immediately rushed into his brain. He knew that every second they did nothing increased the danger to Rosa. But he still wanted as many shifters as were stationed at Ft. Lukman right now to participate.

And when he was finished describing what he had in mind, he was relieved to hear Drew say, "Good plan. I don't need to waste time telling you my idea. Let's do it."

Rosa realized it hadn't been very long since Valerie had contacted Liam. Even so, it felt as if hours had elapsed.

Hours in which that gun remained aimed at her.

At least Valerie kept talking, so maybe she had a shred of sanity left that was large enough for her to want to justify all that she had done.

Not that talking about it truly helped her achieve that. But it was keeping Rosa alive for now.

"So I tried in so many ways to be nice to those people Liam works with," Valerie was saying. "Making sure they were served their food quickly and nicely when they came into the restaurant and I was there. Smiling and chatting with them and even kidding around a bit, since they knew I was also a shifter. I hoped my niceness would convince them that I deserved to be in their experiment with their damned elixir, too, but it didn't work that way. And so I got mad."

Mad? She surely was psychologically mad, but Rosa knew she meant angry. "I understand," she told Valerie, to keep her talking.

"And of course I did something about it." She whisked her silvery hair away from one side of her face in a strangely proud gesture that once more made Rosa shake inside.

"What was that?" she had to ask, partly because she knew she was expected to, and partly because she wanted to know.

"Well, I told you I'd been experimenting with something on my own before I even heard of that damned Alpha Force elixir. And like I said, it never worked. In fact, it sometimes caused problems when I took it—not a drink like that elixir, but some powders I blended together that had some similarity, but not enough."

"I see," Rosa said. She could in some ways understand the woman's frustration, but—

"No, you don't see. But you will." This time the grin on the face of the woman who looked so much like her sister was broad and seemed evil, almost devilish. "You know that both that Drew guy and Liam happened to be at the restaurant early on evenings before the moon turned full, right?"

Oh, no. Rosa could guess where this was heading. "Yes," she said tentatively.

"Well, I just happened to add a little flavor—and more—to what they ate. And guess why they weren't able to shift back to human form?"

Chapter 23

The bad thing was that Chuck and Carleen lived in a planned development containing streets lined with houses.

The good thing was that their home was close to the only park in that development.

That was where Liam stood now, and he wasn't alone. No, two wolves and three regular humans were with him—members of Alpha Force who had drunk the elixir and were assisted in shifting, thanks to their aides who were with them.

Liam hadn't shifted yet, but he would do so soon. His own aide, Denny, had accompanied him, and held out a vial of the elixir that Carleen's sister had demanded he bring.

Well, he had brought some. Just not for her.

"Are we all ready?" Liam asked. He received confirming head bows and growls from his two shifted comrades, and a yes from all the aides. "Then let's go."

It was dark enough, fortunately, that they weren't obvious as they all walked in shadows of trees and houses toward the home that was their target. Then the two shifters and all the aides walked quietly onto the porch of that home and crouched down behind the partial wall at its outer end so they wouldn't be readily visible to neighbors.

Liam rang the doorbell. He heard Louper bark inside.

A minute later the door opened, and Rosa stood there. Her eyes lit up immediately, then grew frantic, although the tone of her voice didn't show it. "Well, hello, Liam. Thanks for coming."

He saw all sorts of questions in her expression, but neither of them could talk about anything that Valerie wouldn't overhear.

"Please come in," she finished, although he saw a slight shake of her head, as if she didn't want him to accept her invitation.

"Thanks." He immediately saw why she didn't want him to come in, but having Valerie right behind her, revolver barrel thrust against Rosa's back, wasn't a surprise.

"Yes, come in, Liam." Valerie's voice was much too sweet, and Liam had an urge to attack her with all the one-on-one combat skills he had learned in the military. But he wouldn't necessarily be fast enough to prevent her from shooting Rosa.

No, he would wait and get involved in a conversation with her—and find a way to open a door or window to let his comrades in.

First thing would be to put her off guard as much as possible, although he had no doubt she wouldn't trust him any more than he trusted her.

"So," he said, after the door was closed behind him, "I don't understand, Valerie. Why are you doing this?"

"You do understand," she contradicted. "Did you bring the elixir and light?"

He nodded. "What you asked for is in my car, right outside." Well, not far down the street, but he'd be able to point it out to her if she insisted.

He wished he could reassure Rosa that he was lying, because her scared look took on an angry glint for a moment. "Valerie was telling me before," she said, "that she'd been trying to come up with her own kind of shifting formula—and that she'd put some in your food and Drew's at different times before the recent full moons."

He felt a cold wave shoot up his back. "And that's what prevented us from changing back."

"Exactly." Valerie sounded so proud he wanted to throttle her. Heck, he wanted to throttle her for so many reasons. "Now go out and get that damn elixir of yours."

"In a minute," he said. "Could we go somewhere and sit down and talk? I'm really impressed by your skills and want to know more. How did you come up with that kind of formulation?"

He saw Valerie take a deep breath as she stared at him, and then another. "Okay," she said. "Let's go into the kitchen, but just for a minute. I'll tell you that and more. I'm damn proud of who I am and what I've done, and I'm mad that your stupid Alpha Force wasn't nicer to me. But I've gotten back at them…and you."

Keep her talking, his mind said. And he actually wanted to. Got back at Alpha Force? How?

They soon were seated at the familiar square plastic table in the kitchen—at least Rosa and he were. Louper was in there, too, pacing around. Valerie remained standing, and she kept the .357 Magnum trained on Rosa, damn her. That made it harder for him to do anything at the moment.

But he would. Soon.

"You're going to go get that elixir and bring it in here," Valerie said as she leaned toward Rosa, sticking the gun into her side hard enough that it made her wince—another reason Liam had to prevent himself from acting. "But first, I want to tell you one more thing, since we won't be seeing each other again after this. I didn't only get back at Alpha Force by giving you and that Drew guy stuff to harm you. You know I'm aware somewhat of what you do for that stupid military unit, working with their online stuff to protect their reputation, such as it is, since you try to keep it secret. Well, I knew about it thanks to Carleen. And since they were so unkind to me, I figured I'd be unkind to them. You know of my background with computer technology as well as science, don't you?"

Vaguely, he recalled that Carleen had mentioned her sister's multiple skills, although she hadn't gone into detail. But he wished now that he had pressed Carleen to say more—since he suddenly knew where this part of the conversation was going.

This shifter was versatile. And clearly quite smart.

But so was he. Now, all he had to do was prove it—and make sure Rosa remained okay.

"Yes, I know," he said, biting the inside of his

mouth. "And I'll bet you're the one I've been looking for—one of the people who've hidden their identities but blabbed about Alpha Force's shifters and lied about what they do during a full moon."

"Exactly," she crowed, fluffing her silvery hair away from her face with her free hand. "I'm Orion. Or at least I'm that Orion. I met the guy around here who calls himself that, liked his name and adopted it myself. And sometimes I'm Diana or others, although I don't take on too many female goddesses' names since I don't want it too obvious I'm a woman. But I've been really good at hiding my background, don't you think? No, don't answer. I know I'm great at this stuff, but figure you won't admit it."

Again Liam had to hold himself in check. Had the Alpha Force members with him moved around the house at all? Any of them? Could they hear this? Could Drew hear this?

"I see," he made himself say calmly. "I'll admit that you're definitely skilled in many things." *And I'm going to shut you down*, he promised himself—and Rosa. She was watching him and undoubtedly recognized the fury within him despite how cool he attempted to keep his expression.

Well, enough of this. It was time to act.

"Okay," he said. "I think we need to end this now. Let me go out to my car and get the elixir and light." And backup.

"Very good. But just remember I'll be in here with your sweetie, Rosa—or whatever she is to you."

He didn't like that Valerie watched him so closely. That she remained so near him just then.

He needed a good way to get his backup into the house. But he'd been unable to open any doors or windows.

Still, he'd had a chance to look around—and knew what he was going to do.

"I'll be right back," he told Valerie, aiming a wink at Rosa. Of course they followed him to the front door, so he couldn't leave it ajar.

He had an idea now how this should go, especially after he scanned the area while standing at the door. "Are you going to wait for me back in the kitchen?" he asked, hoping the answer was no. "It seems appropriate, and—"

"If you like it, then forget it. We'll wait for you in there." Valerie flipped the gun toward the living room beside them, then back toward Rosa again.

"Oh. Fine." Liam tried to sound just a touch perturbed, even though her response was what he'd hoped for. "I've got several bottles to remove from my car, as well as the light. I'll be as quick as I can."

He would definitely be as quick as he could, but not doing what he had told her.

He'd be doing something else—something that would allow him to shut her down, and in a way that might teach her a lesson, as well. Or not.

He had to stop this malicious shifter who could only harm her wonderful race, as well as the regular humans they lived among.

Stop her now.

He put his hand on the doorknob, looked at Valerie as if asking permission, then slipped past Louper, who was pacing again—probably aware that there were other beings nearby. Liam went out the door and down the walkway to the street, after trading glances with the shifted wolves who crouched there.

They'd be waiting.

Liam headed past his car—and went quickly into the nearby woods, where Denny waited for him with elixir and a light.

And very quickly, behind trees so as not to be seen, Liam began to shift.

Rosa wondered what would come next.

She knew Liam wasn't going to obey Valerie's command and return with elixir for her. But a little time had passed, and—

Louper stood up, looking around, at attention. The sweet dog had barked just once before, when Liam had rung the bell. He'd seemed uneasy a lot, such as when Valerie had made Rosa accompany her out of the living room to greet Liam. He had acted interested in going outside then, but Valerie had ignored his unspoken request. Rosa half figured the dog would reach a point and then leave a puddle in the house, but that hadn't happened yet.

He'd been in the kitchen with them, then followed them once more to the front door. And when Liam walked out, Louper had seemed agitated once more.

"You may want to take poor Louper outside," Rosa told Valerie, as the woman shooed her back into the living room, the gun, of course, still pointed toward her. "I think he needs a potty break."

"I don't give a damn what he wants," Valerie shouted. "You're not using that as an excuse to get away. If he goes inside, so what? I won't be here much longer, anyway."

Her nasty gaze suggested Rosa wouldn't, either.

Rosa decided to shut up and wait. Sitting on the red-covered sofa again, she nevertheless scanned the room for any kind of shelter, any cover where she could duck if—when—Valerie decided to pull the trigger.

"Where is that damned soldier buddy of yours?" Valerie glanced down at the watch on her wrist. "He's taking too long."

"There's a lot of stuff he needs to bring in," Rosa said. "He may need to figure out the best way to carry it."

"But he got it in the car before. How hard can it be—"

Louper stood up just then and barked—even as the large front window, behind thick draperies, shattered.

Valerie screamed.

Within moments, three wolves resembling the dog who belonged there leaped in. The first one grabbed the heavy curtains in his mouth and yanked them down to cover the broken glass, as the others, following him, sped directly toward where the two women sat in the middle of the room.

Shifters. Rosa knew it. Alpha Force members who'd shifted outside the full moon.

She threw herself onto the floor, hoping Valerie, who hadn't stopped screaming, would be too distracted to shoot her.

Then she couldn't shoot. All three wolves leaped onto her, knocking her down, and one grabbed her wrist in his mouth. Valerie dropped the gun. Another wolf jumped onto her back, holding her in place. That one looked at Rosa, and she knew it was Liam. She had seen him shifted often enough to recognize the silver-and-black markings of his fur. She also recognized one of the others: Drew.

Louper stayed back, but barked.

Rosa assumed there were aides outside, so she called out over Valerie's voice—swearing now—"They've got Valerie under control. You can come in." Too bad Valerie had hidden Rosa's phone somewhere, or she'd use it to call Liam's line, assuming Denny would answer.

"Great!" yelled a voice from outside. "Denny here. Can you open the door?"

Rosa hurried to the front door and opened it. Denny stood there with Captain Jonas Truro and Sergeant Kristine Parran. Jonas was Drew's aide, and although Kristine helped several shifters, Rosa figured that the other shifter in wolf form was Captain Patrick Worley.

The aides hurried in, guns drawn, and immediately aimed at Valerie once they'd called off the wolves—which they didn't need to do, Rosa figured.

These particular wolves had human cognition.

"Okay," Jonas said, securing Valerie's arms behind her back as he lifted her from the floor. "You're under our control now, Ms. Corland."

And she was.

Rosa gave a huge sigh of relief, dropping to her knees to hug the wolf who was Liam.

It was over.

Chapter 24

"This meal is on the house," Chuck said, as Carleen and he served burgers and sides including salads and fries. The group, mostly in camo uniforms, was seated around the large table once more created by pushing a lot of small tables together at the rear of Fastest Foods.

Which was a nice thing for his brother and sister-in-law to do on a night after the latest full moon, Liam thought, as he took a sip of some wine that had been brought in special for this occasion.

It was also nice of them to close the place early for this party, which included all members of Alpha Force currently stationed at Ft. Lukman. After all, they'd closed the restaurant early last night, too, since they'd shifted, as had about half the people there.

Though he understood why they did it tonight. This was definitely a celebration for them.

Despite what they had been told before, Chuck and Carleen had been permitted to use the elixir. Drew had told them that morning, when shifting was over with no problems at all, that the experiment had gone well enough that they were going to get some elixir for every full moon for the foreseeable future—and the experiment would also expand at some point to allow them to use the elixir outside a full moon.

They were thrilled—even as they remained embarrassed and very sorry about all that Valerie had done. Carleen, tears flowing from her eyes, had apologized over and over for her sister's actions—and for her own failure to see even a hint of what had been going on.

"So," Drew said, standing at the head of the table. "Let's toast Alpha Force and all this wonderful military unit does."

"Hear, hear," called a lot of those who were there— and Liam heard a couple additional female voices behind him do the same.

One he'd anticipated hearing. Had been eager to hear—and to see the lovely, sexy, wonderful woman it belonged to.

He turned.

Sure enough, Rosa was there, just entering the place holding the hand of Drew's older child, Emily. Melanie was with her, carrying Andy.

Good. Liam had known Rosa would come. She had told him so.

She had told him a lot since he had helped to bring down Valerie—and prevent the insane shifter from doing further harm. A lot of what Rosa had said was "Thank you." But it included "I'm so glad she didn't hurt you, too," and "I'm also happy that you now have your answers about who posted all those nasty things online about Alpha Force."

They'd spent a lot of time together since then, too—although Valerie's attack had been only a few evenings ago. But those nights together... Liam felt his body move as he thought about them.

And after the shifts to wolf form during the full moon, Rosa had been there in her veterinarian role in case medical assistance had been needed. Which it hadn't, fortunately.

Without Valerie around to spike their food or whatever, all the shifters had changed back right on time.

Liam saw Rosa's gaze scan the table—and light on him. He grinned and motioned toward the empty chair beside him, which he had saved for her.

She walked to the other side of the table, where Drew was, first. The unit's commanding officer had saved seats there for his family, and Rosa turned Emily over to her daddy.

Then Rosa headed to Liam's side. He wanted to grab her in his arms and give her a huge kiss. But this wasn't the right time. Instead, he just took her hand and basked in the glow of the big smile she gave him as she sat down on that saved seat.

"Hi," she said.

"Hi back."

But before Liam could say anything else, Drew spoke. "Welcome to my family, and welcome to all of you. Tonight is special in many ways. All went well last night—and thanks to the capture of the person responsible for our prior problems, all should continue to go well."

"What's going on with Valerie?" prompted Denny, who sat at Liam's other side.

"She is awaiting trial, in federal custody at a covert maximum security prison," Drew responded. "One with special solitary confinement facilities—so she shifted all by herself last night."

"And back," Patrick added.

"Anyway," Drew said, "we've got a couple of surprises pending for later. But for now, let's eat. And drink. And be merry."

There was a buzz of conversation as everyone quizzed him and others on what he was talking about, but he wouldn't explain. Not yet, at least.

Although Liam hoped for one very special thing...

As everyone finally got settled and continued eating their meals, Liam turned to Rosa. "Everything okay at the vet clinic today?"

"Sure," she said, looking him deep in the eye as she smiled at him. "But I did happen to be a little tired. I stayed up late last night."

He laughed. "Me, too."

"And everything okay online about the world of shifters?" she asked him.

"Everything was fine—mostly because there was almost no mention online of shapeshifters over the past few days, including today, and none at all making accusations against some bizarre military unit of shifters hurting people."

"Good," Rosa said, giving a crisp nod.

"Yes, good," Liam said. Were regular humans finally accepting the existence of shifters? Maybe, and maybe not.

But he still hoped for that to be reality someday.

* * *

Rosa was so pleased to be here with Liam and with his whole local Alpha Force gang. She felt part of it despite not being a shifter.

But heck, she liked shifters.

One more than the rest, of course.

In fact, she knew now that she loved Liam.

Although it was premature to let him know that. But he was smart, sexy, techie yet tough, and he had saved her life.

And she wanted so much to crow about that to the world, even though this group already knew it.

She also wanted to melt into Liam's arms and stay there. Forever.

But for now, she just ate her burger and salad and drank her wine.

Liam and she talked about what it had been like on the night of the full moon for both of them—him as a shifter at the edge of Ft. Lukman, and her there, too, observing him and the other wolfen Alpha Forcers.

They weren't relating anything new to each other, but continued to have a good conversation, sometimes including Denny or Melanie or Drew or anyone else.

When they were done eating, Liam said, "There's something in the kitchen here I'd like to show you."

"Some new appliance Chuck bought?" Rosa was teasing. She figured Liam, like her, wanted to share a kiss, despite all the other people here, who didn't need to see it.

That was more than fine with her.

They both stood, and he held her hand as they slowly made their way past the others, some of whom turned to talk to them. But soon they were in the kitchen.

Then Liam led her out the back door and onto the parking lot driveway. "It's quieter here," he told her. "And maybe a little more romantic."

She laughed. "Oh, I like that last part. Romantic." She took a step toward him, wanting to throw her arms around him. But he stepped back.

"Wait a minute," he said, and she felt hurt.

But only for a moment, since he reached into his pocket...and pulled out a small box.

She gasped. It surely wasn't...

But it was. He opened it. It contained a ring. One with a lovely, nice-sized diamond.

Liam did the customary thing and got down on one knee. "Rosa, I love you. I've been fighting it because I figured you might like shifters, but forever with one? So...I'm not really sure you feel the same way, but just in case—"

"I do," she interrupted, and realized those words might have a different meaning someday in the future, assuming he was proposing.

For when he asked if she would marry him, she immediately said yes.

He rose, put the ring on her finger and gave her the deepest, sexiest, most loving kiss she had ever experienced.

Then another one.

And when they finished the third, Rosa said, "We'd probably better go back inside. Did Drew know about this? He mentioned something about some surprises tonight."

"I told him about the possibility," Liam said, grabbing her left hand where his diamond now sparkled as he began leading her back inside. "I told him not to hold his breath, since I wasn't... But boy, am I breathing well now."

Rosa laughed and followed Liam. She determined to ask Melanie about the shifting capabilities of her kids, since she might need to know that someday soon.

Back in the dining room, someone Rosa vaguely recognized was talking. "Isn't that—" she began in a whisper.

"That's General Greg Yarrow, the highest commanding officer of Alpha Force," Liam whispered back. "He must have come in from the Pentagon today."

Like many of the others, the general was clad in camo, although his uniform had a lot of stripes and medals on it. He appeared to be a senior, although his hair was dark black. His voice was strong.

"I'm here to thank all of you again for being members of Alpha Force," he said, "and also to greet Chuck and Carleen and congratulate them for participating in our experiment. There may be more changes looming for Alpha Force, though that's not certain yet. But you can be sure your group is considered very special to those of us in Washington who know about you— including some like me who wish at times I had your shifting skills."

The group laughed, then everyone raised their glasses as Greg did and toasted Alpha Force.

And when the general sat down, Rosa saw Drew look directly at Liam, who nodded.

Drew rose. "Let's again toast the future of Alpha Force," he said, and they all did. And when they had finished, he added, "Let's also toast some very special people around here, one of our own, and one who's my dear wife's wonderful assistant. I believe that Liam and Rosa just became engaged. Right, Liam?"

"Absolutely," said the wonderful man beside Rosa, who was now her fiancé. He also stood and drew Rosa to her feet. "I'll certainly drink to that." Which he did, looking her straight in the eye.

"So," said Drew, "let's all toast Liam and Rosa and the future. May they have a wonderful life together."

"Hear, hear," came the call, and everyone with wine took a drink.

Then Rosa, still standing, rose on her toes and gave Liam a brief but sexy kiss. She lifted her glass. "To Alpha Force, and to my Liam, and to all of you. Here's to a wonderful future for all of us."

She took a long sip, again gazing into Liam's eyes— and looked forward to later that night…and forever.

* * * * *